THE CZAR BOMB

Dennis Meredith

Glyphus

For information about this title or to order other books and/or electronic media, contact the publisher:
Glyphus, L.L.C.
2947 Mesa Grove Rd., Fallbrook, CA 92028
www.glyphus.com
editor@glyphus.com

ISBNs:
Print: 978-1-939118-32-5
Kindle: 978-1-939118-31-8

LCCN: 2025916605

Cover: Ryan Meredith

EXPLORE THESE OTHER BOOKS BY DENNIS MEREDITH

Science Thrillers

Angelians (Angelians.com)
Attack of the Food Zombies (FoodZombiesNovel.com)
Mythicals (MythicalsNovel.com)
The Neuromorphs (TheNeuromorphs.com)
Solomon's Freedom (SolomonsFreedom.com)
The Cerulean's Secret (CeruleansSecret.com)
The Happy Chip (TheHappyChip.com)
The Rainbow Virus (RainbowVirus.com)
Wormholes: A Novel (WormholesANovel.com)

Non-fiction

Explaining Research: How to Reach Key Audiences to Advance Your Work (ExplainingResearch.com)

The Climate Pandemic: How Climate Disruption Threatens Human Survival (ClimatePandemic.com)

Earthbound: The Obstacles to Human Space Exploration and the Promise of Artificial Intelligence (EarthboundTheBook.com)

To E. J. Hunter

Contents

PROLOGUE

October 30, 1961

A 50-50 chance of surviving. That was all Soviet Air Force Major Andrei Durnovtsev and his crew had of living through the thermonuclear blast from the superbomb slung beneath his TU-95V "Bear A" bomber. The nuclear scientists had warned that the airmen might be incinerated into charred corpses inside a flying crematorium. On the other hand, Durnovtsev knew that there was a 100-percent possibility that if the bomb failed to detonate, they would receive bullets to the brain. Their murder would ensure that a failure would not be made public to tarnish the Soviet Union's reputation for nuclear success.

After all, Nikita Khrushchev and the other Soviet leaders saw detonating the largest man-made explosion in history as not only a technological achievement. It was to be a propaganda coup of the highest magnitude for the Soviet Communist Party.

But Durnovtsev was prepared to die, as a dutiful son of the Soviet Union. So, bundled in a thick leather jacket against the icy, gray dawn of Olenya airfield in northern Russia, he set about meticulously inspecting the 26-foot-long, silver-painted bomb.

He paid particular attention to the huge bundle attached to the bomb's tail. It held the 1,800-pound parachute that he hoped would be the savior for him and his crew. The parachute canopy would deploy as the bomb was released, in hopes of slowing its descent to give time for the bomber and its accompanying TU-16 Badger observer plane to escape.

While the bomb was highly experimental, Durnovtsev had confidence in the plane and the skills of him and his crew. He had trained assiduously on the TU-95V, with its long, slim fuselage and swept-back wings.

The Bear A bomber with its 164-foot wingspan and 151-foot length was the only craft that could possibly carry the bomb, code-named Vanya. Even so, the engineers had made major modifications to strengthen its structure. Durnovtsev meticulously inspected those modifications—the reinforced suspension and release mechanisms, and the heavier bomb rack attached directly to the plane's weight-bearing beams.

A major problem was that the bomb was so bulky that the engineers had removed the bomb bay doors and slung the bomb beneath the plane. So, besides the huge risk of just taking off with the 30-ton load, the protruding bomb spoiled the bomber's aerodynamic shape.

The technicians had also taken steps to enable the plane to survive the hellish temperatures from the blast that was to come. They had sprayed its metal surface with white paint in hopes of reflecting at least some of the searing heat.

Even with such precautions, none of the engineers, technicians, scientists, or supervisors had the guts to be on the flight to witness first-hand their success or failure. They huddled in the command post with Major General Nikolai Pavlov, Chairman of the State Commission. They nervously drank coffee, smoked cigarettes, and monitored the test, as Durnovtsev and his crew would fly into history. Or to annihilation.

His external inspection complete, Durnovtsev and his crew climbed aboard the plane, settled into the cramped cockpit, strapped on their harnesses and oxygen masks, and ticked through their preflight checklist.

Durnovtsev then ended the early morning calm by starting the four 15,000-horsepower turboprop engines. They roared obediently to life making the plane deafeningly loud. He shoved the throttles forward and began the taxi.

The plane rumbled down the runway for a seemingly interminable distance before finally heaving itself into the overcast sky. Durnovtsev banked toward the northwest and set a course for the Mityushikha Bay Nuclear Testing Range 600 miles away.

During the flight, radio messages between his plane and the Badger were terse, as were communications with the ground. The crews immersed themselves in their mission, trying to ignore the potential consequences of the holocaust that was to come. Or the lethal consequences of failure.

Finally, the target slid slowly into sight 34,000 feet below—the snow-covered terrain of Novaya Zemlya Island. The next moments were beyond Durnovtsev's control. The ground control transmitted the radio signal that automatically triggered the three bomber locks, releasing the bomb.

Freed of its load, the bomber lurched violently upward, and Durnovtsev slammed the plane's controls into a banking turn desperately racing for a safe distance of at least 30 miles. Thankfully, he saw the parachute deploy.

At 11:32 am Moscow time, a blinding flash lit up the clouds, its ethereal light expanding, causing the clouds to glow and become transparent. An immense, fiery orange ball emerged from a gap in the clouds—a sun born on earth, expanding, expanding, expanding.

Eight seconds later, the blowtorch of a blast wave slammed into the plane, driving it into a plummeting uncontrolled dive of more than half a mile. Smoke filled the cockpit, as the plane's electrical circuits sizzled and shorted out.

Durnovtsev strained at the controls, fighting for the craft's, and the crew's, survival. Finally, he managed to recover the plane, and in the distance, he could see a rising, roiling mushroom cloud the magnitude of which no human had ever witnessed. It thrust relentlessly upward, reaching forty miles into the stratosphere.

The blast ionized the atmosphere, blocking radio communication for forty minutes, so Durnovtsev could not report their survival or determine the fate of the Badger observer plane. Finally, to his relief, he heard a report from the Badger that it had survived, and he contacted the ebullient and relieved scientists, engineers, and party officials.

He eagerly anticipated what would come next: promotion to the rank of lieutenant colonel, being named Hero of the Soviet Union, and very, very large quantities of vodka.

***

Although the bomb detonated at 13,000 feet, the thermonuclear inferno scorched the rock-strewn terrain of the island beneath it like a gargantuan blowtorch.

The blast completely destroyed the village of Severny 34 miles from the blast, even its brick houses leveled. More than 100 miles distant, wooden houses were flattened and stone dwellings lost roofs and doors. Witnesses 170 miles away felt the heat of the blast, and it shattered windows in Norway and Finland, hundreds of miles distant. The light flash was visible more than 600 miles away. The shock wave circled the Earth three times.

An American observation plane nearby, scorched by the blast, managed to measure its size, at the equivalent of 58 megatons—million tons of TNT.

Later, the Soviets would revise that figure to 50 megatons, making it by far the largest man-made explosion in history—1,500 times larger than the bombs dropped on Hiroshima and Nagasaki combined.

January 16, 1963

Still exulting in the successful thermonuclear detonation more than a year earlier, Nikita Khrushchev boasted with great fanfare that the Soviet Union had constructed an even more powerful 100-megaton bomb. He declared that it was hidden somewhere in East Germany. The Soviet people proclaimed their new superweapon, "Tsar Bomba," the Czar Bomb.

CHAPTER ONE

Khalid Rasul pushed his way warily through the thick brush shrouding the broad hill, clutching his Tabuk assault rifle, scanning the surrounding German woods. He didn't like forests. He was used to the broad rocky expanse of the Middle Eastern desert, where he had so often stalked and killed an enemy. At least the forest was quiet, except for the dull thunk of picks and shovels, as his crew dug into the earth below. He had chosen where to dig by picking the most likely spot to reveal an entrance to what might be hidden beneath the suspicious hill the size of a warehouse.

Working from historical records, Rasul had located the hill and identified it as an artificial feature, possibly the resting place of their prize. The hill was distinctly different from its surroundings. Only brush grew on it, no trees, probably because some structure beneath the soil prevented their roots from taking hold.

The crew did not speak, as they had been so instructed. Voices would carry in the silent woods, and Rasul did not want visitors to their project. The crew was silent because they were loyal to Rasul and his friend and master, Iraqi shipping oligarch Saadallah bin Shadid. They were also quiet because they knew that Rasul was perfectly capable of instantly silencing any who disobeyed. Permanently.

Rasul knew he could not count on his disguise in the coveralls of a German railroad worker to allay any intruders' suspicions. His swarthy features, thick beard and dark, curly hair marked him as not a German. And his muscular physique was distinctly different from the doughy form of so many Germans.

He had planned his response to an intruder. He would give him a friendly greeting, find out if he was alone, and slash his throat. Rasul knew how to do it cleanly, expertly, and silently, as he had done many times in the service of bin Shadid. It required a single vicious, arcing slash that severed both arteries and the voice box. And, he knew to give the victim a shove to launch him backward, so Rasul avoided any spatter from the gush of blood.

But he didn't expect to need this skill during the crucial assignment with which his master had entrusted him. The nearest people to the dig site—the staff of the Stasi Bunker Museum half a mile away—had been warned to keep people away because the supposed railroad construction crew might be blasting to make improvements on the right-of-way. It was a very useful fiction.

Fortunately, it was a fiction Rasul did not have to sell to the railroad. He had bribed the middle-aged local stationmaster of the Leipzig-Dresden railway line to clear the way for him and his crew to do their work. It took only a satchel containing approximately ten times the stationmaster's annual salary, and a subtle threat.

He moved to overlook the crew below, also disguised in railroad coveralls, as they hacked their way through the root-clogged earth into the side closest to the nearby railway line. The workers, smuggled from Iraq, had already chopped through decades of thick overgrowth.

Suddenly, rose the faint clank of metal against metal, followed by an excited, hushed babble from the men. Rasul climbed down from the hill, commanding them in Kurdish to concentrate their digging at that point. He curtly dispatched a guard to the top of the hill to take over the watch.

The workers redoubled their exertions, and in an hour, sweating and panting, they had excavated a section of what appeared to be a huge steel door.

Now mindless of the noise with the prize so close, Rasul summoned the backhoe from the flatbed truck out on the main road.

The waiting men slumped against nearby trees, drinking water, devouring fat German meat loaf sandwiches from backpacks, and dozing.

After half an hour, its engine growling, the machine advanced ponderously through the brush, crushing bushes and flattening small trees. It began to claw large chunks of damp earth away from the hillside, revealing the full extent of two rusting steel doors. They were encrusted with soil from decades of being buried.

At Rasul's command, the workers roused themselves and finished clearing the soil around the doors. They brushed away the final clods of dirt on the doors' surface to reveal a thick chain wound around its handles, secured with a rusted lock.

One worker brought up a cutting torch taken from the backhoe. He donned a welding helmet and ignited its blue flame, applying it to the chain. With hissing and sputtering, the flame cut its way through the rusted metal. After only minutes, the chain parted, dangling from the door's handles. The workers ran a thick steel cable from one of the door's handles to the backhoe.

With a roar of its engine, the backhoe lurched back tightening the cable. With groaning metallic complaint, the door slowly gave way, opening up a crack.

Holding a flashlight, Rasul squeezed his way inside. He coughed at the musty, dust-filled air that likely had not seen ventilation for decades. The flashlight played about the chamber, revealing it to be a huge concrete bunker holding only a metal boxcar resting on rails.

Rasul circled the boxcar, playing the flashlight beam over its surface, inspecting it. At first glance, it resembled any other boxcar. But on closer inspection, it was unlike any other he had ever seen. Its doors were not really doors, but door-like panels welded to heavy metal walls designed to be lifted completely away. The boxcar had a multi-sectioned roof fastened by heavy latches, so they, too could be completely removed. He smiled in satisfaction when he saw that its sides were stenciled with Cyrillic characters. This was a *Soviet* boxcar!

He climbed a ladder at the end of the boxcar, peering across its curved roof. He could see no access hatch. He would have to lift one of the roof sections to see what was inside. He shone his flashlight upward to see mounted on the ceiling a hand-operated crane. It would allow him to lift a roof section. Things were looking promising!

Lowering himself back to the floor, he found a ladder in one corner of the chamber and climbed it to reach the top of one of the boxcar's side walls. He was about to pull one of the roof latches open, but abruptly stopped, his brow knitted in suspicion. Any ordinary thief would not have hesitated to open the latch, lured by the prospect of stealing the gold or other valuables the thief would believe were locked in this elaborately hidden bunker. But Rasul was no ordinary thief. He had not survived on Baghdad streets mined with buried IEDs without an acute sense of danger.

Shining his flashlight at the latch, he could see that it was fitted with electrical contacts, as were the others. He smiled wryly at the cleverness of those who had hidden the boxcar.

He called two of his most trusted guards into the chamber, cautioning them about the electrical contacts and dispatching them to carefully scout the bunker. They moved off, their flashlight beams playing over the gray concrete walls and ceiling.

Rasul launched his own exploration and quickly discovered wires leading to the electrical contacts on the latches. The wires led down to the concrete floor of the bunker and ran along the inside of the steel rails on which the boxcar rested.

A call from one of the guards brought him to the other side of the bunker, his flashlight revealing a row of small black boxes spaced out along where the wall and floor met. The boxes ringed the bunker, each attached to wires connected to the ones Rasul had discovered.

He instructed the men to leave. He would be the only one to die if he made an error. Bin Shadid would want to know of the circumstances of his death.

He gently pried open the lid of one of the metal boxes to see it filled with blocks of black material labeled with "PVV-5A." It was explosive. Each block had a wire running from it, all gathered into a sheaf connected to a battery. He gently traced the wiring, and his experience told him that opening a latch on the boxcar would complete a circuit and detonate the explosives. And he had no doubt that any one detonation would set off all the explosives in the bunker.

Even more worrisome was that the wires were corroded, and the battery was encrusted with white crystals, having deteriorated over decades entombed in the bunker. Thus, the circuit might be unstable, with even the slightest disturbance setting it off.

He took a deep breath, bracing himself for whatever was to come. His master badly wanted the device that was believed to rest in this bunker. He would get it for him, or die trying. He reached down and ever-so-gently pulled the lead off the battery.

Nothing!

He blew a sign of relief, sat down on the cold concrete floor, and whispered *"Alhamdulillah,"* the Muslim prayer of thanks. He proceeded from one metal box to the other, kneeling and detaching the battery leads. With each act, he braced himself for a blast and oblivion.

Finally, he had disarmed all the boxes. He hauled himself back up the ladder. He took a deep breath and unlatched the first latch holding one of the end roof segments to the boxcar wall. Again, no explosion!

He continued the process, one by one opening the latches holding down the roof. He called the guards back in and mounted the roof, directing them to crank down the crane's cable and attach the cable's hooks to the four rings on the roof segment. As the guards cranked the segment up, he shone his flashlight down into the boxcar's depths. The light revealed a massive cylindrical object, shrouded in gray canvas, nearly filling the boxcar. He lowered himself into the boxcar and lifted back the canvas. He gasped and uttered once more "*Alhamdulillah!*"

He had found it! He had done his master and friend the great service of finding it! He quickly snapped photos with his cell phone, replaced the canvas, and climbed out of the boxcar. He had to make sure that none of the workers saw inside the boxcar. He directed the guards to replace the roof, instructing them to make sure that no worker entered the bunker. He tapped his assault rifle, an unspoken instruction about the consequences of such a transgression.

After taking more photos of the dimly lit chamber interior, he followed the rails on which the boxcar rested out of the chamber and into the afternoon sunlight, where they went underground. He directed the men to begin digging along the path outside the chamber. Again came the clank of metal shovels striking buried metal. They were the rails. The builders of the structure had laid the rails leading to the main line in a shallow depression, so they could be buried once the railroad car was in place. To hide the connection to the spur line, the builders had removed only the section of rails connecting at the main line.

So, it would be an easy task to reconnect the spur to the main line and remove the boxcar. He would post his trusted guards on the site overnight. Over the next days, the crew would dig out the rails and reconnect to the spur line.

The bribed stationmaster would be persuaded to route a freight engine along the spur line to connect the boxcar and route it to its destination. Rasul dispatched a guard to obtain the necessary paint and identifying information to disguise the boxcar as an ordinary German freight carrier. In a few months, the pudgy German stationmaster would be found murdered, amid evidence that he had been a drug smuggler.

To further erase any sign of the operation, Rasul would then bring new batteries, reconnect the explosives and detonate them to bring down the structure. Should anyone figure out what the bunker had held, they would believe that it had been buried beneath tons of rubble.

As the crew dug their way along the rails to uncover their length, Rasul took out his cell phone and encrypted the images he had taken, transmitting them.

He sent with the images a text message in Kurdish that said simply, "We have found Vanya." He found grim satisfaction that he had given his master the instrument of revenge for the soul-crushing horror he had suffered. Americans had killed his master's family. Millions would pay the price.

***

Wenzel Fischer slumped in the worn armchair sipping his tea, his bony hand trembling slightly, his walker beside him. He liked to take afternoon tea in the small German community center and watch the elderly ladies at their knitting. They sat at the long wooden table, their crafts piled before them, gossiping and making the baby booties, shawls, and other items to sell.

But today he was not at his ease. Today, the anxiety over the newspaper article gnawed at him. He had said too much to the reporter. He had showed the reporter his wooden box full of the yellowed pages from his time as a supply clerk for the East German Stasi.

He cursed his stupidity! True, he had asked the reporter not to put anything in the article about his role in the mysterious construction project in Machern. But the reporter did, anyway.

Frau Richter had noticed his worried expression and come over to comfort him. "You are all right, Wenzel?" she had asked, patting his stooped shoulder. "You look uncomfortable."

He merely nodded, so she had asked him what was causing his worry. "The article. It had things in it. About my time back then. I didn't want that. I didn't want that." Then he pointedly went back to his tea. She smiled and understood that he wished not to talk further, and went back to her knitting.

But he couldn't forget that time. He sat and sipped his tea and remembered ordering the huge amount of cement and steel reinforcement for the project. And the explosives, the large amount of explosives. Since he worked for the Stasi, none of the suppliers ever questioned the orders.

He remembered particularly the massive steel doors he had been tasked to procure. As with the other suppliers, the owner of the foundry knew better than to question the order.

But Wenzel Fischer was curious, as young men foolishly are. He remembered going to the site during construction and telling the foreman he only wanted to check whether the materials were being delivered properly. He was ordered away with an ominous warning not to return. But he realized that things were not right when he heard the construction workers speaking Russian.

This was *not* a German crew, and he suspected that the guards were KGB. In fact, it was a Russian-accented guard with a Russian AK-47 assault rifle who had threatened him.

Still, he was so curious that when the supply orders had stopped, and he was sure the construction was complete, he had sneaked out to the site at night. He had made his way cautiously through the thick woods, until his flashlight revealed a massive mountain of new compacted soil. He had circled it, looking for some sign of a structure, but there was only the mountain. He had climbed to the top. He only realized that he was standing on a buried structure when he had picked up a stick to dig down in the dirt and it struck concrete.

He was making his way back through the woods, when another discovery revealed the horror of what had happened at the site. Taking another route back, he had come upon a clearing in the woods. His flashlight revealed an area of freshly turned earth maybe ten meters long and ten meters wide. He stood puzzled for only a moment when the realization struck him. *It was a mass grave!*

As he sat in his chair decades later, he still shuddered at the recollection. A voice brought him out of his reverie.

"You are the man in the newspaper article?" The questioner was a wiry man with a thin face in a hooded jacket, wearing a canvas knapsack. The man smiled, but his smile was as frightening as if he had pointed a gun at Fischer. And his eyes were dead, like those of a snake Fischer had once seen at the zoo.

Incongruously, the man held in his hand a rag doll that he had apparently bought from one of the ladies. Despite his ingratiating purchase, they were all glancing suspiciously at him.

"Uh. . . I don't want to talk about it," said Fischer, putting down his teacup. As the man loomed over him, the wolfish smile still on his face, Fischer took up his walker, beginning the arduous process of pulling himself up. He had to escape this man!

"But it was fascinating that you worked for the Stasi. . . ," said the man. ". . . that you helped them with construction. Could I ask you more about it? About your records?"

"No, I have to leave. I need to take my medicine." With a grunt, Fischer began to hobble away.

"Perhaps I could come to your apartment, and we could talk. Where do you live?"

"I need my medicine. I need to go."

The man looked back at the women, who by now were staring at him with open suspicion. "Ah, well, perhaps later," he said.

Wenzel Fischer fled as fast as his walker would allow. He had to get to his apartment. He had to get to the box that had rested under his floorboards for many decades. He had kept the box for so long because he had been haunted by that project and the mass grave. His conscience told him that he should keep those records to preserve the memory of whatever went on. He was only a minor player in that dark history, but no matter what happened to him, he felt a responsibility to preserve evidence of it.

And he knew how to do that.

***

The thief had quickly left the community center under the glare of the old women. Those gossipy old women would likely tell the police if he showed up again. He didn't want them to see him following the old German, so he had walked out the front door, but circled the quiet block to enter the courtyard behind the building. The old man was slow, so the thief arrived in time to see which apartment he had entered.

It was late afternoon, so the thief went to a nearby Brauhaus to drink beer and have dinner. He really didn't like this particular job. He was a thief, not a murderer, he persuaded himself, although he had killed two men in the course of his career. But those kills were in furtherance of a job, making them a necessity. So also would be this kill. So he was still primarily a thief, not a murderer really. Besides, the pay was very, very good.

He continued to nurse a mild unease over the job, as well as several beers, until late in the evening. He checked that the community center was closed and the women gone. He picked up his knapsack and made his way back to the courtyard and up to the apartment door. All was quiet. Old people go to bed early.

He tried the door. It was locked, so he took his lock picks out of his knapsack and deftly picked the lock as he had done so many times before.

He stepped inside, waiting silently in the dark for any sign he had been detected. There was none. He reached into the knapsack and pulled out the small gas bottle and the attached face mask he had been given.

He stepped quietly into the small bedroom. The sound of rattled breathing told the thief the old man was asleep. In the dim light from the window, he could see the old man lying on his back on a little cot in the corner. He turned the valve on the gas bottle to start the flow of carbon dioxide.

Striding across the room, he straddled the old man, pinned his arms, pushed the mask over his face, and held it there.

He was surprised at the weakness of the response, as the old man writhed feebly beneath his weight. The old man grunted as he struggled, but fortunately, the sound was muffled by the mask.

The thief was also surprised how quickly that struggling ceased, as the old man died. A fetid odor arose from the body, causing him to gag, as the old man's sphincter opened in death, and his bowels emptied. Enduring the stench, he held the mask on for another minute to make sure the old man was dead. Then, he climbed off the corpse, checking to make sure the thin blanket was arranged so as not to look like somebody had crouched on it.

Now he had all night to find the box. Over the next two hours, he searched every possible hiding place in the small apartment. He thought his search had ended when he discovered the loose floorboards in the corner by the small coal stove. But when he pried them up, the niche was empty.

Alter wichser! The thief spat, cursing the old man. The box was not there! He would not get the other half of his fee, even though he had done most of the work for this job in killing the old man. His employers were ruthless and powerful, so he might himself be in danger!

He decided he would do the only thing possible. He would have to watch and wait. Maybe somebody in the community center had the box.

CHAPTER TWO

B enjamin Webber didn't realize he had forgotten his umbrella on the trolley until he reached the steps of the townhouse. His mind was elsewhere, as he walked four blocks from where he had emerged from Berlin's subway, the U-Bahn.

By then, an icy rain of the German winter had begun. It soaked his stocking cap into a cold slab that chilled his head, and his woolen sports jacket into a sodden shroud. He had been neglectful because he had been immersed in thought on the commute from the university to the townhouse rented for his sabbatical. Now he was immersed in rain.

He did have the presence of mind to instinctively clutch his leather briefcase close to his side, as if that would keep it dry. He had critical papers inside, along with his laptop.

He trudged up the stone steps, pausing at the door. He patted his pockets, realizing that unlocking the door would not be possible. His keys were likely still on his desk at the university.

Today, he had good reason to be absent-minded. As an historian, he had made a major discovery that would send his research soaring to a whole new level.

He knocked on the door and expected a considerable wait while Abby came to answer. But the door opened almost immediately.

She stood there grinning at him, holding her cell phone that she had used to track him. She was a pixie of a woman with long auburn hair swept up in an unruly bun, wide brown eyes, a pert nose, and lips charmingly upturned at the edges. She wore those ridiculous fat fuzzy slippers she loved to tromp around the house in. And, she wore a flower-bedecked house dress that didn't quite conceal her pregnant belly.

"*Benjamin*," she declared in mock scolding. "You are one wet puppy."

"Abigail," he mirrored back, smiling with guilt. "I kind of forgot—"

"Come in here, right now, sir," she commanded with amused officiousness. "We need to warm you up."

He stepped inside the hallway and peeled off the wet cap, and she helped him off with his soaked jacket. Then she gave him a long delicious hug, embracing his taut form.

Her soft touch warmed him body and soul, and he breathed in her lovely aroma of shampoo and some undefinable womanly scent. He felt her growing baby bump against his stomach and reached down to pat it.

"How is Schnitzel? Is he a happy little guy?"

"Schnitzel was very busy today," she said, patting her belly. "He was flippin' and flutterin' all day." After learning a week ago that they were having a boy, they began jokingly testing the oddest names they could think of.

She had brought a towel and thoroughly rubbed his thick, curly, black hair and gently patted his face with its fine features. His face dried, they enjoyed a long kiss, which inspired him to ask, "Maybe we can postpone dinner?" He glanced significantly at the stairs leading to the second floor and their bedroom.

"Well, it will be postponed, but not for the reason you'd prefer, my love. We're expecting visitors. I called to tell you, but you didn't answer. I texted, too, about them. . . and to tell you to bring home milk."

"Oh, Jeez, sorry, I had it on vibrate because I was in the Stasi Museum all morning. I forgot to turn the ringer back on when I went back to the office. *Abby, I identified the central monster!*"

"Oh my God, really?"

"Yes, he was a colonel in the Stasi Office of the Minister."

"Tell me all about it after you've talked to the ladies. They're due about now."

"Ladies?"

"The one who called said she and her friends needed to see you about something very important. She asked if you were a *kompetenter Professor.* Competent professor. I told her you were *prima.*"

"*Prima?*"

"Tip-top. The best. I also told her you were a pussycat."

"You *do* make me purr," he said smiling and hugging her. "Thanks for the buildup."

She headed back to the kitchen to make coffee, and he went into his study off the entrance hall to unpack his briefcase and open his laptop. He had just finished the process when a faint knock at the front door brought him back out into the hall. He answered the door to see three women standing on the stoop with grave expressions.

"*Herr Professor Webber?*" asked one, a slim wrinkled woman with a gaunt, stern face.

"*Ja, ich bin er,*" he answered, opening the door to admit them. *Bitte komm herein.*" He helped them off with their matching gray raincoats and rain hats, including one clutching a scarred wooden box, and led them into the living room. It was sparsely furnished with the simple, sturdy furniture installed in townhouses assigned to visiting faculty. A small fire flickered in the ceramic-tiled fireplace.

Ben sat in one of the room's two large armchairs, and the women sat solidly, impassively on the living room couch. The other two sitting beside the slim woman were of the plump variety with short gray hair, who were commonly seen in markets trundling about filling shopping carts. All wore simple print dresses and black sensible shoes with low heels. The plump woman with the box clutched it tightly on her lap.

Abby entered to offer them coffee or tea, and at her urging, they accepted. She left to fetch the drinks.

Ben smiled warmly, asking *"Wie kann ich Ihnen helfen, meine Damen?"*

The slim woman answered his question, introducing them. *"Ich bin Frau Richter und das sind Frau Hoffman und Frau Haas."* She then asked whether he would prefer that they speak English: *"Würden Sie es vorziehen, dass ich Englisch spreche?"*

Ben chuckled deprecatingly. "That would be extremely helpful. I can speak German if it's easier for you, but I confess my German is still not what it should be."

"We will then speak English," announced Frau Richter with the finality of a stern German matriarch.

Abby arrived and served the tea and coffee, then settled in the other armchair, adjusting her body to gain whatever comfort was possible, given her pregnant state.

Ben repeated his earlier question, now in English: "So, how may I help you ladies?"

"You study the Stasi?" asked Frau Richter. She hissed the last word, as did all Germans when mentioning the notorious East German secret police who had terrorized the populace during the Soviet occupation. "We asked at university, and they told us."

"I do," said Ben.

"Why?" asked Frau Richter. "Why would you want to study them?"

"They were one of the most brutal, oppressive organizations in history, along with such groups as the Nazi SS, the KGB, and the Juntong in China. As an historian, I became interested in why they were so brutally effective. If we can understand that, we can understand how to fight them, to stop groups like them."

"And you are finding why they are effective?" asked Frau Richter.

"I think so. I'm drilling down into the organizations to discover what I call the hidden monsters. Many times it wasn't the most prominent leader that made these groups so effective. It was the lesser-known officers. It's always been said that to kill a beast you cut off its head, but I think we can really undermine, even destroy these organizations by targeting these hidden monsters. Besides teaching at my university, I consult for the US government to help develop strategies to do that."

"And you make *Entdeckungen* . . . discoveries. . . about Stasi?"

"Yes, in fact, today I just identified a major hidden monster in the Stasi hierarchy."

Frau Richter looked questioningly over at the other women, and they nodded back in assent for her to continue.

"We will trust you with some Stasi records that we want to give to someone who can figure out what they mean." Frau Hoffman, tightly clutching the wooden box, raised her eyebrows and peering at him over rimless glasses.

Ben raised his eyebrows, as well. An old box like that could hold important historical documents. "I have to ask, why did you come to my home? Why not my office. And how did you find out where I live?"

"When I tell you about the records, you will understand why we come here. And Frau Hoffman found your address. She is *ein Hacker*."

Frau Hoffman shrugged in modest pride.

"So, tell me about them," said Ben.

Frau Richter paused, clasping her hands in front of her. "Every day, we go to community center in our neighborhood. We have coffee, knit things to sell, just be together. We are mostly women, but one old man, Wenzel Fischer, came just about every day. He lived in an apartment behind the center. He never said much about his past, but one day, this reporter came. A newspaper reporter. He said that he had tracked Herr Fischer, because Herr Fischer used to work for Stasi. The reporter was doing an article on Stasi. Herr Fischer insisted he was not really Stasi, but only worked for them on projects. He said he was only clerk, ordering materials. The reporter interviewed Herr Fischer, and the article was in the newspaper about how he had ordered materials. He showed the reporter papers he had saved. From his time with Stasi. These papers." She reached over and patted the wooden box.

"So, what are the papers?"

"We have looked at them. They were records of a construction project at Stasi bunker in Machern. He told reporter Russians built it. But when he realized what he had said to the reporter, he became very frightened. He begged the reporter not to mention the project or the papers, but it was in the article anyway."

"Do you know why he was frightened?" asked Ben.

"No, but after article came out, a man came to our center. He asked Herr Fischer about the project. We all saw that Herr Fischer was frightened, and when the man saw how we disapproved, he left. That was when Herr Fischer came back and brought us his box. He said if anything happened, we were to give the box to someone who would know what to do with it."

"So, can I ask Herr Fischer about the box?"

"No," said Frau Richter. The women's expressions grew somber. Frau Hoffman began to weep, dabbing her eyes with a handkerchief.

"Why not?"

"He is dead. We think. . . *ermordet*. She paused, looking for the word in English. "Murdered."

***

Ben hunched his slim frame over the scarred oak desk in his study and pored over the papers from the box. The documents were brittle and yellowed, matching the era of the battered wooden box. As an historian, Ben was so accustomed to judging the provenance of historical documents that he did it almost unconsciously. Not only were the documents old, but the box showed decades of grime and scarring, likely secreted away under a bed, in a closet, or in some niche.

The contents seemed mostly prosaic; nothing more than invoices for building materials—including large amounts of concrete and steel girders. One invoice that stood out was for two large steel doors to be produced at a foundry in Leipzig. The most striking order, however, was for large amounts of the explosive, called PVV-5A, used by Soviets during the era.

The materials were to be delivered to someplace called "*Stasi-Bunker Lübschützer Teiche*" in Machern, a village near Leipzig. The English translation of the location was the "Stasi bunker Lübschützer ponds."

He opened his laptop and did a search of Stasi facilities. The bunker was a secret fallout shelter for elite Stasi, hidden away in the East German countryside. It had been built to look like a resort, and was so well disguised that it hadn't even been discovered until decades after the Cold War ended.

As was his custom, he took handwritten notes on a yellow pad as he inspected the contents. Even though he had a computer, scribbling on paper was a way to work through a problem.

"Sweetie, you need to eat," said Abby leaning against the study doorway, her arms cradling her belly, and with her puffy slippers crossed in mock impatience. "We *three* need to eat," she added, patting her belly. "I made currywurst and fries."

He closed his laptop, replaced the sheaf of documents in the box, and followed her into their small kitchen, where they sat at the wooden table and ate the German sausage with its spicy curry ketchup. He washed his meal down with beer, and she drank Apfelschorle—a soft drink of apple juice and sparkling mineral water.

"So, what do you make of the ladies and their box and their murdered friend?" she asked.

"The box seems genuine," he said. "The documents don't seem all that unusual, but they certainly have significance, or he wouldn't have hidden them. As for the murder, from what I can tell that's just their theory. You remember, they said the police concluded it was a natural death. And when I asked about it, the ladies said he was found in his bed, and although his apartment was messy, it didn't seem as if there had been a burglary."

"More important, tell me about your hidden monster. And I'll make you a deal. I'll tell you about my hidden *treasure*."

"I'd rather hear about yours first." He always took great pleasure in hearing about her explorations as an art historian. It was such a relief from his own grim work. And it reminded him how they had met in Washington. She had asked his help in tracking down artworks stolen by the Nazis. Now, she was exploring Berlin for public art neglected by the popular guidebooks, much to the absolute delight of the Berlin tourism bureau.

She spun out her story of discovery of a sculpture hidden away in the courtyard of a restaurant. And he told her of the Stasi hidden monster, as they continued their conversation over dinner. Afterward, he returned to the study to examine the documents in the box.

He puzzled further over the kind of construction project that would require cement, steel girders, and huge custom steel doors. On his second pass through the documents, he also discovered a large order for railroad ties and rails. Why would a concrete-and-steel structure need railroad access? Even more puzzling was the order for explosives. Why would blasting be needed for a building?

He was pondering his notes about the papers when Abby padded in, leaned over, and placed her soft cheek next to his, her silky hair brushing his face. He expected to hear a sweet-nothing in his ear. Instead, in a breathy, sexy tone, she whispered.

"Milk."

He laughed and got up, hugging her. "Yes, dear. Right away, dear."

He put on his raincoat, pulled a dry hat from a hook by the door, picked up Abby's umbrella and opened the front door. He remembered he didn't have his keys, so he left the door unlocked. He plunged into the gloomy, drizzly night, stepping carefully down the slick, wet steps, and headed for the neighborhood market two blocks down.

At the store, he bought a liter of milk from the young, bearded man at the counter and started back toward the townhouse. He kept the umbrella lowered in front of him to ward off a rainy breeze, glancing up only occasionally at the sidewalk ahead.

He was a block away when he looked up to see a dark figure emerging from their townhouse. It was hooded, and it rushed down the steps turned toward him, and then looked up. He saw only a flash of a surprised face and something clutched under its arm. It quickly reversed and ran away.

Puzzlement was giving rise to unease, then a growing dread. The figure had not behaved like an innocent person. He furled the umbrella and quickened his pace, then broke into a sprint. Reaching the townhouse, still grasping the milk, he plunged through the door, pitching the umbrella aside. Entering the warmth of the townhouse, he smelled a faint, unfamiliar metallic odor. His anxiety rose further, clutching at his chest.

"Abby?" he called. No answer. Then "*Abby!*" He looked into the living room, where she had gone to read, but she wasn't there. Then he turned toward the study.

His breath deserted him at what he saw: Abby's feet extending from behind the desk, one clad in a fuzzy slipper, the other bare, a slipper nearby.

With a shocked grunt, he dropped the milk and rushed into the room.

Abby lay on her back, her arms flung out, her eyes open and staring. Her head rested in a pool of blood that had flowed from a deep gash in the side of her skull.

His mouth gaped open in horror, but no words emerged; only a long, agonized moan. He collapsed to the floor beside her inert body, gathering her into his arms, not knowing what to do. He took her face in one hand, then tried to cover the wound, feeling the wet sticky blood that covered the side of her head.

What to do? What to do? He began to sob, as he felt her neck for a pulse. *None!* Tears filled his eyes, as he reached down to feel her chest for a heartbeat. *None!* Then he looked down to see her round belly, and loosed a searing, soul-deep scream.

***

"Herr Webber?" asked the stocky police officer. "*Herr Webber?*" he asked again.

Ben didn't answer. He slumped on the couch, head bowed, sobs racking his body, his face buried in blood-caked hands. He still wore his raincoat, now stained with blood.

He looked at his hands, at her blood on them. The blood would wash way. But not the horrific memory. And not the guilt.

"It's my fault," he breathed to himself.

"Herr Webber, what do you mean?"

He looked up at the officer, not really seeing him. He turned to look dully out at the hallway and across at the people in the study where Abby's body still lay. The flash of a camera periodically lit the room.

"I left the door unlocked."

"On purpose?" asked the officer, who was dressed in a dark suit and black tie. Two other similarly dressed men stood beside him.

"Yes . . . well I mean I didn't have a key," answered Ben. "I left it at the office." He vaguely recalled phoning the police. He had first punched in 911, then remembered he was in Berlin and called 112.

Meine Frau! Meine Frau ist verletzt!" He had exclaimed "*Bitte komm! Bitte senden Sie Hilfe!*" But at first, he couldn't remember his address, finally stammering it out.

Within minutes, emergency technicians had arrived. He didn't remember answering the door. Immediately afterward came uniformed officers, and after that the men in the suits.

"So, you are saying that would be the reason there was no sign of a forced entry. That is your story?"

"Who are you?" asked Ben dully.

"I am detective Koch with the LKA."

"LKA?" asked Ben.

"*Landeskriminalamt.* Criminal investigators."

"Oh."

"Herr Webber, let us start at the beginning. Tell me what happened." said Koch.

"My wife was killed. Somebody killed her."

"Herr Webber, did you have a fight with her?"

"What? No. There was a man. I saw a man."

"In the house?"

"Coming out."

"What did he look like?"

"I don't know. It was dark. He wore a hood."

"So it was a burglary?"

"I guess."

"What was taken, Herr Webber?"

Ben looked vaguely around. "I don't know."

"Where were you during this?"

"I was out. I got milk. Down the street."

One of the men said to Koch, "*Es lag ein Liter Milch auf dem Boden.*"

Koch replied, "*Fragen Sie den Verkäufer im Geschäft,*" and the man left.

To Ben, he said, "We see that you had milk. So, you got milk from the store and came home. Did you get angry?"

"Angry? Why would you think I got angry? A man broke in."

"Herr Webber, you are saying a man just came in. But we have no witnesses who saw an intruder. My fellow detective will go with you to clean up and change. Then, Herr Webber, we will take you to our headquarters to be questioned."

"Am I under arrest? I need to make a call."

"No, this is just questioning . . . for now."

"I need to call my sister, my lawyer."

"Yes, you can make both calls."

"It's just one. My sister is my lawyer."

***

Saadallah bin Shadid never exited his jet on the tarmac. He always waited until the sleek Gulfstream G650ER had been towed into a hangar, its gleaming surface reflecting the overhead lights. Bin Shadid wanted no visual record of his personal travels, even though his jet's flights were tracked, as were all aircraft.

So his jet rolled into the rented hangar at the Berlin Tegel airport, and his men hurried down its steps and closed the hangar doors.

Bin Shadid stepped out of the plane, a wiry man with a caramel complexion and a precisely trimmed beard that exactly followed his jawline. He wore a pinstripe suit, a dark blue tie with a University of Oxford pattern, and a red- checkered traditional Middle Eastern headdress.

His guards stood stiffly behind him as he regarded the man standing before him with the impassive expression of one looking at an object of only mild interest. Under his cold gaze, the thief dressed in a dark hoodie shifted nervously from one foot to the other. He grasped a battered wooden box flecked with red spots. He opened his mouth to speak, but was stopped by a frown and a slow shake of the head from one of the guards.

They stood silently for a long moment, then bin Shadid said quietly, "What did you bring me?"

"Um. . . these are the papers that the old man had kept. I killed him as I was instructed . . . . with the mask." The thief held his hand over his face, showing how he had placed the inhalation mask over the face of the sleeping old man and fed carbon dioxide from the small gas cylinder into his lungs. Such a murder would leave no trace and no sign of a struggle.

"But you didn't find the box at his apartment, I have been told?" asked bin Shadid.

"Um. . . . well . . . No. I searched thoroughly his apartment. There was nothing there. I kept watching the center where the old ladies were. I came back the next day and waited all day. That night, the women came out carrying the box. They were hurrying."

"Then how did you get the box?" asked bin Shadid, motioning for one of his men to take it from the thief.

"I followed the women. They went to a house. A man came to the door and let them in. After a while, the women left without the box. So I thought I would break in late at night and get it. But then the man left. It didn't look like he had locked the door. So I went ahead tried it and got in. I thought I could sneak in, but a woman caught me. I didn't know she was there."

His security chief Khalid Rasul approached him and whispered in his ear, then moved away. Bin Shadid frowned and raised his hand.

"You killed the woman," he stated to the thief.

"She saw me," the thief replied, shrugging to indicate the necessity of his action. "I had to do something. She could identify me. It was unfortunate, but I got the box like you wanted."

"What is that on your face?" asked bin Shadid.

The thief touched the two long red scratches on his left cheek. "She struggled. She fought."

Bin Shadid turned to Rasul and nodded, uttering only "Šamšir." Rasul nodded back at the Persian nickname he had proudly given himself decades ago. He was his master's "sword." Bin Shadid turned back to the thief. "You will be paid." He made an offhanded wave to Rasul, turned, and boarded the plane.

One of bin Shadid's men approached the thief, taking out a fat envelope. The thief grinned, nodded, and reached out to accept it. He handed the box over to the man, not noticing Rasul looming behind him. Rasul reached up, grasped the thief's head, and with a powerful twist, snapped his neck. The faint crack of the severing spine was absorbed by the vastness of the hangar.

The thief crumpled to the ground, his head lolling on a broken neck. Another of bin Shadid's guards pulled a body bag out of the cargo hold. Rasul retrieved the envelope, as two others deftly lifted the thief's corpse into the bag, zipped it up, and hauled it off to a corner of the hangar, there stuffing it into a four-foot-square crate.

The men boarded the plane, one carrying the wooden box. But Rasul and two of his men remained, stepping away to be out of the departing jet's path. Rasul took out his cell phone and made two calls. One was to a freight company with instructions to pick up the crate for transport. The other was to the Gardener.

CHAPTER THREE

The Gardener, a small, stooped man with a thick, gray beard and a disheveled mop of salt-and-pepper hair, climbed out of the white van. He pressed the button on the outside of the corrugated steel warehouse in the dusty industrial park outside the city of Erbil, Iraq. The overhead door to his windowless building began to rattle open.

He returned to the van and backed it in. His two sons—athletic, dark-haired young men dressed as he was in gray coveralls—climbed out of the van's back doors, waiting for his inspection of its cargo. He always examined crates before unloading them, even though he and his sons had been the ones who loaded them in the first place. They had also inspected the crate when it was unloaded from the private jet, the preferred method of receiving such sensitive cargo.

The large entry room of the warehouse looked like any other gardening shed. It was piled with bags of fertilizer, bottles of pesticide, and gardening tools stacked in one corner. But at the back of the room were two large steel doors, and when the Gardener keyed in a code and opened them, the warehouse's real purpose was revealed. The huge brightly lit room held an array of stainless-steel machines whose combined purpose was to make corpses disappear.

The Gardener held his cell phone in his hand, as he always did when the door to the warehouse was open. Should any intruder appear, he would key in a code to detonate the 14 charges of C4 explosive installed around the warehouse. They were attached to barrels of gasoline, ensuring that the building would be instantly engulfed in flames. But all was peaceful today.

So, he pressed the button to close the outside door, pushed his rimless glasses up on his nose and scrutinized the wooden crate, finally nodding in approval. Bin Shadid's men had constructed it to the standard size that the Gardener required, and there had been no sign of tampering and no leakage. He signaled to his two sons, and they hefted the crate out of the van and onto a dolly.

Back in his office, the Gardener didn't bother to check his laptop to see whether the standard disposal fee for the crate's grisly contents had been deposited in his Swiss bank account. This job was gratis because this package came from bin Shadid. After all, his master had set him up in this business.

The Gardener had, indeed, served as bin Shadid's head gardener, and he still supervised the gardens at the oligarch's six estates. But one landmark day, bin Shadid had asked him to do a very special, private favor. One of bin Shadid's security men had killed an employee who had made the deadly error of stealing from the oligarch. The man's body needed to be disposed of. The Gardener had readily agreed to the task, given his absolute loyalty. A meticulous man, he had done a particularly efficient job of erasing every vestige of the thief's corporeal existence.

Over the next year, the Gardener was called upon not only to dispose of bodies for bin Shadid, but to vanish numerous inconvenient corpses produced by other of bin Shadid's associates. Those associates included Middle Eastern warlords, with whom bin Shadid had a particular interest in currying favor.

As the demand for disposals grew, bin Shadid provided the Gardener the capital and protection to set up what was now a lucrative—and for bin Shadid politically advantageous—business. Its efficiency was evident in this day's disposal of the corpse from Berlin.

The Gardener's sons pried open the crate and pulled out the packages of dry ice that surrounded the cargo. They lifted out the body bag, zipping it open, extracting the thief's corpse. By now, the sons were able to tolerate the lingering stench of dead bodies. This corpse, however, was neater than many they had handled. There was no sign of torture, no blood. Only a broken neck.

They hefted the body onto a stainless-steel gurney. They stripped away its shoes and clothes and bundled them off to be disposed of, along with the crate. They also removed three bejeweled rings and a watch.

The watch would be ground into metallic dust, but the Gardener and his sons were allowed to profit from any other jewelry, as long as they melted the metal down to sell as anonymous ingots. They could also keep any gems to sell, as long as the diamonds were not engraved with an identifying serial number. The Gardener took the jewelry to his work table, where he began prying out the gems. For the remaining metal, he used a small furnace and chemicals to extract the gold to make pure gold bars.

In his business's early days, the Gardener had realized that simply burying bodies was out of the question. Informants could reveal their location. And corpses held clues that could be followed. He had first resorted to cremating bodies on piles of wood and later dismembered in a furnace. But as his throughput grew, he realized that incineration was a cumbersome method. And the emissions from such fires might be noticed, not to mention rumors that his building was a crematorium. And besides, incineration was polluting. So, he had found a less conspicuous, more environmentally friendly disposal method.

That method was water cremation. It used a cylindrical, stainless-steel chamber into which the sons slid the thief's pale, naked body. One son sealed its door, and the other pushed a red button, triggering a whooshing sound, as the machine filled with a corrosive alkaline solution. The solution, pressurized and heated to 300 degrees Fahrenheit, would dissolve the corpse's tissues into a tea-colored liquid that would be flushed down the drain. No telltale DNA would survive the process.

While the chamber did its job, the sons went about bleaching the clothes and the crate. They fed them into an industrial shredder, reducing them to a compacted mass that would go out in the trash.

They returned to the chamber after 90 minutes and emptied it of the skull and bones, ignoring the cloying, pungent aroma of the alkaline solution wafting out of the machine. They took care to look for metal implants and bullets. There were none with this corpse, but if there had been, they would have been melted down.

The sons loaded the skull and bones into a commercial clothes dryer, which clattered noisily away for half an hour. They then ground the skull and bones into a coarse gray powder using a cremulator—an industrial-size blender. After sifting through the powder to pick out stray metal dental fillings, they bagged it.

The Gardener instructed his sons to ship the bag to bin Shadid's villa in Baghdad. The gardens there needed fertilizing, and the human bone meal was quite excellent. The Gardener smiled in satisfaction. He was very proud that bin Shadid's gardens were famous for being particularly lush. They had won awards.

He called Khalid Rasul to inform him that the "package" had been received and processed. The security chief told him that bin Shadid would spend the next day in his Erbil villa tending his business interests. Then, he would fly 2,400 miles to a private airstrip in Bulgaria. The Gardener was told to expect more packages.

***

"You went to get milk, you came home. For some reason you got angry. And you killed her," said Detective Koch, standing beside the steel table in the interrogation room.

Ben sat across the table in the gray-walled room, his head in his hands. He looked up, his eyes puffy, his cheeks tear-stained. His hair was unkempt, his clothes rumpled from spending the night on a cot in a holding cell after hours of questioning. And now, the next morning, more questioning.

"Dear God, why would I do that?" he asked, his voice choking. "I loved her. I loved her so much. She was carrying our baby. Our son." He lowered his head back into his hands.

Koch sat down, his expression softening. "I understand how hard it is to have a wife who nags you, who is pregnant and demanding."

Ben said nothing, just shaking his head slowly. "There was a man," he said tiredly. "I've told you all night. I've told you over and over there was a man."

"And he just came in a door you left unlocked. Did you hire a man to kill your wife? Did you not want to be a father, and hired a man?"

"God no! But there was a man!"

"We looked at cameras in the area. But it was dark and rainy. None of them showed anything. And nothing was taken from your house."

After a long silence, Ben looked up, his brow furrowing. He held up one hand, waving it back and forth to pause the interrogation. He said quietly, "On the desk. The desk in the study. Was there a box? A wooden box?"

Koch took out his cell phone and began swiping through crime scene photos. "No, just papers."

Ben sat back and took a deep tremulous breath. "*Oh, dear God! He took the box! The box with the papers! Oh, God! He killed her for the box!*"

The detective swiped through the photos, spreading his fingers to zoom in on some. "There was blood on the desk where her head hit the corner," he said, continuing to swipe through the images. "There's a void in the blood splatter. A rectangular void."

"Yes, that was where the box was! I told you about the women who brought me the box and what they told me about it. Frau Richter,

Frau Hoffman, and Frau Haas. I told you they would tell you I was not angry at Abby. Have you contacted them?"

"My colleague went there." Koch punched a number into his phone, and when his call was answered said, "*Hast du schon mit den Frauen gesprochen?*" He waited for the answer, then muttered "*Ja wirklich? Bist du sicher?*" He ended the call, scowling.

"The women are missing," he said. "Would you know anything about that?"

***

"*Fakakta putz!*" exclaimed the tall, black-suited woman as she swept into the interrogation room. Her thick, black hair was swept up in a tight bun, and she carried a leather briefcase, and a large red handbag slung over her left shoulder. Her sharp features and thin lips were formed into an angry scowl, her brown eyes glaring at Detective Koch. It was late afternoon, and the remnants of lunch littered the table in the room.

"Who are you, and what did you just say?" demanded Koch.

Ben looked up from the table, an expression of relief on his face. "That is my sister, and she called you a blithering idiot."

"I am Azariah Webber-Friedman, and I am also his lawyer," she said. "You will free him immediately."

"You are an American—"

"How very observant you are, Herr Detective."

"You cannot practice law in Germany."

With a commanding flick of her wrist, Azariah beckoned outside the interrogation room door, and three men entered. Two wore conservative business suits, and a third wore a black pullover sweater and khaki pants.

"But these two lawyers can," she replied gesturing at the suited men. "They will arrange for my brother's immediate release. You have already kept him twenty-four hours. And this man. . ." she gestured at the man in the sweater ". . . is one of Germany's foremost forensic experts. You will have him escorted to the morgue, where he can review the evidence and examine the. . ." she paused, her expression changing to one of sadness, her head bowing ". . . examine Abby."

Koch began, "Mr. Webber will remain in custody until we can"

"*Kish Meine Touchess, Herr Detective,*" interrupted Azariah.

Ben translated, "She said you can kiss—"

"I know what she said," said Koch.

"You may leave us, so we can confer with our client," said Azariah. Scowling, Koch gathered up his files and left.

"Yiddish, Azzy?" Asked Ben, standing up from the table and embracing her. "You cursed him in Yiddish?"

"It's a tactic I use with adversaries, dearest brother," she said hugging him tightly. "It throws them off balance." She held the hug for a long moment, whispering, "My heart breaks for you, Benjamin. Oh, dear God, my heart breaks. Abby was such a wonderful. . ." she could not finish the sentence. She stepped back, her eyes moist, and paused to recover herself.

Her expression returned to its combative glower. She sat in the chair across from him, beckoning to the two German lawyers to do the same, and they pulled up chairs. She introduced them, as Herr Berger and Herr Sommer, then said,

"Thank God you called me the instant you were detained! I immediately called my firm's Berlin office, retained these gentlemen, and got the next flight to Germany. Now, tell us everything that happened. You can speak English. Herr Sommer can translate for Herr Berger."

***

Azariah sat on the bed in the hotel room, her head bowed, clutching her phone. She tapped the send button to transmit the photos she had taken of Ben's arms and face to the German lawyers, Sommer and Berger. "The police will want to examine you in person, but these should hold them."

"She fought the killer," Ben said sadly. "Abby fought." He rolled down his sleeves and slumped down in a chair in the room, a sleekly modern suite in a downtown Berlin high rise.

"Yes, she did, indeed. The skin the forensic examiner found under her nails showed that, and so did the bruises. And your lack of scars shows you could not possibly have been her attacker."

"It was my fault, Azzie. I left the door unlocked."

"We Jews are good at guilt, but dear brother, this is not a time to feel guilty. Think about this: The guy was a professional burglar. He was obviously hired to get that box. So, whether the door was locked or not made no difference. Do you understand?"

"I will still feel guilty. If I hadn't accepted that box. If I hadn't left the door unlocked—"

"*Ben, it was not your fault!*"

Ben shrugged his shoulders. "Logical as always, Azzie. What happens now?"

"We'll get her body released as soon as possible. I've contacted a synagogue, and they'll arrange a burial society to prepare her. We'll take her back to Philadelphia. That's where her folks want the funeral to be. . . her hometown. You can sit shiva with them. That okay?"

"Whatever gives them some measure of comfort."

"Mom and Dad will come. Then, you can go back to DC?"

He looked up at her and shook his head decisively. "No, I'm coming back here." He rose up and went into the bathroom, scrubbing his face, leaning over the sink, his head down.

"Why? Surely the university would excuse you from the fellowship."

He emerged from the bathroom, his expression grim. "Oh, I won't be returning to the fellowship."

"Then what?"

"I'm going to find whoever killed Abby."

"That's not a good idea, Benjamin. Let the cops do their job. They know how—"

"They don't know how to do what I can do." Ben took a deep breath. His expression had transformed from one of grief to a clenched-jaw look of determination.

"What can you do?"

"I know how to research historical records better than they do. And that box was a starting point."

"But the box is gone."

"Not my notes. They were on the desk." He put on his coat. "I'm going back to the house. I'm going to get them. You need to get me access to the crime scene."

"Ben, just what do you think you're going to do when. . . or *if*. . . you find who did it?"

"I'm going to kill them."

CHAPTER FOUR

B in Shadid donned the tattered cloth cap and exited out the door of his jet and into the gathering gloom. His disguise also included a worn, brown cloth jacket and black work pants with holes in them. His precisely shaved beard was the only incongruous contrast to the shabby appearance he sought.

There was no hangar at the small Lesnovo airport outside Sofia, Bulgaria, but he didn't worry about attracting curious gossip with the landing of his jet. Besides the protection of the descending darkness, Bulgarians had learned under decades of Soviet rule not to ask questions.

Instead of his usual limousine, he climbed into the faded yellow van labeled with a plumbing company logo. His driver, also dressed as a common worker, drove onto the narrow road of cracked asphalt leading to his destination. The flat, brown landscape faded into night as they drove the 15 kilometers to the large railroad repair shop near Kazichene Railway Station. The long-abandoned three-story structure was a rusty patchwork of tin sheeting that bin Shadid had bought through a shell company, and it served his purpose well.

The interior was lit by overhead incandescent lights whose yellow illumination revealed a grease-stained concrete floor, piles of rusting engine parts, and a railroad track leading from the nearby spur line. The factory smelled of oil and dust. On the track nearest the huge sliding doors sat a rusting PM 36-2 type antique steam engine. It had been hauled in with great public fanfare, so that the locals would accept the cover story that the building was being used to restore the train by a wealthy businessman and railroad buff.

But farther into the building, hidden behind a newly built floor-to-ceiling wall, was the railroad car that held the factory's real purpose.

Bin Shadid pushed through the wooden door in the wall into the area, to be greeted by his four guards, all armed with assault rifles. They stiffened at his approach. His head of engineering stepped forward, ducking his head and smiling.

Fayez Badour, a rotund, balding man had been with him for decades, serving him faithfully as he had built his Iraqi shipping empire. Badour would continue to serve him devotedly in this new endeavor. He knew what drove bin Shadid's obsession: the utter, soul-shattering tragedy he had suffered.

"Have you examined it?" asked bin Shadid. He scanned the weathered steel railroad car. The sides enclosing the boxcar body had been unbolted and raised on chains into the upper reaches of the factory by a massive overhead crane used to hoist railroad engine components. The removal revealed a massive object shrouded in gray canvas.

"Only to the extent that you instructed," said Badour. "I have not yet uncovered it. Sir, remember, it might not be the real thing. Only a casing. I don't want you to get your hopes up."

"You are always the cautious one, Fayez. I value that."

Bin Shadid climbed up into the railroad car, and Baddour followed. The magnate gestured for the canvas to be removed, and Baddour did so, revealing a gray metal bomb with a black nose cone, black tail, and square guidance fins. The only features on its surface were the brackets that would suspend it in the bomber. It was eight meters long and two meters in diameter.

"It looks like the photographs of Tsar Bomba," said Baddour.

Bin Shadid placed his hand on the bomb, in a touch that seemed almost a benediction. His expression somber, he said quietly, "Yes it does. Open it up."

Baddour reached into a toolbox and came up with a wrench, proceeding to unbolt a side access panel in the bomb's body. The two peered inside.

"That would be the tamper, the fusion part," said Baddour. "It looks like the diagrams. This is hopeful."

"And the primary?"

Baddour moved to the nose of the bomb, calling two of the guards to climb onto the boxcar to hold the nose cone as he unbolted it. As the bolts were freed, they carefully slid the heavy nose cone off and placed it on the floor of the boxcar, revealing a metal sphere connected to sheaves of wiring.

"That is the nuclear bomb that is the fusion trigger," said Baddour. The engineer stood up staring at the mechanism. He blew out a breath of amazement. "Sir, you *do* have a thermonuclear bomb."

His expression grim, Shadid only nodded.

"Now, I cannot say whether it can be made operational," said Baddour, examining the spherical nuclear bomb. "I do not have the expertise. It is probably not working now. It has sat for decades. But even in its current state, you could sell it for hundreds of millions of dollars. Iran or North Korea, they would pay. It would give them an enormous advantage in building their own thermonuclear bomb. It would serve your purpose."

"I do not intend to sell it," said bin Shadid. He waved his hand to send the guards out of the boxcar.

"I do not understand. What do you intend to do with it?"

In a tone of cold-blooded resolve, bin Shadid said, "I intend to detonate it."

***

Ben stood outside the entrance to the stark, gray concrete building, the Berlin Stasi Museum that housed the East German internal security ministry's records. Two months had gone by since Abby had been murdered. Now he no longer suffered devastatingly black periods, nightmares, bouts of tears. But the sorrow still shrouded his spirit. And embedded in his soul like some tumor was the horrific memory of discovering the murdered bodies of her and his unborn child. Before now, that memory had paralyzed him. Now, it drove his action.

During the two months, he had gone to the funeral, sat the seven-day mourning period of *shiva* with her family, and stayed for the month-long mourning period of *shloshim.* They had sat together, along with Azzy and his own mother and father, and memorialized Abby. Her parents told stories about her childhood as a merry, bright little girl and her teen years as a flighty, hilarious adolescent. Ben told of their time together, about her years as a loving wife. And they celebrated her generosity, her kindness, her adventurousness, her industry.

The memories had left him with some comfort, but no sense of closure, of peace. During *shloshim,* as was the custom, he had studied the *Torah*, but his objective was more than mourning and reflection. He was seeking guidance, and even permission, to do what he was going to do.

The *Torah*, and Jewish law, prohibited revenge; prohibited holding a grudge. It instructed him to forgive, to erase vengeance from his heart. But it did not prohibit seeking justice, repudiating evil. The monster was evil who murdered his wife and his unborn child. He had decided that his response was not vengeance, but dispassionate justice, retribution for that evil. Killing those responsible would prevent them from further crimes. Maybe it was a rationalization, but it was one he could live with.

Now, he would begin that quest for justice. He entered the museum to find behind the desk the stocky middle-aged woman he had seen so many times before, when he was seeking the Stasi's hidden monsters.

The archivist looked up, regarding him blankly. She hadn't recognized him at first because he had kept the beard that he had grown during *shloshim*. It made his formerly smooth, fine-featured face more grizzled. Nor, had he gotten a haircut, making his curls shaggier.

But when she did recognize him, she greeted him with a sad warmth. She had read of the terrible tragedy in the newspapers, and expressed her sorrow at his loss.

"I am beginning a new project," he said in German. "I would like to have access to the facilities records for Stasi structures. Like the construction records."

She agreed and led him up the broad staircase and down a wide paneled hallway. She unlocked the door to a room containing dozens of floor-to-ceiling shelves of boxed records and a small oak reading table. Again, she expressed her condolences at his loss.

He set down his briefcase, took out his laptop, and brought up images of his notes he had taken the night of the murder. He could not bear to handle the papers themselves; they were spattered with his wife's blood.

He began scouting the shelves, scrutinizing the typed labels in German. After half an hour, he found the shelf holding records pertaining to Stasi facilities in Machern. He combed through the boxes of records, scanning the construction contracts and material requisitions and orders. The Stasi bunker had been built between 1968 and 1972. It was a massive 16,000-square-foot underground complex meant to protect Stasi officers in a nuclear attack.

But for the mysterious project described in the invoices in the wooden box, the dates were years before that, in 1962. Whatever built on the site predated the Stasi bunker. Fortunately, he had recorded those dates in his notes, for like any good historian, he had begun charting a time line.

He found the records box covering 1962, but it was empty! He pulled down boxes covering the years before and after. They were stuffed with yellowing papers, and he examined them. None covered the mysterious construction; only requisitions for components of a telecommunication tower built on the vacant, thickly wooded 12-acre site.

He put away the materials and made his way back to the archivist's desk, asking her about the missing records. She frowned at first, but then held up a finger denoting a returning memory. She consulted her logs.

"As you know, we do not allow records out of the building. But there was a man who was here for months last year. He came every day, and he was in that room every day. He made many photocopies. Then one day, he left and did not come back. He may have taken the records."

"May I have his name?"

Frowning at the theft of the records she was dedicated to preserving, she called up the visitor records on her computer. She showed him the screen. "We require identification for scholars, and he showed a passport. I scanned it. He is Aman Querishi."

"Can I get your record on him?" he asked, and she transmitted the scanned image of the passport to his phone. The picture was of a dark-haired owlish man with round rimless glasses. The name and passport photo were only a thread. But to Ben, it could be all he needed. He would pull on it to unravel the fabric of the plot that he hoped would lead to the murderer of his wife and unborn child.

***

The two men, their heads shrouded in black hoods, were led by guards out of the yellow van, stumbling into the Bulgarian railroad shop. The guards removed the hoods, and the men blinked and peered around at the grimy, littered interior and at the rusting locomotive.

"We were paid to come here to see a train?" asked the taller of the Iranian nuclear engineers. He was dressed in the shabby workmen's clothes that he had been required to don in bin Shadid's jet. The shorter, rounder engineer was dressed similarly.

"You have come here to see something far more significant," said bin Shadid, who stood waiting with his engineer Fayez Badour. Bin Shadid and Badour led the two men through the door in the wooden wall into a room where the bomb rested on the open platform of the rail car. The bomb's side panel was open, its detached nose cone resting on a stand.

Both engineers were struck mute, standing wide-eyed, staring. Finally, the taller one asked in wonder, "Is that what I believe?"

"It is a one hundred megaton thermonuclear bomb," said bin Shadid. "It was called the Czar Bomb by the Soviets. Three thousand times more powerful than the Hiroshima and Nagasaki bombs combined."

"Ohhhh!" breathed the taller engineer in awe. "Where did you obtain it?"

"I happened to be reading a book on Nikita Khrushchev. I read a quote from him. He boasted there was such a bomb hidden in East Germany. So, on the chance he was telling the truth, I hired a historian to look into it. He found evidence of where the bomb was stored. We found it."

"Was it stored properly? Was it preserved properly?"

"We think it was," said Badour. "It was sealed in an earth-covered concrete bunker, so temperature was cool and constant. And the bunker was above ground so it stayed dry."

Bin Shadid said, "You are here to tell me if it can be made operational."

The taller engineer cocked his head to indicate asking permission to examine the bomb, and bin Shadid nodded. Both engineers climbed onto the railroad car and proceeded to scrutinize the bomb's mechanisms, talking among themselves in Kurdish. After half an hour, they let themselves down from the rail car, and the tall engineer reported.

"We have heard of this design but never seen it before. I am probably telling you some things you already know. It is a three-stage bomb with a Trutnev-Babayev second and third stage. They are called the tampers. The nose houses the first stage, the atomic bomb that triggers the thermonuclear reactions in the second and third stages."

"Yes, I know all that. Can it be restored?"

The engineer paused, but he was not to be distracted from his technical discourse.

"We would have to dismantle it to really be sure. But the second and third stages are lithium deuteride enclosed in cylinders of uranium two-thirty-eight. They would be good even after many decades. The first stage, the atomic bomb, has a plutonium sphere at the core. This sphere is compressed by chemical explosive to create the nuclear explosion that triggers the thermonuclear explosion. The plutonium would also still be good. It has a half-life of many thousands of years. And the Styrofoam that surrounds the components and sustains the fusion reaction would be good. But what worries us. . ." he paused and gave his shorter, rounder engineer Iranian colleague a dubious look" . . . is that the chemical explosive has probably deteriorated over decades. It is called TATB. It could detonate if jarred. It would have to be replaced by new explosive, PBX, and new electric detonators added. But we—"

"*Can it be made operational?*" demanded bin Shadid.

"Yes. It could be made operational." The engineer shrugged before continuing. "But not by us. I will contact my superiors, but I would advise them against our helping you making it operational. Should you use it, and Iran was implicated, we would be drawn into war. However, we *would* advise them to purchase it. They would pay just about any price you would name. You would not have to restore it."

"I am disappointed. We have such good affinity with Iran, I would hope we could have your help." Bin Shadid stared impassively at the two engineers for a long moment. "But your superiors do not know you are here?"

"No. As you required when you gave us your very generous consulting fee, we told no one. Of course, we didn't know why we would be here, or we would have told our superiors."

Saying nothing, bin Shadid turned and walked away, Badour following. He paused beside the guards, speaking to them in a low tone. They nodded. He and Badour climbed into the van. The large door to the factory was slid open, creaking and rattling, and the van drove out.

The faint crack of two gunshots echoing from within the factory barely registered inside the departing van.

CHAPTER FIVE

The sign out front of the small storefront read *"Herbstlaube, Begegnungsstätte für altere Menschen,"* which translated to "Autumn Arbor meeting place for elderly people." Its outside walls were decorated with a colorful mural of painted flowers and foliage. In its windows hung knitted child's sweaters and other apparel.

Ben felt a sharp pang of sorrow upon seeing the tiny clothing, but he took a deep breath, remembered his purpose, and pushed through the wooden door to go inside.

Seven elderly women sat at a long wooden table covered with their knitting projects—sweaters, scarves, hats, baby booties, and skeins of colorful yarn. They pointedly stopped their amiable chatter when Ben walked in.

"Schönen Tag," he greeted them, identifying himself as the man to whom their friends brought the box: *"Ich bin Ben Webber. Ich bin der Mann, den Frau Richter, Frau Hoffman und Frau Haas mit der Kiste besucht haben."* Their expressions of casual curiosity grew tightly grim.

"May I speak English?" he asked.

"Ja," said a small, round woman with gray hair cut into a tight bowl. "I will speak to you. I am Frau Braun. We know about you. We know what happened to . . . to your wife and her. . ." She did not finish the sentence, but bowed her head. "We are so sorry."

"Thank you. I am trying to find out what happened. It would help me if I could find out more about the box. And about what happened to Frauen Richter and Hoffman and Haas."

The women talked among themselves, and Frau Braun answered.

"Herr Fischer would come here every day. He lived in the back in his apartment. He gave them the box after the newspaper article came out and the man came to see him."

"The man? Can you tell me about the man?"

"We thought he was just a visitor. He bought from us a doll he said was for his child. But he talked a lot to Herr Fischer, asking about the article. He asked about Herr Fischer's papers. Herr Fischer became very frightened. The man was *dunkelhäutig* . . . with dark skin. Not black, but dark. Accent like from Middle East. Then Herr Fischer did not come for days, and we found him in his apartment dead. The doctors, the police, said it was natural, but we. . ." she looked at the others and said to them, "*Nicht natürlich.*" They all shook their heads emphatically. She turned back to Ben. "Not natural," she said.

"What do you mean?" asked Ben.

"It just did not seem natural that he would die suddenly right after he talked to the man and was frightened. He needed a walker, but he was very healthy. And we could tell his apartment had been disturbed. We cleaned it for him, so we knew things were out of place. It had been searched."

"Do you know what happened to your friends?"

"After they went to see you, they did not come to the center the next day. . . then for many days. We went to their apartments. They were not there. Some of the apartments looked *unordentlich.*"

"Messy? Like there had been a struggle?"

Frau Braun nodded, her expression grave.

"Could they have gone somewhere? To hide?"

"The police said that. But we do not believe it. Their *Kleider.* . . their clothes . . . were all there." Frau Braun's voice choked with emotion. "Please help us find them. Will you help?"

"I will try. But I must be honest. They may have sacrificed their lives bringing me the box."

***

"It is an open case. We are continuing our investigation," said Detective Koch curtly, in a tone reeking of emphatic certitude. He sat stiffly at his desk in the Berlin *Landeskriminalamt* state police office, the light streaming through its tall windows behind him.

"And what has your investigation found?" asked Ben. "About the death of my wife and unborn child?"

Koch paused. "Our investigation is continuing, and—"

"*What the hell have you found?*" demanded Ben.

Koch's expression hardened. "Herr Webber, it is an ongoing investigation."

Ben leaned over the desk, thrusting his face closer to the detective, glowering. "Their murder has received considerable attention in the media. What if I were to go to the media and tell them you have made no progress because you have neglected the case?"

"That is not true, we have made every effort."

"It doesn't matter that you do not think it is true. The media will take my word."

Koch took a deep breath. "Okay, but you must *not* reveal any of what I will tell you. It will prejudice the case."

"Fine." Ben backed away, still standing.

"The DNA from the skin under her fingernails was from a known criminal. We traced his last known address, and we talked to his associates. But he has disappeared. We have undercover informants in place, who are trying to find out why he targeted your house."

"I know damned well why he targeted my house. He wanted a box of records of a construction project in 1962 in Machern. I went

52

to the Stasi Museum, and there was a man, Aman Querishi, who might have taken the same records from their archive. I want you to trace this man for me."

Koch frowned and shook his head. "Herr Webber, I don't see how that is relevant. We believe that this thief thought the box was an antique, worth something. It's just too far-fetched to think that some old papers—"

"Too far-fetched? Herr detective, people are dying or disappearing that had to do with this box. What about Herr Fischer, whose box it was? He died."

"The autopsy found no evidence of foul play. His heart stopped."

"And the three women who brought me the box. They are gone."

"Now they are considered missing persons. Again, our detective saw no evidence of foul play. No bodies."

"*Bullshit!*" spat Ben. He stood up again, and leaned forward, placing his fists on the desk. "Their apartments showed signs of struggles! You're ignoring evidence! *I'm going to the media!*"

"You will only cause unfounded stories. . . paranoid conspiracy theories."

"There's a saying. 'Just because you're paranoid doesn't mean somebody's not after you.'"

Koch cursed under his breath, then said, "Herr Webber, here is what I will do. I will send all the files. . . on the murder of your wife and child, on Herr Fischer, on the women, on this man at the Stasi Museum. . . to the *Bundeskriminalamt*, the federal police. They will review the case and take appropriate steps."

"*Appropriate steps?*" asked Ben, but he did not wait for a clarification. "You have my cell number. I am staying at the university campus hotel. *Schönen Tag*, Detective Koch." He got up and made his way to the first floor, surrendered his visitor's badge, and left.

A clerk sitting at a desk in a corner of the office took out his cell phone and pecked out a text message, "The person is back." The clerk set down the phone and continued his tasks entering data. After twenty minutes, the phone vibrated, he picked it up, and read the message: "Find out his location. Another consulting fee."

The clerk replied "OK," erased the messages, and brought up his bank record. It showed the deposit of the agreed-upon first "consulting fee" from the anonymous private detective who'd texted him months ago with the lucrative offer to watch for the American.

***

Khalid Rasul stood silently at the doorway to bin Shadid's large office in his villa in the Abu Al-Khaseeb neighborhood of Basra. The walls, floor and ceiling of the office were covered with a colorful array of hand-painted Persian tiles, and bin Shadid sat at his ornately carved desk intent on his laptop computer. The desk's surface was clear, except for his computer and a black-framed picture of a smiling woman and two young children.

The security chief waited for his superior to look up from his computer. When bin Shadid was concentrating on a business issue, he did not want to be interrupted.

After ten minutes, he finished his typing and looked up, cocking his head in an unspoken question.

Rasul knew what the question was, and answered it. "The two packages from Bulgaria have been delivered to the Gardener. Like the three from Berlin, they have been processed." He paused, hesitating to deliver the next piece of news that would likely anger his master. "Webber is back in Berlin," he said. "He went to the police station. We have made further inquiries and discovered he also went to the Stasi Museum and to the old people center."

"You have his location, where he is staying there?"

"We will have it soon from our police contact."

"Send a man. . . ours, not a local. Only one. Tell the Gardener to expect another package from Berlin."

Rasul turned to go, but bin Shadid raised a hand to stop him. "Bring in the interpreter, my Šamšir, my friend. And please stay. I will be making important arrangements, and I want you to be here."

Rasul left and returned with a young woman dressed in a black hijab, the headscarf commonly worn by Arab women, and a long black abaya. At bin Shadid's direction, she sat primly in a chair close beside him, and Rasul sat a chair across from him.

Bin Shadid typed commands on his keyboard, and on a wall-screen display appeared the stern visage of a North Korean officer, dressed in a brown uniform decorated with a sheaf of ribbons.

"Greetings to you, sir," said bin Shadid, and the interpreter translated his words in the Korean Munhwaŏ dialect. She continued to translate their conversation between Kurdish and Korean.

"We have received the images of the device," said the officer. "They are interesting, but you show only the outer casing. They are, thus, insufficient for us to assess the mechanism inside."

Bin Shadid smiled wryly. "You ask too much at this early point in our discussions. You will receive only those images until such time as your engineers have restored the device."

"Then we are at an impasse." The officer reached forward to end the call.

"I think it can be resolved," said bin Shadid quickly. "Give me your best engineers. I will allow them to open the device and conduct all the inspection and documentation they wish, to determine that it is, indeed, a real device. They will confirm it to you. Then, we will hold all that documentation until they have fully restored and improved the device to my specifications."

"And when will we receive the documentation?"

"When the device is successfully . . ." bin Shadid paused, searching for the most euphemistic term ". . . applied."

The officer's eyes widened, his expression transforming into one of shock. "*You intend to use it?*"

"I do."

"Where, when?"

"That is none of your concern. I will just say that it will be applied at a time and place that your government would find advantageous."

"*Applied? You are contemplating a massive attack!* No time, no place would be advantageous! And our Dear Leader would be implicated!"

"No, *I* will be implicated. *I* intend to take sole credit. I will make sure that no one will ever know that your engineers had any hand in restoring the device."

"I must consider this," said the officer grimly, shaking his head.

"No, you must make a decision now."

"But I am taking a huge risk, committing our engineers to such a project." A faint sheen of perspiration glistened on the officer's forehead. "I must consider this," he said again, his voice quavering ever so slightly.

Bin Shadid felt the opportunity slipping away. But a clever businessman knows how to rescue such an opportunity.

"I can make your commitment much more attractive up front," he said. "I have five oil tankers leaving Turkey over the next month. I can redirect them to China and instruct my Chinese customers to divert their cargo through their pipeline in Dandong to your refinery in Sinuiju. So for the modest commitment of several of your engineers, your government will receive a huge windfall of oil upfront."

A faint smile slowly dawned on the officer's face. He cocked his head in thoughtful agreement. "Dear Leader would be pleased."

"Indeed, he would. And in the end, the reward to your nuclear development program will be immense. You will have the details that will enable your program to make a great leap forward, to create your first thermonuclear weapons."

Bin Shadid pressed the key to end the call before the officer could reply. The officer, head of North Korea's nuclear weapons program, would approach his superiors with a proposition that would no doubt greatly elevate his standing with the mercurial North Korean despot.

CHAPTER SIX

*H*ow *strange*, thought Ben to himself. *How very strange* that this green, sun-dappled landscape of fields and woods outside the German village of Machern might hold some secret for which his Abby and their unborn child were murdered. He paced back and forth, puzzling over what he might find, as he waited outside the nondescript structure that looked like a modest vacation cottage.

The gray stucco building concealed the entrance to the sprawling underground bunker built decades earlier to protect the officers of the East German Stasi from a nuclear attack. It was a high-security area during the Cold War, perfect for the Soviets to build a structure to house something valuable and secret. Something worth killing for. But what? Gold? Chemical weapons?

He had already taken the guided tour of the 16,000-square-foot bunker, with its stark living quarters, Soviet-era phones, and other old equipment. Now, he waited for the tourists to clear out, so he could talk to the guide alone.

The last of the stragglers left, strolling away down the wooded path. Finally, the slim elderly guide and caretaker exited, locking the door behind him.

"*Bitte, darf ich mit dir reden? Sprichst du Englisch?*" asked Ben.

"Yes, I would be happy to talk to you," the old man answered. "And I do speak English. How may I help you, young man?"

"I'm interested in the construction at this site? This bunker was built between 1968 and 1972?"

"Yes, it was."

"Was there construction before that? Like in the early 1960s?"

"Well, there was a radio tower. But I'm not sure. . ." His voice trailed off, his brow wrinkling in concentration. "Well, this is a large site, so there might still be something underground that we have not found yet. The crew that was here last year might have uncovered something."

"Somebody was here last year? Really?"

"Ah, yes, from the railroad. They were upgrading the rail bed on the spur line over there." He waved his hand across a broad field at a distant, thickly wooded area.

"Did you see what they were doing?"

"Oh, no, they would not allow visitors. It turned out, it was a good warning. There was the blast."

"They blasted?"

"Once. *Mein Gott, it was a huge explosion!* It shook the ground and made a lot of dust in the museum bunker, even this far away!"

Ben thanked the guide and began a hike away from the Stasi bunker. He crossed the sprawling open field, plunging into thick woods. He pushed his way through the undergrowth for a quarter mile when the terrain abruptly changed. He found himself at the edge of what looked like a large area that had collapsed. The brush was a jumble of vegetation, and the ground was uneven.

He stepped into the disturbed area, finding that in some sections, his foot abruptly sank into the ground. In others, chunks of concrete protruded from the soft earth. It was treacherous going, so he backtracked and circled the section. On the other side, he found himself standing beside two huge steel doors lying on the ground. They seemed to have been blown away from what might have been some kind of underground structure. Leading away through the forest was a pathway of loose dirt, cleared of trees.

He heard the faint rumble of an approaching train, and since the path led in that direction, he followed it. He realized that he was walking along hastily buried railroad tracks when he found a short section of steel rail protruding from the soil.

After perhaps five hundred meters, he came to the edge of the forest and the main rail line. He examined the ground leading to the tracks. There had been rails laid connecting the spur line, but they had been removed. He leaned against a tree, thinking.

A dull thunk by his head startled him out of his pondering. Something had slammed into the tree. He froze, confused for a moment, but then a chunk of the tree exploded away, splattering him with slivers of wood. Then he realized it!

Someone was shooting at him! Barely missing his head!

The metallic clatter of the approaching train had masked the sound of gunfire. He ducked down and a clump of earth erupted beside him. Gauging the direction of the shooting, he leaped behind a large oak, peering out to see a man running toward him. It was pointing a pistol at him!

He leaped up, trying to figure out where to run. The only clear path was along the railroad tracks, so he bolted out of the forest, running as hard as he could, his heart thudding in fear. The train overtook him, and as he was running, stumbling alongside it, a searing pain ripped through his left arm. He grunted and glanced down to see blood flowing from a wound, soaking his jacket sleeve. Energy drained from him, and panting with pain and exertion, he looked quickly back to see that the figure was holding up the pistol, aiming. It was a muscular, dark-haired man dressed in a brown jacket, holding a semiautomatic pistol.

He jerked to the right closer to the train, and with a metallic clang, a gash appeared in the metal of the tank car that was rumbling along beside him. Another bullet!

Unless he did something drastic, the next bullet would kill him! He had no escape into the woods, because now he was stumbling along a section of the track that ran in a deep cut. He was trapped!

He decided on a likely suicidal act. Blood streaming from his arm, he judged the speed of the train, judged how quickly he could move while wounded. As another bullet ricocheted off the tanker car, he slammed onto his stomach and rolled under it, aiming just behind the front wheels. The gravel tore at his skin, but he kept rolling. With a deep grunt, he shoved his body to the right, barely clearing the track as the huge rear wheels of the tanker car thundered past.

He laid there for a moment, taking a desperate, panting breath, feeling the pain of the wound and the cuts and bruises from his escape. He looked up to see the killer crouch down on the other side of the moving train and take aim. He rolled away from the track and into the brush, as the man took another shot that whizzed over his head.

His gut knotted with fear, as he realized that his escape was only temporary! As soon as the train passed, the killer would cross the tracks and have a clear shot again.

An idea formed, another desperate tactic, a huge risk, but one that might save him. Rather than flee into the forest, he hauled himself to his feet and began running alongside the train, occasionally leaping toward boxcars that had followed after the tanker car. He had to convince his attacker that he was trying to catch the train.

He had to lure the man into trying the same trick he had—rolling beneath the moving train. The man had to believe that to get a clear shot he had to be on the same side of the moving train as Ben was. As the train cars rumbled passed, Ben glimpsed the man sprinting along on the other side, raising his pistol, trying for a shot between the cars.

After several such leaps at the boxcars, Ben no longer saw the killer. He stopped, dropping down to peer beneath the passing train cars. No sign of him.

Ben backed away into the brush, hiding until the train had passed, its rumble receding into the distance. He crept out, peering back down the tracks. He could see a crumpled form in a brown coat. He stumbled back down the tracks holding his bleeding arm.

He found a bloody collection of body parts that had once been a living human. The torso had been crushed in half lengthwise, the bloody, glistening organs spilling out. The man's head was now a pink mush of brain and skull fragments.

Ben bent over and vomited.

***

"Don't take me to the hospital yet," Ben commanded in German. His voice was less than authoritative, weakened from blood loss and the trauma of being shot. He lay on a stretcher in the ambulance, his arm bandaged, an IV tube inserted into his arm. The emergency technician, who had just injected him with painkiller, protested, but made no move to close the ambulance door.

Ben asked for the local detective who had arrived to lead the investigation, after Ben had staggered into the nearest cottage with a blood-soaked arm to report being shot.

The detective, a middle-aged man with a thick mane of gray hair, appeared, asking "You are okay to talk now, Herr Webber?"

"Yes, and you should contact Detective Koch at the LKA in Berlin. He is handling the case. He has also sent the file to the federal police."

"What case?" asked the detective.

"I think the man was sent to kill me because of what I am investigating." He outlined the facts to the detective, finally asking "Have you identified him?"

The detective blew out a sigh. "Well, facial recognition is out of the question. He has no face. And he had no identification on him. We have transmitted his fingerprints and are checking them now."

"Do you have any hints at all who he is?"

The detective frowned, pausing before answering. "Well, I can tell you that his jacket had a label from a clothing store in Iraq. So, we're checking his fingerprints with Interpol."

Ben put his head back on the stretcher as the ambulance pulled out. "Iraq," he said to himself. "That changes everything." As the painkiller brought its soft relief, he began to ponder questions the attack had raised. Why would he be attacked now, given that whatever was in the bunker was either long gone or buried under rubble? And why would the attacker be an Iraqi? They would be mysteries that would propel him to even more aggressive probing, as if he needed more motives.

***

The two North Korean weapons engineers were slight men with matching brush haircuts and dressed in drab worker's garb one size too large. They finished their examination of the bomb, standing next to its bulk on the railroad car, chattering to one another in Korean. Their conference complete, they let themselves down from the platform and approached bin Shadid. He was disguised as before in a brown cloth jacket and black work pants. Standing beside him in a drab dress of the type worn by Bulgarian women was his interpreter.

"We think we can do it," said one of the engineers through the interpreter. "We think we can make operational. We have brought some tools." He gestured at the large duffel bags each engineer had brought. "But we will need specialized tools and instruments, other equipment. We will give list. We will also need PBX, polymer-bonded explosive, for the atomic bomb trigger. The existing chemical explosive, TATB, is still potent even after decades, but PBX is preferable for better dependability.

Bin Shadid, nodded at his chief engineer Fayez Badour, who was busy taking notes. "He will procure everything you need. Now, as to what *I* need. I want you to wire the triggering mechanism so it can be controlled remotely. I want to be able to specify GPS coordinates to trigger detonation. And I want to be able to set a timer to control the detonation."

"So, no altimeter trigger?" asked the Korean engineer.

"I do not intend to drop this bomb from an aircraft," said bin Shadid.

"Then how will you deploy it?"

"That is not your concern. You may now send a simple message to your superiors telling them that the bomb is genuine. Then you may begin documenting its details as you disassemble it."

Bin Shadid felt a dark satisfaction at being able to specify his vision for the weapon that would be one element of his revenge, his triumph. He watched Badour and the two engineers return to the bomb, Badour making notes on a laptop. These men would enable both elements of his two-pronged plot. Both elements would serve to devastate his enemy, the country that had murdered his family and millions of his countrymen. The interpreter pacing demurely behind him, he turned and walked away, stopping to talk in a low tone to the guard. The man nodded. This time the guard kept his pistol holstered.

CHAPTER SEVEN

"Okay, make your case," said Adrian Grinell, the Berlin CIA station chief. The gangly, middle-aged man stared doubtfully at Ben, who sat in on the couch across from him in the simply furnished office in Berlin's US embassy. "Make the case that the guy who tried to kill you isn't alone—"

"A guy from Iraq," Ben interrupted.

"Okay, a guy from Iraq who tried to kill you . . . make the case that he represents a terrorist plot. Y'know, maybe he was just part of whatever ring of thieves broke into that bunker. . . or whatever that mound of dirt was. You said yourself the place might have been a repository for Soviet gold."

Slumped on the couch, Ben slowly, emphatically shook his head. "Look, I've been a field consultant for you people for eight years. I know what you can do. I need to use your resources. I need to know what this is all about."

Grinell let out a frustrated sigh. "Yeah, well, that was at headquarters. I've not worked with you before. You walk in here cold with what you say is a terrorist plot. Okay, I looked at your record. True, you've seen your share of action. And in nasty places. Egypt, Sudan, Colombia, Yemen."

"Yes, and I've proved myself as somebody who knows what a terrorist plot looks like."

"Again, make your case."

"Let's say he was just some thief. He and his gang discover a bunker full of Soviet gold . . . whatever. . . and they loot it. They read a newspaper article that some former clerk has papers that could lead to the bunker. Why the hell would they care?" Ben stood up, his voice choking with emotion. *"Why would they care enough to try to steal the papers from me and murder my wife and unborn son?"*

"Well, it's possible—"

"I'm not finished. Why would they bother to blow up the bunker? Why would one of them try to kill me? It was clear that he followed me out to the site, probably from Berlin. Why?"

Grinell spread his hands and sat back in his chair. "Okay, given that you already have clearance, I'll give you access to our system. But look at you. You've lost a loved one, you've been shot, lost blood, you're traumatized. At least take a couple of days to recover. Let us look into the case, see if we can get more information. Jesus, we've got a dead Iraqi national squashed like a bug, we've got some damned hole in the ground . . . . Give us some damned time."

Ben touched his wounded arm, which was supported by a sling. "Aman Querishi," he said tiredly. "He was the one who traced the construction site. Find out who he is."

"We will do that. We'll put you in a safe house, and you can recuperate."

"Give me a computer and a login to the Agency's historical records of the sixties."

"Go to the goddamned safe house!" Grinell repeated.

Ben stared grimly at Grinell. Finally, the station chief shrugged his shoulders. "Well, hell. Okay, sack out in one of the bedrooms here. We'll get you some food, some coffee, and when you're fresh, we'll set you up."

Grinell had an assistant show Ben to one of the small bedrooms in the embassy, and he laid down on its bed, collapsing into sleep within minutes. Because of the trauma and the painkillers, he didn't move for two hours, during which a tray of sandwiches and a carafe of coffee was brought in. He awakened and found them, quickly eating and drinking to revive himself. Carrying the carafe and a coffee cup, he went back to the CIA offices and got directions to the cubicle he had been given. Sitting down at the terminal, rubbing his haggard face, he began to sift through the CIA historical database, seeking answers to his questions.

He started with his assumption that whoever broke into the bunker wanted to hide evidence of whatever had been there. That they had plans to do something with the contents. That pointed to chemical weapons.

He plumbed records of the Soviet chemical weapons program In the 60s. They had developed the nerve agents tabun, sarin, and soman. The Soviet Institute of Biophysics ran the program and managed stockpiles all over the Soviet Union. But not in East Germany. He could find no hint that the Soviets wanted to put a stockpile in East Germany. No historical records, no phone taps. Nothing.

Dead end.

Then, he found in a phone tap transcript, a single unusual word: Vanya. A man's name. It was a thread that stood out as a distinctly different color in the fabric of data. His experience with the CIA told him it would be useful to pull at that thread. So, he winnowed through more phone tap transcripts, travel records, newspaper articles. He scribbled madly on a yellow pad, trying to discern a pattern, a picture, a truth.

Then the records suddenly revealed a deeply horrifying truth. He whispered to himself, "*Oh, my God! Oh, no!*"

He grabbed his notes, leaped up, and sprinted to Grinell's office, bursting in on a meeting. Sitting at the conference table, Grinell and three other case officers looked up in surprise at the bearded, shaggy-haired man with his arm in a sling, waving a sheaf of yellow pages.

"You're not going to believe this!" he exclaimed.

"Try me," said Grinell, annoyed, motioning for the others to leave.

"They should stay," said Ben. "This is something I'll want everybody's take on."

The men settled back into their seats looking at each other, smiling in amused tolerance, and Ben began to pace as he talked.

"Okay, the chemical weapons theory was a dead end, so I kept looking for an explanation for the bunker. I got my first hint of what was going on when I was reading over phone tap transcripts from back in the early sixties. On December 14, 1962. . . remember that date; it's important. . . the Berlin KGB chief directly called Nikita Khrushchev. The call lasted one minute. The KGB guy just said "Vanya is in his home.""

"So?" asked Grinell. "Maybe it was some guy Khrushchev wanted to know about."

Ben shook his head emphatically. "It was totally out of character. A low-level KGB station chief does not make a one-minute call to the First Secretary of the Soviet Communist Party just to tell him a buddy of his had made it home okay."

"Then what?"

"I kept looking and. . . well, first, you need the context," said Ben. "In late 1961, the Soviets set off a fifty-megaton thermonuclear bomb, called the Czar Bomb. Khrushchev had ordered the bomb built as a show of Soviet nuclear power. Originally, the bomb was to be a hundred megatons, but the air force commanders were afraid a bigger bomb would incinerate the bomber crew. Not good for morale. So, they had the engineers dial back the Czar Bomb from the higher yield. So, it could have been twice as big. After the fifty-megaton bomb worked, Khrushchev wanted to show that the Soviets could build that bigger bomb—one that was not hobbled."

"So, what's your point?"

"The code name for the Czar Bomb was *Vanya*." Ben stopped his pacing and looked expectantly from one man to the other. He repeated, "Vanya."

Grinell shook his head in disbelief. "You're saying that they built a second bomb, a bigger one?"

"Yes, they did. And in early 1963, Khrushchev announced that a second, bigger bomb had indeed been built, and *that it was in East Germany!*"

"Where did he say that?"

"It was at the same UN meeting where he banged his shoe on the table. Khrushchev was a volatile son of a bitch, and he announced that he would show the United States a 'Kuzma's mother.'"

"What the hell does that mean?"

"I looked it up. It was Russian slang that meant 'we'll show you something that will overwhelm you.' *It was also one of the nicknames given the Czar Bomb!*"

"Jesus. You think that's what was hidden in the bunker?" asked Grinell.

Ben shuffled through his notes, as the men gave each other quizzical looks. He held up one page.

"Well, the records match up in terms of a time line. It looks like the bomb was constructed and the bunker was built in 1962."

"Okay, but a huge question is how they managed to keep it hidden," said Grinell.

"The Soviets were ruthless about secrecy. I found transport records then of prisoners from a Soviet gulag taken to Machern. But there was no record of them returning. My theory: they were forced to build the bunker, and then were probably killed. So, there were no civilian witnesses left from the site. But the Soviets didn't kill the Stasi supply clerk, Wenzel Fischer, who ordered the materials. First of all, it would alert the Stasi that something weird went on at their site. And second, they figured Fischer didn't know enough to be dangerous. So, only Khrushchev, the Berlin KGB chief, and maybe a few faithful minions really knew what was there."

"So *why* did they keep the bomb hidden?" asked one of the CIA case officers.

"Khrushchev likely made that decision," said Ben. "He had originally intended to trot out the bomb as a propaganda coup. He wanted to emphasize the Soviets' control over East Germany. But things got complicated. NATO was pushing to put nuclear weapons in Europe. So Khrushchev decided he needed to head off that possibility by hiding that he already had one huge bomb there. What's more, he had started nuclear nonproliferation talks with the US. He realized that revealing he'd built a big damned bomb would make him look like a warmonger. So, he never revealed it, except when he went a little nuts at that UN meeting in 1963, which he was known to do. And he made sure the very few who knew kept quiet, too, under pain of death. When they died, the secret of the bomb died with them. And the bomb was basically forgotten, as hard as that seems to believe."

"So, he let sleeping bombs lie," said the man, chuckling wryly.

"But now it doesn't just lie," said Ben. "Somebody found the bomb. Looks like they're Iraqi."

A stunned silence shrouded the room, except for several whispered curses, as the CIA operatives pondered the cataclysmic implications of what they had just heard.

***

The bearded, elderly Muslim cleric knelt beside Saadallah bin Shadid in the small room in his Erbil villa set aside for prayer. Bin Shadid had replaced his customary business suit with a simple white robe. They finished their recitations, rolled up their prayer rugs and settled onto large cushions.

The imam, gathering his own white robe around him, was the first to speak. "My son, it is a pleasure to be with you. But I have a feeling that you invited me here for more than prayer and socializing."

"I did, Mulla Khadem. I wish your counsel on a mission I have set for myself. It has to do with Qisas, the law of retaliation."

"You are considering retaliation for the deaths of your dear wife, your lovely children? It was a horrible tragedy. My heart still aches for your terrible loss, and I pray for their souls. But retaliation?"

"It was not just a tragedy. It was a crime. The Americans who launched the drone strike knew there were civilians at the event. It was a. . ." bin Shadid stopped, his voice choked ". . . it was a *wedding! They were trying to kill a fighter, but they knew it was a wedding!*"

"And that is your rationale for revenge?"

"The law of Qisas says it is permissible."

"More importantly, my son, our religion is one of choosing forgiveness over retaliation. The prophet Muhammad consistently chose forgiveness over retaliation. Even though the crimes against him were often vile and demeaning, he took Allah's words literally and chose kindness over anger."

"But I have a broader reason, Mulla Khadem. I am seeking more than retaliation for my own loss. Two million Iraqis were killed in the American invasion. Two million souls. And the Americans invaded after ignoring the possibility of negotiation. And the *Quran* says 'an eye for an eye.'"

"That is not the whole of the *Quran*'s direction," said the Imam, shaking his head sadly. "The passage does hold revenge as legal retribution. . ." The Imam quoted words from the holy book to give his position more weight. "*But if anyone remits the retaliation by way of charity, it shall be for him an expiation.*' So, dear son, Allah's true way is forgiveness."

Bin Shadid leaned forward, tears welling in his eyes. "Mulla, the *Quran* also says "punish with an equivalent of that with which you were harmed. My nightmares are haunted by the image of my family's bodies wrapped in white in their graves. My wife Faiza, my little son Hakeem, my daughter Isra. . . so loving, so innocent." His voice failed him, and he bowed his head and sobbed.

The Imam clasped bin Shadid's hands gently in his, and answered, "But the book also says 'but whosoever forgives and makes amends, his reward is upon Allah.'"

"Mulla Khadem, I must—"

"My son, let Allah punish those who harmed you. . . those who harmed our fellow countrymen. I beseech you, leave it to Allah."

"Perhaps I am to be his instrument."

"That is for Allah to decide."

Bin Shadid did not reply, removing his hands from the Imam's grasp. He had decided that continuing their discussion would only serve to agonize the gentle cleric. Studying the holy documents, bin Shadid had decided they told him that forgiveness is not the way if it results in humiliation of the Muslim, or if it encourages the aggressor.

He already decided to be the instrument of revenge against the aggressors, not only for the loss of his own family, but for all the losses suffered by his people.

He had the means to that revenge. He would use it.

***

"We need more tools, more instruments," said the North Korean weapons engineer, as he climbed down off the rail car holding the bomb. Still crouched over the bomb was the other engineer, taking images with a small camera. The two had unbolted all the bomb's metal coverings, revealing the spherical atomic bomb trigger at its nose and the cylinders toward the rear marking the thermonuclear bomb mechanism.

"Why would you need more tools?" asked the head guard, Rahnim, a muscular man with a thick beard. He was dressed in the tattered coveralls that hid his identity as one of bin Shadid's most adept enforcers. He was not sure of some of the words because they were speaking in broken English, a language they both knew.

"Tools, instruments. We need more to proceed with restoring the bomb. We must go into the city to obtain them." The other engineer finished his photography and let himself down from the rail car. He slipped the camera into the pocket of his coveralls.

Rahnim paused, his expression dubious. "I had thought you have all you need. You gave a list."

The engineer shrugged. "When we opened the bomb, we realized there were operations that would require different tools. We need those tools. We will take the van into the city. He hefted up his duffel bag onto his shoulder, as did the other engineer. They began walking toward the door of the factory.

"I will send a driver with you," he said.

"Oh, do not bother. You need all your men here," said the engineer over his shoulder.

"You are too valuable to be left alone," said Rahmin, more emphatically. He signaled to a guard, who followed the engineers out the door.

To Rahnim, their exit was just a little too hurried. He took out his satellite phone and called bin Shadid's engineer, Fayez Badour. He told Badour of the engineers' insistence that they leave for the city.

"Do not allow them to leave until they give you a list of the tools and instruments they need!" Exclaimed Badour. "They gave us a list, and they should not need anything else!"

Rahnim ran to the factory door, and slammed it open, beckoning for the guards to follow him. The van was already departing, now nearly to the road, a hundred yards away. He shouted for it to stop, directing the guards to pursue it. Wielding their assault rifles, they ran toward it.

The van stopped for a moment. The faint crack of a pistol sounded from its interior, and the driver's body was shoved out the van door onto the dirt road.

"SHOOT THE TIRES!" bellowed Rahnim, as the guards reached the van. "TAKE THEM ALIVE!" With bursts from their rifles, the guards deflated all four tires, drawing near the van.

A thundering, fiery blast blew the van into shards of flying metal, shredding the bodies of the guards into unrecognizable masses of charred flesh and bone.

The blast wave launched razor-sharp shards through the air, one slicing through Rahnim's arm, sending a stream of his blood flowing onto the ground.

CHAPTER EIGHT

"**Y**ou were an expensive 'consultant' when we first started paying you. Now you are dangerous one," grumbled the Russian oil executive Arkady Yahontov to bin Shadid. They sat in the Russian's plush penthouse apartment in Erbil, its glass wall showing a view of that city's green, forested Sami Abdulrahman Park.

Bin Shadid took a slow sip of his lemonade and let the silence settle over his conversation with the vice president for Iraqi operations of the Russian oil company.

"Indeed, I have been expensive," he said quietly. "But our business relationship has been valuable to you, no? Through my influence you have received lucrative Iraqi oil contracts?"

"*Da*," grumped Yahontov. But—"

"And you welcomed the proposition I offered . . . to sell me the plans for the Status-6 weapon. The transaction will make you rich. And it will make your friends at the Ministry of Defense rich."

"We *do* need the money," said Yahontov, shaking his head in disgust. "Putin's *spetsial'naya voennaya operatsiya* . . . special military operation . . . in Ukraine has left us all in poverty. But we do not want to be rich and *dead*. You have taken precautions?"

"Of course. Nobody knows I am dealing with you. And I take it nobody knows who you are giving the plans to."

"Nobody," said Yahontov. "Not even the Ministry of Defense officials. They only know they will be handsomely paid."

"So, shall we proceed? Shall we transfer the money first?"

The obese oil executive with the carefully sculpted gray pompadour loosed a raucous laugh, raising his glass of vodka in a salute.

"Indeed, once I have the money, you have the plans." Yahontov reached into the vest pocket of his suit and pulled out a thumb drive. He held it up, grinning. "Amazing that such a small thing is worth sixteen billion rubles. But that is a pittance to you, little more than your last consulting fee."

Bin Shadid handed his tablet computer to Yahontov. "Enter the account number you wish to have the funds deposited to. I leave it to you to disburse the appropriate amounts to the Ministry people."

"Oh, I will make them happy," said Yahontov, keying in his account number. He handed the tablet back to bin Shadid, who made the transfer and returned the tablet to Yahontov. The Russian's thick eyebrows arched upward in pleasure, and he handed bin Shadid the thumb drive.

"I still don't understand what you want with the plans for this thing, this Status-6 weapon. Are you planning to put them on your tankers to make them into warships?"

"Actually, I will only build one."

"Well, I don't care how many you build. I got my money." Yahontov raised his glass of vodka once more, grinning.

Bin Shadid rose to go, then stopped at the door to Yahontov's apartment. "Well, actually, there's more to come. To commemorate our long association, I am sending you a special gift. You will be surprised."

***

The bearded, round-faced professor Aman Querishi sat alone in the CIA interrogation room fidgeting, his eyes darting to the door, occasionally biting his nails.

"Is he ready?" asked Ben. He stood with Adrian Grinell, the Berlin CIA station chief, in the observation room of the interrogation complex, looking through the one-way glass.

"I would say so," said Grinell smiling wryly. "He's been stewing in there an hour. I'll call Khan. He interrogates any Muslims we bring in."

"Let me try first," said Ben, staring steadily at the nervous Querishi. He knew he could get to the fearful academic in a way no CIA interrogator could. He wielded the scalpel of his knowledge of the man's psyche. He was ready to use it.

"No dice," said Grinell with finality. "You've never done this sort of thing. We've only got a few hours. Snatching him wasn't strictly legal. His family or coworkers will find out he's gone, and if the local cops link the grab to us, we'll have a little bit of an international incident."

"Look, Khan won't even know what questions to ask. We're both academics. I can draw him out. Give me an hour, then you can send in your goon."

Grinell gave Ben a steady appraising gaze. "Our goon? Our *expert*, you mean." He let out a resigned sigh. "Okay, you got an hour. And I know how motivated you are. Just don't get too motivated and beat hell out of him."

"This is a mind-game situation," said Ben. "It's what I know how to play." He took a deep breath and entered the room. He stood silently inside the doorway, letting the silence raise tension in his quarry. It worked. The professor regarded him with frightened eyes.

"Who are you?" asked Querishi tremulously. "You've kidnapped me. Right off the street. What are you going to do?"

"I know what you've been doing," said Ben.

"*Doing?* I'm a teacher. . . history. Is this about something I said wrong in class?"

"You worked at the Stasi Museum for months. I'm an historian, too. I know what you were researching. I went through the records there. I know what you stole. And I have other records that you don't."

Ben knew the last statement would strike at the heart of Querishi's confidence. For an academic to have inferior data was debilitating. Indeed, the pudgy middle-aged man shifted nervously in his seat, his eyes widening.

"I was doing research on Stasi history. That is all."

"You were tracing Stasi construction projects in the sixties. You identified one that you reported to the man who employed you. A key project. We know somebody paid you a lot of money for the information. We have your bank accounts. Who paid you?"

Querishi bit his lip, pausing for a long moment. "I won't. . . I can't—"

"I went to that site. I know what was done with the site."

Querishi shrugged. "All right, I know, too. It was artwork that the Stasi had stolen. That's what I was told."

"Who told you?"

"He said not to reveal his identity because he intended to sell the paintings and sculptures on the black market."

Ben took out his phone, bringing up a picture of the Czar Bomb, holding it in front of Querishi. "It wasn't artwork. It was a thermonuclear bomb. I suspect you knew that. The man who hired you is a terrorist. That makes *you* a terrorist!"

"*I'm not! I'm just a professor of history! I needed the money!*"

"WHO WAS IT?" Ben thrust his face into Querishi's.

"He's a *terrorist?*" whimpered Querishi. "*He'll kill me if he finds out!*"

"It'll be *when he finds out* if you don't cooperate. It'll be *when* he finds out that we have you. You'll be killed. You're only hope is us. We'll protect you. And, we'll protect your family. You'll get a new life."

Querishi began to sob, tears coursing down his face and into his beard. He finally choked out "An Iraqi shipping magnate. Saadallah bin Shadid. Protect my family! My wife, children, mother! Please!"

Ben turned and left the room to find an outraged Grinell. *"Goddamnit, why did you do that? Why did you tell him about the bomb? We'll have to take him to a black site. And what the hell do you think you were doing offering him a new identity!?"*

"It was the only way to get him to talk," said Ben quietly. "Now you go do what you do and find out who the hell this bin Shadid is and what he's up to."

With a mixture of anger and resignation, Grinell said, "You're off this mission. You're the loosest of cannons. You can't handle this mission dispassionately. I'm bringing in a nuclear expert from Langley. He'll take over. Go home. Mourn your loss."

***

Rahnim's hand trembled as he tried vainly to wipe the blood from his hands. He took out his phone amid the scene of carnage in the Bulgarian railroad factory. The phone was smeared with blood because his jacket was soaked with blood as well. It came from his wound. And also from putting the dead guards' lifeless bodies into body bags. He took a deep breath, drawing on the same soldier's strength that had carried him through the violence and blood of the Iraq war.

He snapped orders at the other five guards, some of whom were still staggering or retching from the explosion and its bloody aftermath.

He directed two guards to haul the body bags into the factory, punching in a number on the phone with trembling fingers. His master answered, and in a shaking voice, he told the horrific tale of the explosion. The response was immediate, and the guard answered:

"Yes, the device was unharmed." The security man knew Saadallah bin Shadid well enough not to expect any expression of sorrow over the dead. After all, they were servants. "What do you want me to do?" he asked.

He listened for a long while, put away the phone, and turned to two guards.

"Keep the police and fire brigade away as long as you can. Tell them. . ." Rahnim paused and bowed his head, crystallizing the story that he would tell. "Tell them that the explosion was fuel. Say that there is still the danger of explosions from fuel." To other guards, he ordered, "Gather the debris of the van into a pile and cover it." The warbling sound of a siren rose in the distance.

Fortunately, the only officials likely to show up would be easily deflected locals. When they were told the lie that there had been no casualties, and that the fire was out, they would leave. Even if they got a look at the site, they would likely not be experienced enough to recognize that a car bomb had gone off.

He turned to other guards. "Secure the nose cone and the parts on the rail car. Load the bodies beside the bomb, then lower the boxcar body back down over it and bolt it to the platform. Make sure the doors are locked. Let no one near it."

He turned to two others. "Go to the freight yard. Get a locomotive to pull the rail car. Do whatever you have to."

He handed one guard a case holding Bulgarian currency. He indicated the alternative strategy, by patting the pistol in his shoulder holster. They rushed away, and shortly the sound of their car starting up could be heard, and the car sped away.

Rahnim took out his phone and began planning their travels over the next week. The factory was no longer a viable site for restoring the bomb. So, he had been instructed to transport it to Istanbul and load it onto the rail ferry that ran between Sirkeci and the port at Haydarpasa. There, it would be loaded onto a cargo ship.

That ship would be its home and the workshop where it would be transformed from an antique mechanism into the most fearsome weapon in history.

***

"Hello, I'm Carrie deLong," said the petite young woman, holding out her small, pale hand. She smiled warmly, her fine lips upturned fetchingly at the ends. She had long auburn hair and wide, brown eyes.

Adrian Grinell took her hand and replied, "Been expecting you. Heard a lot about you from Langley. You're considered their best nuclear weapons analyst."

"Yeah, well, that's debatable," she chuckled. "There are some very smart people at Langley."

Carrie took a seat across from Grinell in the CIA Berlin station chief's office. She pulled out her tablet computer, tucked back her long hair, and began to scan its screen. "Real shitshow you've got here, that's for sure. I've analyzed the historical data that Dr. Webber provided. I've consulted with Los Alamos." She looked up, shaking her head, the smile transformed to a grimace. "The goddamned thing could work!"

"What do you mean?"

"The techs told me that even after decades, a one hundred megaton thermonuclear bomb of the type detonated by the Soviets could still be made operational today. In the US, we stockpile warheads for many years, and they remain viable. There's no reason the Soviet bomb couldn't be, too."

"What would it take?"

She took in a deep breath and blew it out as an emphatic sigh. "Hmm, good question. Bin Shadid would need really expert nuclear weapons engineers. Where would he get them? Maybe Iran. Maybe North Korea. Maybe even renegade Russian engineers. We'll need operatives doing some legwork to figure that out."

"What about the bomb itself? What would determine its viability?"

"Well, for one thing, the conditions under which it was transported and stored. And how it might be different from the first bomb. I need to talk to Dr. Webber. He knows the history. He's also seen the bunker where it was stored."

Grinell shook his head. "Not possible. I took him off the mission. I didn't think he had anything else to contribute, and he was kind of a loose cannon."

"You mean given that his pregnant wife and unborn child were murdered?"

"Yeah, that would make him erratic."

Carrie leaned forward, smiling tolerantly at Grinell. "That would also make him committed. And, he would be invaluable because of his historical insights, research ability, and field experience."

"Well, I made the decision to—"

Carrie shook her head slowly and emphatically. "Not yours to make. I'm heading this mission now. You get him the hell back, okay?"

Scowling, Grinell started to object, but paused, shrugged and picked up the phone, punching in Ben's number. He waited for two minutes before hanging up and turning to Carrie.

"He didn't answer. Maybe he's got his phone off. Maybe he went to the safe house, like I told him." Grinell called the safe house, and after a brief conversation hung up. "He's not at the safe house."

"You have a tracker on his phone, right?"

"Well, it doesn't work if it's off."

"Okay, you have someone shadowing him, right?"

Grinell made a call, then hung up, his expression exasperated. "He seems to have evaded—"

"You lost him? Seriously? Given his state of mind, who knows what the hell he could be up to?"

***

The Chinese CIA operative, wearing an orange hardhat and gray coveralls to blend in, crouched low behind the 48-inch steel pipe. Taking advantage of the cover of the early morning fog hanging over China's Yalu River, he sprinted along the pipe toward the small stucco building. It housed the instruments monitoring the oil pipeline that ran from Dandong, China, across the river to North Korea.

He tried the rusty steel door. It was locked. He knew if he didn't get inside quickly, he would be caught by the guards, arrested, inevitably shot. He had to get in, but he couldn't leave any trace that he had been there. But he had made this intrusion each month for two years, so he knew how to pick the lock efficiently.

His high-priority mission was to record data on the flow of crude oil from China to the North Korean refinery in Sinuiju. He quickly made it inside the control building and moved to the computer terminal. With practiced keystrokes, he brought up the flow records from the previous month. He took out his cell phone and snapped an image of the screenful of numbers.

He stopped and stared at the screen, knitting his brow in consternation. He usually didn't pay much attention to the numbers because they were fairly steady month to month. The pipeline carried ninety percent of North Korea's oil supply, and China was meticulous about maintaining a controlled flow. They sold North Korea just enough to keep the country's military and political elite supplied; but not so much that its tyrannical "Dear Leader" would feel emboldened to become more aggressive.

But this month's numbers showed a huge spike in the flow. Why would China increase oil shipments so much? Somewhere up the supply chain, somebody had injected a massive amount of crude meant for North Korea.

The CIA operative shook his head and resolved to highlight this fact to his handler in Beijing. As usual, he would code the image into an innocuous-looking family photo and post it online. The ubiquitous Chinese Internet censors would miss it, but the CIA chief would decipher it and likely be puzzled, if not alarmed.

The fog was lifting, and the operative hurried out the door. Soon, he would start his day job running a boat along the river for Chinese tourists seeking a glimpse of the shabby buildings, smokestacks, soldiers, and farmers on the North Korean side.

***

Holding his wounded arm, still supported by a sling, close to his chest, Ben trudged down the broad concourse of the Istanbul airport. As he walked beneath its soaring arched roof and past the busy, colorful kiosks, he asked himself, *Was he walking to his death?*

His answer: *Possibly, even likely.*

But it was a mission he was driven to undertake. He had to confront the man who had caused the death of Abby and his unborn son. He needed to confront the man who now had in his possession the most fearsome weapon on the planet.

But his barely controlled rage was tempered by a cold-blooded strategy. As an historian, he had learned to go to the source, wherever possible. Most of the time, his sources were long-dead. This one was alive—for now. By getting a first-hand assessment of the man behind a terrorist plan, he could gain insight into stopping it, even killing its architect.

He wound his way through the chattering crowd of prosperous-looking travelers to an imposing, bearded man holding a sign with his name on it. From there, they walked to a waiting black limousine, and he climbed in to find himself sitting beside another imposing man who made only passing acknowledgment of his presence. He adjusted the sling, as an occasional sharp pain reminded him of his wound. He had stopped taking pain pills. He needed to remain sharp. And the physical pain reminded him of the pain in his soul.

He would not be killed right now, he guessed. The terrorist would want to see him first—to take his own measure of his enemy.

The limousine accelerated onto the straight freeway that ran through the flat, featureless terrain outside Istanbul. Finally, it pulled up to the marble-covered portico of a luxury hotel, and the taciturn man led him to a private elevator. They ascended to the penthouse suite and outside the elevator the man grabbed his shoulders, standing him still, as he winced at the pain, and subjecting him to a thorough pat down.

The man escorted him past two guards to a massive mahogany door. He directed Ben through the door, into a sprawling, luxurious penthouse opulently appointed with oil paintings, sculptures, Persian carpets, and brocaded wing chairs and a sofa.

Saadallah bin Shadid stood by the floor-to-ceiling window, dressed in a pinstripe suit and wearing a red-checkered traditional Middle Eastern headdress. Behind him, the glimmering, azure waters of the Black Sea stretched away to the horizon.

Ben felt a cold satisfaction at finally confronting this hated man. This was a man who could kill without remorse. The man's expression was one of mild, detached interest, his dark eyes regarding Ben as one might view a trivial objet d'art. Bin Shadid smiled coolly.

"Dr. Webber, I'm glad that you were willing to fly to Istanbul while I am here on business. But I am a bit puzzled as to why you would want so much to meet with me." His tone was soft but commanding, like velvet-on-steel—portraying a man whose power was never questioned, whose commands were submissively obeyed. His diction was precise, his accent refined, with only a slight middle-Eastern accent.

Ben remained by the door, glowering at bin Shadid. He became conscious of a muscular, black-suited man, probably the magnate's head of security, looming behind him.

"You *know* why I wanted to see you," Ben said coldly.

"I am afraid I do not. You are hurt?" he asked gesturing at the sling. "An accident?"

"You know it was not."

"Again, I am at a loss to understand your meaning. May I offer you refreshment? Tea, perhaps?"

"If you did not know why I asked for a meeting, why did you agree?"

"When my assistant received your request, I had him research you. You are a noted expert on terrorist organizations . . . their structures, their weaknesses. 'Hidden monsters' is what you term the principal architects in such organizations. I am interested in such organizations . . . in how to cope with them, even thwart them. I have to deal with them in my business. So, I thought meeting with you would be useful."

"You killed my wife, my pregnant wife, my unborn son." His fists clenched, Ben took a step forward, but the security man stepped forward as well.

Bin Shadid raised his hand in placation. "Dr. Webber, I have no idea what you are talking about. I am a businessman. I transport oil to customers. I do not—"

"I have traced the murders to you. And I know why. Aman Querishi gave me the information. I went to the site in Germany, where the bomb was hidden. That's where your man tried to kill me." He held up the sling supporting his arm.

"Bomb? Kill you? Dr. Webber, I understand you are distraught. My researcher showed me the news accounts of the terrible tragedy that befell you. But you are laboring under a terrible mis-impression, even delusion. I can understand why—"

"*You can understand? You can understand? You have no idea—*"

"I do. I lost my entire family," interrupted bin Shadid quietly, sitting heavily into an armchair. He looked up at Ben, his expression somber. "An American drone strike."

Ben stared at him for a long moment. "I didn't know." He almost said he was sorry, but remembered who he was talking to.

Bin Shadid shrugged and said, "So, yes, Dr. Webber, I can, indeed, understand your loss."

Ben's fleeting expression of sympathy returned to one of accusation. "So, you have the bomb. What are you going to do with it?"

Bin Shadid also recovered his equanimity, smiling wryly. "Again, you speak of this bomb? Sir, you seem to have spun out a fantastic scenario in which I am some kind of monster. Are you looking for a shaytan?"

"A what?"

"It's what they call a demon in my religion."

"No, I've found him. What do you intend to do with this bomb?"

"Dr. Webber, our meeting is concluded. I thought we would have an informative discussion. I was in error. I think we should call someone to come and help you. Who knows you are here?"

"People. People know I am here."

"Really? I would propose that you would never have been allowed to come if you had asked permission." Bin Shadid gave the security man looming behind Ben a slight nod. "I would propose that nobody knows you are here. Nobody knows you came to see me."

Ben quickly brought up his phone, snapping a picture of bin Shadid. He tapped the screen to transmit the image. He tapped again to display a map with a dot marking his location at the hotel. He showed the map to bin Shadid.

"Now they know."

CHAPTER NINE

"Welcome back," spat Adrian Grinell, his voice drenched in a brew of sarcasm and disgust. He stood behind his desk, leaning on it with his knuckles, glaring at Ben. Nearby stood the CIA nuclear weapons expert Carrie deLong.

She extended her hand, smiling. "Yes, welcome back." Her tone was kinder. She introduced herself, then said, "Adrian is perhaps less charitable than me about your foolish adventure, because I have a feeling I better understand why you did it."

Grinell sniped, "He did it because he was going off the rails. It shows he needs to be severed from this mission."

Carrie gave Grinell a long, stern look. "And I have overruled that decision. I am in charge of this mission, not the station chief. Dr. Webber, you will remain on this mission, but you *will* do so under my express direction, is that clear?"

"Okay, okay, I'll agree. As long as you recognize that, while you know the technology, I know the human factor."

"And your wound? Is that troubling you?"

"*I am fine,*" said Ben emphatically.

"Well, then, okay," said Carrie.

"Not okay," said Grinell. "Someone who is so emotionally biased should not—"

"Sure, I'm emotionally *invested,*" shot back Ben. "But that visit was strategic. . . *research.* . . I wanted to find out what his motives were."

"I could call his motives nuts," said Grinell.

"I know what his motives are for going after the bomb. And, I have a sense what he intends to do with it."

Carrie motioned for him to sit, to lower the emotional temperature in the room. She and Grinell sat as well.

"So, what are his motives?" she asked.

"Revenge. His family was killed in an American drone strike. We need to find out what happened. That's primarily what drove him. . . what *drives* him."

"He has other motives?" asked Carrie.

"He is Iraqi. He lived through the invasion. Like so many, he bears deep anger over the huge numbers of Iraqi civilians killed."

"And what does your insight as an historian tell you about those motives?" she asked.

"His culture is one of dedicated tribalism. It values family honor, the honor of his religion, his sect, and national honor. These values, along with his personal need for revenge will make him implacable. He will use every bit of his considerable resources to get revenge."

"So, he has no intention of selling the bomb?"

"He'll seek not only to use it, but I suspect he'll try to give the technology to any nation or group that could use it to harm the United States and its allies."

"Jesus!" breathed Grinell. He seemed to deflate in his chair. "Everybody could end up with a hydrogen bomb. So, what do you need?"

"Like I said, we need to find out more about the drone strike that killed his family," said Ben. "That goes to the heart of his motivation."

"That would mean getting into military records. Tough, but doable," said Grinell.

"We also need to track his movements," said Ben.

"Already done." Grinell typed commands on his computer keyboard, bringing up on his office's wall-sized screen a sequence of closed-circuit camera scenes. "After you showed up on the GPS feed, we sent our local operatives to the hotel. The security footage showed him leaving the hotel after being there a day. His jet was at Hezarfen private airport in Istanbul, and their footage shows him boarding it. He flew directly back to Erbil, and our agents there report he's been at his villa there ever since."

"He went home?" asked Ben. "The timing doesn't seem right. He didn't go to Istanbul just to turn around immediately and go back home."

"Well, that's what the footage shows," said Grinell. "We're putting a Scan Eagle drone on him out of Ain Assad Air Base. He won't be able to move without us seeing him."

"Any indication about why he was in Istanbul?" asked Ben.

"Business, like he told you," said Grinell. "He met with some oil people."

Carrie interjected, "Look, the key thing is where is the bomb? We need to go through every bit of data we have for any hints about where it might be."

"We are doing everything we can, Carrie," said Grinell. "The only unusual event in the region was an explosion near Sofia. Some kind of accident in an old railway repair shop."

"The bomb was on a railway car!" Exclaimed Ben.

Said Carrie, "Okay, trace what happened there afterward. See if we can get resources on the ground there. Ben, you need rest. "

Ben smiled wryly. "Well, I do have somebody who will make sure that happens."

Who?"

"My sister. She came here when I was arrested, but she went home. Now, she's back. She flew in yesterday, and she's at a hotel. I called and told her everything that happened. I learned a long time ago that if I didn't, there would be hell to pay, and she finds out everything, anyway. I'm going to see her now."

***

Bin Shadid climbed from the battered gray Renault still wearing his black wig, glasses, and tattered green jacket. He kept his head down, striding up the gangplank and onto the deck of the ship. The vessel appeared to be a rather shabby, rusty freighter that hauled general cargo from one small port to another. The only distinguishing characteristic was heavy reinforcement of one of the cranes installed on the deck. Any knowledgeable observer would have wondered why such a crane, meant to lift far heavier objects than the usual cargo, would have been necessary.

When bin Shadid descended the narrow metal stairs, he entered, not the usual cavernous freighter cargo hold, but a workshop crowded with a lathe, drill press, grinder, a metal-slicing plasma cutting table, computers, and electronic testing equipment. The low rumble of the ship's engines reverberated in the workshop, which held the clinging, musty smell of decades of service as a cargo carrier.

He removed his disguise, nodding to Rahnim, the guard who had led his men at the railroad repair shop. The hulking, bearded man still wore the haunted look of someone who had seen his fellow soldiers blasted to unrecognizable bloody pulps.

Bin Shadid gave him only a brief sympathetic look. "You did well, Rahnim." he allowed. "Clearly, it was a suicide bomb. The North Koreans knew that if captured, they would be tortured and killed. Their government would believe they might give up information. But by committing suicide, they knew they would be seen as heroes. Their families honored and taken care of."

"Agha bin Shadid, the packages from Bulgaria reached the Gardener," said Rahnim. He addressed bin Shadid using the Persian title of respect. "The Koreans' remains are being processed. Our people are being prepared for burial in our faith."

"Make sure the bodies arrive at their homes as soon as possible. Tell the families they died honorably, in battle. And contact my financial bureau. The families are to be taken care of generously."

"Yes, Agha bin Shadid."

"And Webber?" asked bin Shadid.

"He is at CIA."

"Is he vulnerable?"

"No, he is too guarded. We are following him. He is now with his sister. She came from America."

"But most importantly, the bomb?"

"Successfully transferred." Rahnim gestured to a separate walled enclosure in the cargo hold. Bin Shadid made his way to its doorway and through, to find the bomb resting on a steel cradle, its nose cone sitting nearby. His engineer, Fayez Badour, crouched beside it, peering into its interior.

"I know you cautioned me about transporting the bomb too much," he told Badour. But the factory was needed as an isolated place to safely store and assess the bomb. . . until the ship was ready. So, did the transport affect it?" he asked Badour. The little man stood and shook his head tentatively.

"As far as I can tell, no damage. The mechanism seems not to have been affected in transport. But it would be up to a nuclear engineer to say for sure. There could be internal cracks in the secondary uranium tampers or in the fusion fuel, the lithium deuteride."

"Then we will procure more experts. Continue your examination. Take the measurements and images and take them to Basra to use for our . . . *other* . . . purposes."

Badour nodded knowingly. He knew that the "other purposes" were not to be discussed, even in front of their own workers.

Bin Shadid stood for a long moment, silently contemplating the bulky casing of the bomb. Then, followed by Rahnim, he made his way into the quarters constructed for him off the main workshop. The space included an office, a living room, and a separate bedroom, all fitted with luxurious furniture, carpeting, and wall hangings. The low thrum of the ship's engines coming to life was barely discernible.

He changed into a white silk caftan and launched a video call on the large screen that hung on an opposite wall. The image of his security chief Khalid Rasul materialized. The man bowed his head, his expression impassive. Standing beside Rasul was an absolute twin of the multibillionaire Saadallah bin Shadid. The double was dressed in the same characteristic tailored pinstripe suit and wore a red-checkered keffiyeh. The only discernible difference was that the double gave a servile bow to his master.

"The journey from Istanbul went well?" asked bin Shadid.

"Yes, Agha bin Shadid," said Rasul. "Faisal gave a good performance."

"I would expect so. He has been my double long enough."

"It has been my great honor Agha bin Shadid," said Faisal, grinning and bowing again.

"Faisal, you are to remain at the villa. You are to go about normal activities, making yourself seen. . . but of course avoiding anyone who could recognize that you are not me."

"Yes, of course."

"Now leave us."

Faisal quickly left, and to Rasul bin Shadid said, "Make it known that I have decided to remain largely in seclusion, for a period of prayer. I will conduct business remotely from here. The virtual network will make it seem that I am conducting business from Erbil."

"I will."

"And as for the Russian, Arkady Yahontov, I captured his bank login information when I transferred the money to him in Erbil. His bank account will show that he received an extremely large sum of money. And now, he will disappear, and the money will disappear from his bank account. And the Gardener will receive another package."

"I will arrange it," said Rasul.

"You should have no problem getting to him. I told him he would be receiving a surprise gift from me." With a rare smile, bin Shadid ended the call and instructed the guard Rahnim to summon his interpreter. The young woman padded quietly in, dressed in a black hijab and a long black dress. She took her place close alongside bin Shadid. He typed a command on his computer, and there shortly appeared on the screen the grim image of the crisply uniformed director of the North Korean nuclear weapons program.

Before he could speak, bin Shadid said, his tone one of cold fury. "You tried to cheat me. Nobody does that. Your men tried to steal the information on the bomb. They failed."

The director's grim expression gave way to one of wide-eyed anxiety. He waved his hands in a gesture of placation. "You must understand. We did not—"

"You did not count on such an utter failure. But that failure gives me leverage. Unless you send me engineers who will restore the bomb, I will make it known to your 'Dear Leader' that you lost the chance to have its plans. Surely you know what that means."

Bin Shadid was certain the director knew that he would be executed in the grisliest way possible. Perhaps, as had been rumored, he would be strapped to the barrel of an artillery piece and his body blasted to pulp. And, bin Shadid knew, the same fate would wait all the members of his family.

The director's answer showed that he fully understood the consequences, as well. "Yes!" he exclaimed. "Absolutely! I will send our best! And they will be at your disposal! They will be at your disposal."

Bin Shadid knew now was the time to add a carrot to the stick. "I will continue the oil shipment. And I will send you a few images of the bomb. You may show them to your superiors as proof that you are making progress."

"Thank you!" exclaimed the director. "I am—"

Bin Shadid ended the call, and followed it with messages to his agents arranging for smuggling the replacement nuclear engineers from North Korea, and the dispatching of tankers to China to deliver the oil to the Chinese pipeline to North Korea.

During his tasks, the young interpreter remained seated at his side. When he finished, he turned to her and smiled, nodding toward the bedroom. She smiled back.

She said quietly, "I marry you myself."

"I accept," he replied. He handed her a chocolate to seal the bond of their Mut'ah marriage—a temporary "pleasure marriage" condoned by many Shiite Muslims. They had played out the intimate ceremony many times before, and it had become a warm, endearing ritual. She placed her hand on his, gratified at being able to comfort the tragically widowed man.

She sensuously opened her mouth and took a bite of the chocolate, rising, and padding toward the bedroom. There, she would remove her hijab and dress, and slip modestly under the sheet, to be joined by him. He watched her go with appreciation. Then he remembered one last task. He took up the phone, calling his agent in Berlin.

"The man Webber," he said tersely. "He will not care about his own safety. But he will care about his sister. . ."

***

Azariah hugged her brother for a long while, careful to avoid aggravating his wound. To explain the length of the hug, she whispered, "This is for me, this is for Mom, this is for Dad."

When she finally released him, her expression was darkly accusative. "They tried to kill you. Then you went right to the goddamned killer? Benjamin, what were you thinking?"

Ben sat slowly down onto the armchair in the hotel room, adjusting his sling. "I needed to see him. I needed to take his measure. . . find out who he is."

"And did you, brother?"

"I saw a man driven by the deepest of rage. Dedicated to revenge. I saw a man with unlimited resources. Azzy, I just don't know how he can be stopped."

"Maybe you don't know now, but you will. I just know you will. That's why I'm here. To help you get justice for the scum who killed Abby and your baby. Mom and Dad told me to come here to bring you home. So, you can heal. And they said to let the police do their job."

"You know that's not going to happen."

Azariah shook her head, smiling knowingly. "Yeah, well, I didn't tell them that. So, what do you know? And what do you need me to do? I'll be your left arm."

For the next hour, Ben gave her every detail of his discoveries, watching his sister's expression transform into one of utter shock when she learned of the existence of the thermonuclear bomb. He pointedly did not tell her of his work with the CIA. That had been his secret for almost a decade.

Swearing her to secrecy, and asking her to stay in constant contact, he left her sitting at the desk in the room, tapping away on her laptop.

Shadowed by the CIA security man assigned to him, he walked down the hall to the elevator. They passed a man dressed in a porter's black uniform with gold braid and pushing a large serving cart. The porter waited until the elevator door closed to whisper into a cell phone pulled from his pocket.

Shortly, another man, also dressed in black, appeared from behind a service door. Peering up and down the hall for any guests, they moved toward the door to Azariah's room.

***

Grinell brought up the first image on the wall screen in his office. He narrated, as photos flashed on the screen from the Global Hawk drone circling high above bin Shadid's villa.

"Here he is by the pool; here he is getting into his limo; here he is with who we think is his security chief, Khalid Rasul. He never goes anywhere without Rasul."

"So, it's business as usual?" asked Carrie.

Said Grinell, "Well, not quite. He seems to be keeping to himself. No business meetings, no socializing."

"What do you think that means?" asked Ben.

"Well my gut feeling is that he's trying like hell to look like he's absolutely not up to anything. That makes me think he's up to something."

"And the elint?" asked Carrie.

"The electronic intelligence shows he is conducting business by email and video from his villa. But like I said, no personal meetings either outside or at home."

"So couldn't you get more clues if you got people near him?" asked Carrie.

Grinell "Well, If strangers show up, it'll arouse suspicion."

"I asked you about the drone strike that killed his family," interjected Ben. "What've you found?"

Grinell abruptly grew silent, taking a deep breath.

"Well?" asked Ben.

"The thing is. . ." Grinell grew silent again.

Carrie spoke up. "Adrian, what did you find out? I sense that you're conflicted. You'd better not be holding anything out. . . given that there's the possibility of a devastating nuclear attack, and you've got intel that could help understand what's going on."

"Well, I called in a lot of favors. Did a lot of back-channeling—"

"Good for you, Adrian," said Carrie. "You get a gold star for effort. *What the hell did you find out?*"

"The strike procedure was, um, suboptimal."

Carrie turned to Ben, declaring sarcastically. "Dr. Webber, as you likely know, in military vernacular that means that somebody screwed up bigtime."

Ben riveted his gaze on Grinell. "*What happened?*"

Grinell sighed resignedly. "Okay, the target was in Iraqi territory that our intelligence said was ISIS-controlled. A Predator drone had spotted a priority ISIS target and followed him to a building outside Baghdad. It was thought to be an ISIS meeting place, so it was considered fair game. The command went through the authorization process, the 'kill chain.' . . . through the lawyers all the way up to the top and got approved."

"So, it was sanctioned?" asked Ben.

"Yes, but a day later, they got better intel on the ground that the building wasn't an ISIS headquarters. It had been a headquarters. But now, it was used as a banquet hall, a wedding site. The officer-in-charge took a day off, and his second didn't know about the intel. So, the intel didn't make it up the chain of command. And in tracking the target, the drone arrived on station too late to pick up the wedding party coming in."

"So it was a massive intelligence failure."

"Tragic. Our intel has revealed that bin Shadid's family was at the wedding."

A shroud of stunned silence settled on the room. Finally Ben said, *"That failure could end up more than 'tragic.' It could be catastrophic, leading to the deaths of millions!"* He vaulted from his chair. *"I can't be here!"* He stormed from the room, taking out his cell phone. He needed to be with his sister to recover.

Azariah did not answer her phone.

***

The Chinese CIA operative furrowed his brow in puzzlement. The North Korean patrol boat was in the wrong place along the Yalu River. The low-slung gray boat was docked where it shouldn't be. But as the operative, a slight young man in a white shirt and baggy pants, worked his day job of taking tourists up and down the river, he studiously avoided going near the heavily armed boat.

He stood at the wheel of the glass-domed tour boat, giving his usual spiel to the tourists crowded in the cabin. Only occasionally would he steal a glance at the patrol boat.

He instantly stopped that practice when he saw one soldier standing, peering back at him. His stomach knotted in anxiety, even though he knew the soldiers were no threat to a Chinese citizen on the Chinese side of the border.

He did notice that the soldiers were otherwise trying to look casual. One had his head poked out of the hatch in the small cabin, chatting with another sailor. Another was hanging t-shirts to dry on the line strung from the stern to the cabin. Yet another sat eating from a bowl.

But their attempt at a casual air did not work, because the patrol boat was docked, unusually, near a gate in a walled military compound. The craft normally prowled up and down the river, warning boats that came close to the invisible border in mid-river separating China and North Korea.

The operative knew that another sign of abnormal behavior would be if the boat continued its presence after nightfall. As darkness fell, the boat would usually return to port, giving smugglers an opening to ferry their illicit cargo from the Chinese side. Waiting on the North Korean shore would be a soldier assigned either to take a share of the cargo if it was something they wanted. Or to accept the usual bribe.

The CIA operative had monitored the nighttime smuggling quite often. So, he was familiar with the process and only mildly anxious at spying on it. Besides, such spying was worth it. Sometimes the illicit cargo, particularly human cargo, had significance that his CIA handler would be interested in. He decided that tonight he would see if the patrol boat was carrying out some clandestine mission. He would lurk below the Sino-Korean Friendship Bridge on which also carried the huge oil pipeline from Dandong across the Yalu River.

As the afternoon wore on, he kept to his tourism routine. He took two more loads of tourists for the hour-long ride. Then, he docked his boat and headed for his small apartment. On the way, he stopped at the Starbucks on Jinshan Street to pick up a Venti Frappuccino. He would need the caffeine. He'd avoided the place until recently because he thought it might brand him as a western sympathizer. But when he saw police there, he figured it would be safe to indulge.

In his apartment, he downed the coffee and changed into dark-colored coveralls. Buzzed from the drink, he waited until late at night, when the tourists would have retired to their hotels. Whatever the soldiers had planned wouldn't happen until then.

Just after midnight, he skulked along darkened side streets back to the river front, taking care to avoid the Chinese army patrols in their hulking, black armored vehicles. He took up a position beneath the bridge, hunkering down against a pylon, where he could see across to where the North Korean patrol boat was docked. Taking comfort at the cloak of darkness, he took out his binoculars and peered through them. Fortunately, the sky was cloudless and the moon was three-quarters full, so he could see the patrol boat in the distance, as a mere smudge on the horizon.

He had waited patiently for two hours, when he detected movement on the boat. It accelerated away from the dock, heading for the Chinese side. It veered downriver throwing up a wake that glimmered in the moonlight. He was fairly sure where it was going. There was a deserted area of the river bank overgrown with thick brush. Ideal for landing surreptitiously, and a spot that had been used by smugglers.

His pulse quickened at the anticipation of the hunt. It was a welcome, albeit frightening, change from his humdrum days as a tour guide. He stole quickly away from the river to a parallel street, so he could sprint downstream under cover of darkness. He reached what he thought was the likely landing spot and turned back toward the river, pushing his way through the brush. He took several deep breaths to recover from the run and to quiet his panting.

Sure enough, the patrol boat was pulling into a cove hidden from view upriver and down by thick brush. As the boat beached, he moved closer to get a view of the passengers. The North Korean soldiers were helping three men off the boat and onto the shore. These were no usual passengers dressed in the usual shabby North Korean garb! They wore black coveralls and carried metal cases. They were met by two men dressed in windbreakers and khaki work pants, who helped them unload several large metal crates. This would make for a report to his handler that would bring him praise, maybe more money!

Intent on the unloading, he took out a small camera that had night-vision capabilities and aimed it at the scene. His finger was poised over the shutter button. He had the mysterious passengers perfectly in frame.

From behind him, a hand gripped his forehead and jerked his head back. A knife sliced viciously across his throat, severing both arteries, sending forth pulsating streams of blood. His mouth gaping open, his eyes wide in shock, he collapsed lifeless to the ground, his flowing blood staining the tan earth.

His killer, a spare Chinese man dressed in a windbreaker and khaki work pants, stepped quickly back to avoid getting blood on him. He removed rubber gloves he had donned just moments ago, when he had first seen the intruder. He always brought rubber gloves in case he had to make such a mess. He really didn't need all the glove fingers, since both his little fingers had been cut off long ago as a punishment by his clan leader in the Chinese crime syndicate, the Triad. Similarly, he was missing his left ear.

Backing away from the bleeding body, he stared impassively at it for a while, watching to make sure his knife had done its work. Satisfied that his intruder was dead, he bent down, wiped the knife on the corpse and returned it to its sheath beneath his windbreaker. His jacket had the orange and red sunrise logo of the China National Petroleum Corporation.

The killer scanned the area to make sure nobody had seen his kill. He moved quietly through the brush to the river's edge where the patrol boat was being unloaded. He instructed the North Korean soldiers to load the corpse onto their boat after everyone had left. They were to drop it in the river, where it would float far downstream. He warned the soldiers that the North Korean nuclear engineers his men had just transported were not to see the body. The soldiers readily agreed. They were faithfully obeying orders from their superiors. And their cooperation was cemented by the thick envelope of cash the killer gave to their sergeant as a bonus for their night time mission and their discretion.

The engineers were quickly whisked away with their cases to waiting SUVs on a nearby road. The killer knew the trip would be uneventful. It was only ten miles to Langtou Airport, where a jet owned by the Iraqi shipping magnate awaited them.

The killer took out his phone and notified his Triad clan leader that the engineers had arrived and there had been no significant problems. He didn't consider the kill significant. His clan leader would be pleased, and thus would be the oil company executives who had hired the Triad for the job. After all, the night's work would bring a million gallons of Iraqi crude oil into the Chinese oil company's reserve over the next month.

The killer also notified his Triad leader that he could ask the oil company for an extra fee for the night's work. There was always an extra fee when he or his men had to kill. The fee was part of the secret agreement between the oil company and the Triad. The agreement was kept in force by the reality that the Triad was perfectly willing to exact a penalty for nonpayment. In the past the penalty for deadbeat clients had left them floating in the river, along with their families.

***

"*Blood!*" gasped Ben, as he stood at the bedroom door of Azariah's hotel suite. "*Too much blood!*" He stared in horror at a large bloodstain soaking the gray carpet of the room at the foot of the bed. Speckling the bed itself, and even the room's walls were splatters of brown, dried blood. Smaller blotches in the carpet led out of the bedroom and into the living room, where they stopped.

Ben started forward into the bedroom, but Carrie gently held him back. "We need to get a forensics team in here. There may be clues to what happened to her." She took out her phone and made a call, as Ben backed away into the living room, slumping against the wall.

"But there's so much—"

"Ben, Ben, just consider this. This is hard to say, but just listen. If they had killed her, they would have left her body. It would have been too much trouble and no reason to take it out. Something else went on here. Something—" She stopped, her gaze going to a side table near the hotel room entrance. She took a tissue from the bathroom and carefully picked up a cell phone that had been left there. "Is this your sister's? It looks like a burner phone."

Ben shook his head, unable to speak. Carrie touched a button bringing its small screen to life. She tapped a key to bring up a text message. She showed it to Ben.

It said simply, "Stop."

CHAPTER TEN

The gale from the helicopter's blades whipped at bin Shadid's coveralls, and he clutched his baseball cap as he peered upward through his sunglasses.

The helicopter loomed above the freighter against the blue sky and eased down onto its helipad. The roar of its engines abated, and its rotors spun slowly down to a stop. Three men climbed out of its doorway. One hurried toward bin Shadid, while the other two hauled out large metal cases.

The chief North Korean nuclear engineer reached bin Shadid and introduced himself, extending his hand, smiling and bowing. Bin Shadid took it briefly. The wiry man merely glanced at Rahnim standing beside bin Shadid. The engineer said in halting English, "We are most eager to help you in your task, as our director has promised. Please, if you will have men take our equipment below, and we will follow."

Bin Shadid instructed members of his ship's crew to handle the cases, and he led the three Korean engineers down metal stairs into the depths of the cargo hold, and into the large workshop. There, the bomb rested on its cradles, surrounded by metalworking machines, electronic consoles, and workbenches cluttered with an array of tools. The bomb's covers had been removed and its nose cone taken off, revealing the sphere of the thermonuclear-triggering atomic bomb and the other components.

The three Koreans chattered excitedly among themselves at the sight of the 27-ton bomb. They began peering into its innards and typing notes on tablet computers.

After fifteen minutes of inspection, the chief engineer returned to bin Shadid's side. "We have received your requirements from our director," he said, in a breathless tone that reflected his awe at seeing the bomb. "You want to restore mechanism, add remote control and timer and GPS trigger, and so forth. We can do these things. But it will take time."

"You will not have much time. You will make the bomb functional quickly if you have to work around the clock."

"But it will take time to—"

"Around the clock," interrupted bin Shadid. He glanced over at Rahnim who regarded the slight engineer impassively, as one might a creature of little consequence.

The engineer's eyes widened. Having lived under a cruel, despotic rule, he knew the dire significance of such a glance. He was also acutely aware that his director had not told him of his predecessors' fate. The others had just disappeared, which undoubtedly meant they were dead. So, he was particularly emphatic when he declared, "Sir, we will meet your every expectation, your schedule requirements. I pledge this to you." He bowed and began to back away, but bin Shadid stopped him.

"Can you tell whether the bomb suffered from transport?" he asked.

"We are hoping there is no damage. But we will repair. I *promise* we will repair. It is unfortunate that device had to be transported to this ship."

"Not unfortunate at all," said bin Shadid. "It was to end up here, anyway. I merely accelerated my plans."

"This ship will take bomb to target? Then detonate from this ship?"

"You do not need to know my plans, except that there will be a delivery vehicle. You will receive details on it. Installing the bomb in it will require some engineering on your part. The vehicle will arrive in a couple of weeks. Meantime concentrate on restoring the bomb."

The chief engineer smiled and ducked his head in agreement. "I will report to you soon on our plan." He scurried off to join the others, as they began unlatching their cases and hauling out tools and electronic parts.

***

"The CCTV shows that something peculiar as hell happened in that hotel," said Grinell. He shook his head in puzzlement, as he stood with Carrie and Ben, showing them the security footage of the hotel hallway.

"What do you mean?" asked Ben. "Does it show Azzy being taken away?" He scrutinized the computer screen as if the intensity of his gaze would somehow yield the secrets of his sister's abduction. His clenched jaw betrayed his emotional witches' brew of anger, fear, and guilt.

"Well, maybe. Just watch this." Grinell clicked the mouse to speed through the footage. He described the scene. "Okay, here's your sister going into her room. Then, here's this hotel guy shows up with a cart and knocking on her door. She opens it. He pushes the cart in, but it looks like he leaves the door ajar and another guy comes in right behind him. Okay, there's nothing for maybe fifteen minutes."

"Azzy didn't come out?" asked Ben.

"Not so we could see. Here is where it gets weird. The second guy comes out pushing the cart. Not the first guy, who brought the cart in. He's pushing the cart like it's heavier now, like it has something. . . or somebody. . . stuffed underneath."

"Azzy! That's how they got her out!"

"Maybe. There is other footage of the cart headed toward a freight entrance of the hotel. We don't see the vehicle it might have been loaded into. But look at this." Grinell fast-forwarded the scene. "Here's the guy coming back to the hotel room, this time with yet *another* cart. And we see him come out a second time with the new cart with something. . . more likely *somebody*. . . hidden in the cart. Maybe two bodies went out!"

"I'm calling her husband," said Ben taking out his cell phone. "Albert will want to know what's going on."

"I'd suggest not," said Grinell. "If the kidnapping gets out, they could kill her. Better we let this play out first."

Ben took several deep breaths, considering what Grinell had said. Finally, shaking his head, he put his cell phone away. "But I've got to do something. This is my fault." He moved back to the computer screen to replay the footage, seeking any possible clue.

Carrie's cell phone buzzed, and she moved off to take the call. She returned shaking her head, her brow furrowed.

"Okay, some news. The tech guys said the burner phone we found just got a new message. 'Your sister will be returned safely if you go back to America. We are watching you.' The techs didn't have time to trace the location."

"I'm not going anywhere," declared Ben. "I'm going to get my sister back. And if they hurt her—"

"Well, actually, *she* might have hurt *them*," said Carrie, tilting her head quizzically and hmphing in puzzlement. "The lab says that blood all over the room. It's *male!*"

CHAPTER ELEVEN

"**S**how her to me," instructed bin Shadid, peering at the video image on his laptop's screen. The image panned around to show a rusty metal door. A hand reached out and opened it to reveal a bare room with a metal cot and a tray on the floor holding dishes flecked with the scraps of a meal. On the cot lay the small form of Azariah Webber-Friedmann, one wrist handcuffed to the cot.

She jerked her head around at the sound of the door opening and struggled to a sitting position. A purplish bruise covered the left side of her face, and her lower lip was swollen.

"Hello, and kiss my *tuches* on this fine morning," she slurred.

Bin Shadid said to the unseen holder of the laptop, "That's enough. Go back to the other room."

The image careened down the hall, settling onto the laptop's owner, a bearded man with dark eyes.

"Did you beat her?" asked bin Shadid.

The man shrugged. "Only enough to keep her obedient."

"Fool. You are not to beat her again. You are to feed her, give her water. Let her have fresh clothing and to bathe and fix her hair."

"But Agha bin Shadid, she killed—"

"I am quite aware of that. But it has been a week, and we need to give proof of life. I do not want a bad image. It will only encourage Webber to do something foolish. Clean her up, take an image of her showing today's newspaper, and send it."

"Yes, sir."

With the video call ended, bin Shadid left the luxury of his rooms in the depths of the freighter and made his way out to the cargo hold workshop. The kidnapping was but an annoying necessity to rid himself of the meddling academic. His real obsession rested in the middle of the workshop. He felt a deep sense of cold satisfaction as he regarded the bomb and the two weeks' progress by the driven North Korean engineers.

The bomb sat on its cradle, wired to electronic test instruments. Two of the Korean engineers crouched at the front of the bomb, adjusting a sheaf of wiring that separated into individual strands fastened around the surface of the sphere that was the atomic bomb trigger.

The chief engineer bent over one of the workbenches, intent on a metal box with a multitude of small sockets. He glanced up, and seeing bin Shadid, came over to him, smiling eagerly.

"All is going very well," he announced, his voice tinged with anxiety. "We have finished fitting new explosives around plutonium core of the atomic bomb. Now we are wiring detonators and timing mechanism. We have used our own technology to make very, very precise timing. As you know explosive charges must be very, very exact in timing to efficiently implode plutonium."

"And the controls?"

"Ah, yes, they are coming next. We have made them." He led bin Shadid to the workbench, taking up a tablet computer. Ducking his head, still smiling, he showed bin Shadid the display of an array of buttons and numerical displays. "See, this is interface that gives you full control."

"And I can trigger detonation from anywhere?" asked bin Shadid.

"Yes, absolutely, with touch screen. We are building extensible antenna into bomb casing. You can determine countdown time to detonation, or GPS location for detonation, or both. . . telling device to detonate even if target area not reached."

111

"I want to go over the controls in detail, with practice runs."

"Yes sir. We will show you everything. You can practice."

"The next phase of your work will begin soon," said bin Shadid. "The delivery vehicle will arrive. Then you will install the bomb into it and integrate maneuvering controls with the interface."

"So, bomb will be mobile?"

"Very mobile. Undetectably mobile."

"How, may I ask will it be mobile? Can you tell us more?"

Bin Shadid paused in thought. "All right, now you can have the plans I purchased from the Russians for the Status-6 vehicle. We have built it, and that will allow you to prepare for its arrival." He handed a thumb drive to the engineer, who bowed again and moved off to talk to the others.

Bin Shadid returned to his quarters, sitting back at his desk and launching a video call. Shortly, the image of his head engineer, Fayez Badour, appeared on the screen.

"Are *they* ready?" asked bin Shadid. He made sure not to say anything specific, given the possibility that even his coded communications were being intercepted.

"Yes sir, and they are perfect. Detailed. I had our best engineers make them."

"Then start them on their journey as we discussed. And the vehicle?"

"It is being built according to the plans," said Baddour. "Our most trusted and able engineers are doing it."

"Thank you, my friend. You are doing well." With a sense of exhilaration at his coming triumph, he ended the call and stood up. He fetched the prayer rug he had been given as a boy and spread it on the floor. He took out his smartphone and brought up the app that would tell him the Qibla direction, where he would have to kneel to face toward Mecca. He would recite his prayers. Then, he would sit quietly, mulling over his plans for revenge, seeking to identify any flaws. So far, he had found none.

***

The guard shoved open the metal door with a screeching sound, and the stench rolled out of the concrete-walled room where Azariah had been kept for a week. She sat on the metal cot, her right wrist handcuffed to it. A waste bucket sat on the floor beside the cot. She was dressed in the same dirty, beige pants suit she had worn when she was kidnapped. It still bore the blood stains from the attacker she had killed, as well as from the beating they had given her.

The muscular dark-haired man, one of her three captors, wrinkled his nose at the fetid odor in the room, scowling at the woman who had killed his friend.

"Maid service in this place is lousy," she said to him. "You won't get a tip."

"We will allow you to clean yourself up," said the man with a thick Persian accent. "We will give you clothing. We are going to give proof of life. If it was up to me—"

"But it's not, is it? It's up to your master who was at the other end of that video call, eh?" She rattled the handcuff that bound one wrist to the metal cot. "How do you expect me to wash up and make myself presentable and dress when you've got me attached to this bed?"

"We give you wet towels. We give you clothing. You stay there."

"Look at me. I'm filthy. I need a shower, and to comb my hair, and to dress myself properly. Y'know, I could just refuse and look like hell. I'd bet your master wouldn't want that."

"We give you—"

"Look, you are a big, strong guy. You got a gun. I'm injured, starved. Afraid I'll hurt you?"

113

The man glowered at Azariah for a long moment before digging a key out of the left pocket of his black pants and pulling his pistol from its holster. He pitched the key to Azariah. He backed away toward the door, leveling the pistol at her.

"Uncuff yourself," he said, "I take you to shower. You dress. If you try to escape, if you try to attack, I shoot you."

Through her swollen lip, Azariah Webber-Friedmann gave a furtive, crooked half-smile. She whispered to herself,

"Sucker."

***

"This *has* to be the ship carrying the bomb," said Grinell emphatically. "The Iraqi freighter *Adaliana* passaged through the Strait of Gibraltar into the Atlantic last week and turned straight south."

He stood in his office along with Ben and Carrie. They stared intently at the wall screen showing an overhead drone image of a ship plowing through the steel-gray waters of the Atlantic, churning a foamy wake.

Grinell continued. "It's owned by one of bin Shadid's subsidiaries, a shipping company. The manifest says it's carrying general cargo to London. But it just changed turned south."

"What does that mean?" asked Carrie.

"It could go anywhere. Maybe even through the Panama Canal."

"How long would the ship take to reach the canal?" asked Ben.

"Probably another week. But it won't get there. The SEAL team landed in Lisbon last night. They're mounting an assault in an hour, after it's dark."

"I'll need a real-time view of the op," said Carrie. "And brief the team not to touch *anything*. If the bomb is there, we don't know its status. Could be operational. And the terrorists might have rigged it to blow. I'll want me and my team to do an examination after the take-down."

"Done and done," said Grinell. He called in an aide and began to give instructions.

Throughout the conversation, Ben stood staring at the screen, his expression one of brow-wrinkled puzzlement.

"You're quiet," said Carrie. "What's going on in that historian brain?"

Ben shook his head slowly. "Actually, not my brain. My gut. Just a gut feeling so far. This situation just doesn't feel like him. Look, consider this: bin Shadid is a multibillionaire, one hell of a business strategist. He's managed to get incredibly wealthy in a country that's lousy with corrupt politicians, terrorists, militia groups, and American military. And he's driven by cold-blooded revenge. I've studied people like him. They are very strategic in seeking their goal. This whole situation has odd elements."

"Specifics?"

"Well, for one thing, the ship is formally registered to his company. It was too easy to find. And for another, it makes no sense for him to be in Erbil and not on the ship. He would absolutely want to be on that ship."

"Well, let's just see what we see."

After an hour, the wall screen lit up with eight night-vision video feeds from the SEALs' helmet cams. Four of the feeds showed undulating views from an inflatable boat cresting waves, approaching the dimly lit bulk of the freighter. Four others showed steadier scenes of SEALs crouched inside of a MV-22 tiltrotor Osprey in flight.

"Can I talk to them?" asked Carrie.

"I can relay any messages to their commander," said Grinell.

"Not good enough. They may have to react quickly. Give me a direct link."

Grinell shrugged and made a call, handing the phone to Carrie. "This is as good as I can do. The op commander at base will tell the men immediately what you tell them."

Carrie shook her head ruefully and took the phone, telling the commander, "Your guys need to know that if they make the wrong move, they could be vaporized, along with a large chunk of ocean. They've got photos of the bomb. Just hope that's what it still looks like."

"Azzy could be on that ship!" exclaimed Ben. "Tell them that!"

Carried nodded and relayed the message, describing Ben's sister.

The helmet videos from the inflatable boat showed the SEALs scaling the side of the freighter. They reached the deck, and in one scene the dark figure of a crewman loomed. The crewman pulled a gun, but immediately crumpled to the deck, shot dead. More figures appeared in the scenes, filling the screen with the flash of muzzle fire and careening images of battle.

The videos from the Osprey team showed the SEALs rappelling from the hovering craft's rear door ramp onto the deck and fanning out. A burst of tracer bullets from the Osprey's 50-caliber machine gun spewed into the night above the ship—a persuasive signal to the crew that surrender was the best option.

Carrie's gaze quickly jumped from one image to the other, scrutinizing them. The video showed the ship's crew raising their hands and shouting. The SEALs herded them to the main deck and handcuffed them.

One image showed a SEAL descending into the cargo hold. It showed sitting in the middle of the hold, surrounded by crates and workbenches, a massive object shrouded in canvas. The SEAL team member pulled off the covering to reveal the bomb.

"*Holy shit!*" exclaimed Carrie. "*Okay, back off! Get out! Don't touch it until I get there with my team!*"

"Until *we* get there," said Ben.

"You shouldn't go," said Carrie. "The fewer people in jeopardy, the better."

"Trust me, I need to be there."

"Look, I know this has to do with your loss, but—"

"Trust me, okay?"

Carrie shook her head decisively, as Ben's phone buzzed, and he answered it.

"*Azzy!*" he exclaimed. "*My God, are you okay?*" He listened for a long moment, then turned to the others, his face showing utter surprise. "*She's okay! She escaped!*" He turned back to the phone, asking Azariah where she was. "I'm sending a car," he said.

***

"Ow, not so hard!" exclaimed Azariah, as Ben hugged her tightly. "I'm kinda banged up." They stood in the lobby of the CIA headquarters, surrounded by dark-suited security guards. Azariah had arrived dressed in men's baggy black pants, a men's black pullover, and men's boots that were three sizes too large.

Ben relaxed his embrace and regarded her bruised and swollen face with anguish. "What did they do to you? How did you get away? We need to get you to a hospital."

"Yeah, but I've got kind of a key question. Is this the CIA? What the hell are you doing at the CIA?"

"Well, I haven't been able to tell you, or anybody else, but I've been working for them for quite a while."

"Jesus, brother, you're a spook? Wow!"

"Well, spook-*ish*. I was recruited from the university when they saw that I was doing work on terrorist psychology. They trained me in field work, weapons, and so forth, and I've been helping them."

Azariah shook her head in wonder. "And I thought I was the family badass. For so many reasons, I need a drink."

His arm around her, he walked with her to the elevator. They took it to the conference room adjacent to Grinell's office, where he introduced himself and immediately gave her a tumbler of bourbon. She took a relished gulp. Her gaze turned to Carrie, who had joined them and she stuck out her hand.

"Azariah Webber-Friedmann," she announced. "Call me Azzy. I'm the pain-in-the-*tuches* sister. And you are. . .?"

Carrie stood and took Azariah's hand. "I'm Carrie deLong."

"And what do you do, Carrie deLong?"

"I'm not at liberty to say."

"Well, given that we're here in a spook palace, I gather it's secret stuff that has to do with why dear sweet Abby was murdered."

"I can say that it does."

"Then we're sisters in this business."

"Looks like we are," said Carrie. "So, you escaped?"

"Well, I escaped *myself*. First of all, there's a body somewhere with a tactical pen embedded in his neck. It's the guy I took out in the hotel room before they zapped me. I want it back. It's my lucky pen."

"Tactical pen?" asked Carrie.

"Yeah, it looks like a pen and writes like a pen, but it's a weapon, solid metal. I stabbed him with it."

Said Grinell, "That explains the two transports from the hotel room. One was the body."

Asked Carrie, "How on earth did you escape?"

Azariah took another healthy sip of the bourbon. "Well, they had me cuffed until their boss apparently told them I had to be cleaned up."

"That was bin Shadid," said Ben.

"Is that their boss's name? Okay, so, I tell the guard I needed to take a shower. The sucker uncuffs me. Dumb move. Takes me to the shower. I figured he's Muslim, so seeing me naked is a no-no. So, he lets me go in the shower room alone. I strip down, soap up. Then open the door."

"You were naked?" asked Ben.

"Yeah, shocks hell out of, him. Stops him cold for a bit. Gives me an edge. And being all soapy made me slippery."

"But still, he was big. You could take him down?" asked Carrie.

"Well, as my dear brother might remember, I spent a couple of years in the Israeli army in my twenties. See, my Ben liked books. At least until a few minutes ago I thought he was just a bookworm." She gave her brother an accusing stare. "Anyway, I liked action. The army gave me Krav Maga combat training. It paid off. I gave the guard an uppercut that snapped his neck back and knocked him down backward. His skull hit the floor, killing him. Got his pistol, then I screamed like a girl. The other two came running not knowing what the hell was going on. They came in, and there I stood naked. I don't think they even noticed I had a pistol. Popped them both."

Smiling and shaking his head, Ben put his arm around her to take her to the hospital.

"Ben, I can go by myself," she protested. "You obviously have spook stuff to do. Tell Albert what happened, but to stay put. I might need him to do some things for me in the States." She asked Grinell to have one of the agents take her, so she could give a debriefing statement on the way to the hospital.

Seeing Ben's look of worry, Carrie said, "Ben, she'll be fine. How about we go look at a bomb?"

CHAPTER TWELVE

B en shook his head in wry amusement at the memory of Azariah's relentless interrogation of him over the phone call from the hospital. His dear, indefatigable sister had, for some reason, decided she needed details about his confrontation with bin Shadid. Even what his beard looked like. So, the memory of her quizzing him was a pleasant distraction, as he sat in the tiltrotor Osprey roaring through the sky toward the ship that could carry a thermonuclear bomb.

Their CIA jet had touched down only an hour before at Naval Station Norfolk and boarded the Osprey, with its 38-foot rotors mounted on engines that rotated to hover vertically or fly horizontally. The Osprey had just returned from deploying the SEALs on the ship *Adaliana*.

Ben and Carrie strapped themselves into the fold-down seats in the Osprey's passenger compartment, along with Carrie's CIA nuclear weapons team. The three men and two women of the team, sat stiffly in their seats, some wide-eyed, some clasping their hands in anxiety. The data analyst, the nuclear weapons engineers and the nuclear physicists were used to sitting at desks at Langly, poring over data, not roaring through the sky seeking to disarm a thermonuclear superbomb. But their deep knowledge of nuclear weapons was critical to the mission.

They all sat at the rear of the passenger compartment, whose ceiling was festooned with a profusion of cables and hydraulic lines. Near them sat the flight engineer manning the craft's 50-caliber machine gun, swivel-mounted so that it could swing into place to fire out the back when the ramp was open.

As the aircraft skimmed over the dark Atlantic waters, Ben told Carrie, who sat beside him, "Azzy demanded I tell her everything that's going on. . . about bin Shadid, the bomb, him being in Erbil." He spoked through the headset over the roar of the craft's huge engines and the loud chop of its rotors.

Carrie shrugged in resignation. "Well, I know you were violating security protocols. But she did deserve to know, given what she got landed right in the middle of. And it would give her context to be a better source of intel on her kidnapping."

"She was injured pretty bad," said Ben. "I hope she's okay. I should have stayed."

Carrie placed a comforting hand on his arm, smiling warmly. "She wouldn't have wanted that. And we do need you. You bring new eyes to the problem." She left the hand resting on his arm.

He looked down at her small hand and said. "Um, I should say that any kind of personal. . . well. . . relationship is not. . . I can't—"

She shook her head. "Ben, it's not like that. I'm just being a friend. You need support to help you through all this. Besides, I'm gay."

"Oh. That's a relief."

She chuckled. "Gee, never got that reaction before. I'm married to a wonderful woman, Beth. We have two amazing kids, a girl and a boy. She's staying home for now, but will go back to work when the kids are older."

"What does she do?"

"NSA analyst. We met on a joint mission six years ago. Love at first sight, probably like you and Abby."

"Yeah, it was." He patted her hand in appreciation of her sympathy.

121

Their talk turned to the mission at hand. Carrie began to go over the details with her team of how they would analyze the bomb. As the dawn began to break, they checked their equipment. They paid particular attention to the bomb-defusing robot, a squat, black machine on treads, fitted with two spindly, jointed arms.

After two hours, the engine noise changed, and the Osprey slowed, as its engines smoothly rotated to vertical to bring it to a hover. The passengers peered out windows at the ship below as the Osprey settled onto the deck of the aircraft carrier. As the Osprey refueled, the crew hauled their black metal cases out its rear ramp and down into its hangar deck. They stowed the cases in the aircraft and shortly, they were airborne again. After an hour, they touched down onto the *Adaliana*'s helipad with a gentle bounce, barely fitting onto its small surface.

The rear hatch opened and its ramp whined down to rest on the deck. Ben, Carrie, and three of the team members rushed out. The fourth team member took up a control box and began maneuvering the bomb disposal robot slowly toward stairs leading down to the cargo hold. They passed SEAL team members holding the crew, as well as other SEALs scouting for crew members who might have evaded them.

Ben stopped at the crew, saying, "I need to check something out."

Carrie gave him a puzzled look. "More important than finding the bomb?"

"Could be," he said, crouching beside the crew members and beginning to question them in a low, urgent tone. As he went from one man to the other, each shook his head decisively, some crying piteously. His questioning finished, Ben rushed away toward the crew quarters in the stern of the ship.

Carrie and the other team members reached the cargo hold, entering to find a massive object shrouded in canvas. They slid the canvas off to find that the object, with its metallic body and black nose and tail, to be the twin of the bomb shown in old images of the original Soviet Czar Bomb.

"We need to look inside," said Carrie. "Can you see how to get into the access panels?" The nuclear engineers nodded and began to take out the necessary tools.

"Don't do it! Don't touch the bomb!" Warned Ben, appearing at Carrie's side.

"Why not?" asked Carrie. "We need to see its mechanism. To see how operational it is."

"Look, there is absolutely no sign that bin Shadid was ever on this ship. I asked the crew, and I checked out the living quarters. No sign at all."

"Okay, maybe he wasn't. So?"

"I know him. This is personal for him. This is personal revenge. He would absolutely have been here supervising the bomb's restoration. I talked to the captain. He said some engineers. . . he thought Iraqi. . . loaded the object onto the ship in port, installed some cameras, and told him that nobody was to touch it. The crew didn't even know what was under the canvas."

"Well, maybe he's lying. Maybe he and the crew were paid to lie. And maybe the work is finished, and he had all traces of his presence erased before going back to Iraq."

"Carrie, don't take that chance. Like I said before, this is too easy. This is not like him. I beg you."

Carrie stared at him, her lips pursed in determination. "We really need close-up, personal inspection of the bomb."

"*Please!* You can always come back after it's opened."

She gave Ben an exasperated look. *"Damn! Well, damn!* Okay. We'll do the opening remotely. We'll get out of a thermonuclear blast radius. Once the bomb's open and disarmed, we'll come back."

The nuclear engineer controlling the robot nudged the joysticks on the control box to send the squat machine trundling into position inside the cargo hold. Other team members fanned out installing cameras around the ship.

Then the team, along with the SEALs and the handcuffed crew, boarded the Osprey, which lifted smoothly off the helipad. It rotated its engines, propelling its bulbous body to accelerate away across the sunlit waters.

Within two hours, it touched down on the heaving carrier deck, amid rolling, sunlit seas. Carrie and the engineers hauled their cases down metal stairs to one of the ready rooms, with its rows of seats.

The team set up the robot's control box on a table beneath the room's wall-sized video screens. They were quickly joined by the captain and other officers, who needed to monitor the mission.

Carrie sat before the joysticks and donned the virtual reality headset that would give her a real-time, three-dimensional view of the scene. The others would monitor the robot's view and the scenes from the ship cameras on the wall screens.

"Are we outside the blast radius?" asked Ben.

One of the physicists, a doughy young man in a baseball cap, consulted his laptop. "For a one hundred megaton ground burst, fireball radius would be eight kilometers; some blast damage out to fifty-five kilometers. Third-degree burns at sixty-four kilometers. We're hundreds of kilometers away, but we'll certainly get a seismic signal. We're good on radiation. The winds will spread radiation westward. It'll be real damn nasty, given that the bomb would vaporize the ship. Lots of bad radioactive metal shit."

"Well, let's hope it doesn't come to that," said Carrie taking a deep breath and clutching two joysticks to propel the robot forward.

It slowly approached the bomb, and Carrie transferred her grasp to control its arms and grippers. She had the robot pick up a screwdriver, gingerly fitting it into one screw after the other, holding the panel in place. After twenty minutes, the panel dropped away to reveal sheaves of wires and several metal boxes.

Carrie raised the robot's cameras on its boom and advanced closer to peer inside.

"Wish I could see farther forward in the bomb," she whispered, as if a louder voice might somehow disturb the bomb. "That's where the fission trigger is, that's where... SHIT!"

She jerked back in her chair and tore off the virtual reality headset, as the robot's camera view on the large screen abruptly went to static.

The group gasped and cursed in unison as one screen showed the ship's massive overhead cargo doors explode off their hinges, vaulting into the air. Other cameras throughout the ship jerked, some going to static, as the ship was rocked by an explosion. The cameras that remained operational showed flames and smoke erupting from the hold and the ship listing to one side as it began to sink.

"*What the holy hell!*" exclaimed one of the engineers.

"*It blew up! The bomb detonated!*" shouted another.

Carrie sat frowning, staring at the robot controls as if they would yield some understanding of what had happened. She finally said,

"No, no, no, it wasn't nuclear. That was the chemical explosive trigger going off. The bomb was a dud! Jesus, it was a dud."

"Nope," said Ben quietly, sitting down in one of the seats, rubbing his bearded face tiredly.

"What do you mean 'nope'?" asked Carrie.

"It wasn't a dud. Bin Shadid would never let work be done that would result in a dud."

"Then what?"

"It was a decoy. A lethal one."

***

"The Americans didn't die," said bin Shadid, handing the tablet computer back to the chief North Korean engineer. "The bomb only destroyed a robot." Bin Shadid's interpreter quietly translated the comment. They stood at a workbench near the real thermonuclear bomb on bin Shadid's ship, the *Trireme*.

The engineer smiled uncomfortably at bin Shadid, nodding noncommittally. He knew not to disagree with the ruthless oligarch. He reminded himself that he was serving the Dear Leader in this project. Success would bring rewards. Failure death.

"But it was good test of control interface," he declared, hoping for a sign of approval. "It tested satellite link and explosion timing mechanism, too. Implosion was precisely coordinated. . . Nanosecond-level. Perfectly symmetrical. If that was real bomb, detonation of atomic trigger would have been accomplished, thermonuclear fusion ignited."

The bomb now sat in its cradles stripped of its outer casing, revealing its steel skeleton. That metal framework supported both the sphere of the nuclear bomb trigger and the squat cylinders of uranium that would ignite to produce a thermonuclear blast. The other two engineers were welding brackets onto the framework for the next phase of their work.

His expression impassive, bin Shadid turned to scrutinize the six video feeds from the sinking *Adaliana* on a laptop sitting on the workbench. Three displayed only static, but the operable three showed images from the sinking freighter, as the waves washed over its deck. The cameras had been installed high in the ship's superstructure, avoiding destruction by the blast in the cargo hold.

"There will be more tests of the controls, more opportunities," said bin Shadid coolly.

The engineer smiled and nodded. He knew that bin Shadid meant not only more opportunities to test the bomb system, but to kill as many of those pursuing him as possible. He took a deep, resigned breath. "Of course, more tests always useful."

"Good." Bin Shadid took out his satellite phone and made a call, conducting a brief conversation in Kurdish. He turned back to the engineer. "I have been told that the Status-6 delivery vehicle will be completed within days. It will be flown to our next port to be loaded aboard. Were the plans you received satisfactory?"

"Yes, sir. We can make delivery vehicle fully operational. And we can integrate it with the bomb."

***

"Damn. It was just about a perfect bomb replica," said Carrie disgustedly. She and the other CIA nuclear weapons team members scrutinized side-by-side images of the Soviet-era Czar Bomb and the one found in the cargo hold of the *Adaliana*. The robot had captured images of the bomb's interior just before the explosion obliterated it.

Also sitting in the ready rom seats in the Azores was the newly arrived Department of Energy National Nuclear Security Administration team.

"Damn big loose nuke!" declared the team's head, a robust man with a bushy gray beard and a bulbous balding pate. "I take it they even put in real explosives."

"Yes, it looks like they were testing the shaped charges that would surround the plutonium core of the real atomic trigger," said Carrie.

"But just imploding the core wouldn't have sunk the ship," he said.

"No, but bin Shadid's people had planted other charges on the hull and set off by the same trigger. The ship went down in waters a couple of miles deep. So we won't be gathering more evidence any time soon."

"Obviously, they linked with the device via satellite," said the DOE engineer. "Can you trace it?"

Carrie shook her head in frustration. "NSA is on it, but there is a lot of traffic on communication satellites. And the communication is coded. They did manage to capture bin Shadid's voice on the phone in Iraq. He was talking with his engineer in Basra. They talked about some devices he was having built. Probably one was this replica bomb. The frustrating thing is that there may be more for us to deal with."

"There will be. He wants to distract you," said Ben, who had been quietly contemplating the images along with the other. "Of course, you'll have to treat them as real. But my advice, look where they *aren't*."

"And that means?" asked Carrie.

"He knows we're hunting the bomb, and he hasn't much time. So, the ship with the bomb is headed directly for its target, and the decoys will be as far as possible from that target."

"And you said he'd want to be on that ship. But he hasn't traveled from Erbil."

"That's a puzzle. That's a real puzzle." Ben took out his cell phone and waved it. "I'm gonna check on Azzy." He moved away from the group and punched in the number of Azariah's new cell phone. She answered quickly. She seemed to be talking over engine noise.

"How are you?" he asked. "What are the doctors saying?"

"They said I'm just fine," she said, her voice raised.

"You were pretty bruised. Your body was bruised. Do you have cracked ribs?"

"Ben, I'm just fine."

"Well, you just rest in the hospital."

"Well, uh, I'm not exactly in the hospital."

"*Azzy, where the hell are you? What's that noise?*"

"I'm on an airplane. Actually, I'm on the way to Iraq. You told me the son-of-a-bitch is in Erbil. Gonna pay him a visit."

Before Ben could protest, she ended the call.

CHAPTER THIRTEEN

"Well, there's another one we'll never get to inspect," said Carrie, peering through her sunglasses in the desert sun across the water, as the Iraqi freighter ship disappeared beneath the Red Sea. The explosion and sinking of the freighter launched a substantial wave that caused the people on the navy patrol boat to brace themselves against its rocking. They watched the rusting freighter go down stern first, its red bow pointing up to the cloudless sky, as its white superstructure disappeared.

"Water's a couple of thousand feet deep here," she said. "We'd need a submersible or an ROV. I'm not inclined to go ask an oil company for one."

"And that's another robot lost," said the nuclear engineer beside her. Crouched around her was her team, dressed in khaki shorts, t-shirts, and floppy hats.

Carrie shrugged. "Better than losing people." She closed the case containing the robot's controls. "And we did get more video to analyze."

As before, Ben had gone along with an interpreter to question the crew taken off the freighter. He returned shaking his head.

"They didn't see bin Shadid, either," he said. "It was just like the *Adaliana* in the Atlantic and the other decoy ship in the Persian Gulf. They said a crew loaded a big shrouded object on board, installed cameras, and told them never to look in the cargo hold."

"Well, at least the one in the Persian Gulf actually came from Iraq. It was headed for Japan. And this one. . ." Carrie pointed an

130

accusing finger at the spot where the freighter had sunk, ". . . was bound for Mumbai."

"So, now we have at least a couple more data points as clues where he is *really* going."

"I'd hate to try to graph it. We really need to get agents into Iraq and put him under closer surveillance. There may be hints at a location for the ship. I'll get hold of Grinell and see what assets we have in Erbil."

Ben took off his sunglasses and rubbed his beard, taking a deep breath. "Well, there is one possibility," he said shrugging. "You won't like it."

Carrie gave him a dubious look. "From that tone, I'm sure I won't."

"We do have an asset in Iraq I didn't want to tell you about."

"Who?"

"Azzy."

"And what the hell does she expect to accomplish there?"

Ben stared grimly at Carrie. "I'm not sure, but I'm worried that . . ." He did not finish the sentence.

Carrie realized the possible import of his unfinished sentence and threw back her head. "*Oh, dear God!*"

***

Havana harbor's smothering shroud of heat and humidity engulfed bin Shadid, as he stood at the railing of the freighter *Trireme*. But he ignored the sweltering weather and the rivulets of sweat running down his face, as he peered expectantly down the dock. He had dressed in his disguise of a wig, glasses, and shabby clothes to avoid even the remote possibility that some Cuban might recognize him.

The road to the dock remained empty. The captain and crew of the *Trireme* were busily loading supplies, but the expected convoy had not yet appeared.

The gently lapping waves made bin Shadid's thoughts turn to a happier time when he had brought his family to his seaside villa in Palm Jumeirah in Dubai. He remembered the lyrical laugh of his beautiful wife Faiza, as she played in the warm Persian Gulf waters with his son Hakeem, then a chubby toddler, and his delicate, sweet daughter Isra.

But as with so many times since their murders, his thoughts then fell victim to the agonizing memory of that horrific day that they died. Of hearing the boom of the explosion as he and Khalid approached the wedding site. Of seeing the rising cloud of smoke against the blue sky. Of running with Khalid toward the smoldering pile of rubble that had been the site of joy and hope, but was now a funeral pyre.

Of being surrounded by screaming, crying people madly tearing away chunks of the cinderblock building, desperate to find loved ones alive. Of finding body after body until late at night, finding the limp body of little Isra. Of Khalid, weeping uncontrollably carrying her from the ruins. And then the final soul-shattering horror of finding Faiza's broken body amid the rubble clutching Hakeem.

His hands gripped the ship's rail, as his heart-wrenching sorrow was overtaken by rage. And that rage drove the determination to carry out this powerful act of revenge. And that rage metastasized to a determination to avenge the larger evil of the murder of thousands of Iraqis by the Americans.

He was brought back from his dark reverie by the sight of three white SUVs and three large canvas-covered trucks coming down the long concrete dock toward the ship. He moved to the gangplank, and the crew immediately stopped their loading to let him pass.

The convoy rolled to a stop, and his engineer Fayez Badour climbed out of the first SUV bowing to bin Shadid, who strode down the gangplank to meet him.

As seven other men emerged from the SUVs, bin Shadid asked, "Everything is in order? All the people and equipment made it? The weapons? And the vehicle?"

"Yes, but. . ." answered Badour. His expression worried, he gestured down the dock at another convoy that had followed them.

Speeding toward them were an army-green Cuban military command vehicle with a mounted machinegun, followed by two troop trucks. The vehicles stopped, and a dozen soldiers armed with AKM assault rifles leaped out of the trucks. From the command vehicle emerged a Cuban army lieutenant, a lean, deeply tanned man, who scanned bin Shadid's convoy and ship with a scowl.

Badour herded his men quickly onto the ship and returned to stand beside his leader. Rahnim joined him, touching the pistol holstered at his side.

A quick summoning gesture from bin Shadid brought the captain and the woman interpreter hurrying down the gangplank. She stood beside bin Shadid, eyes downcast in discomfort at wearing the immodest disguise of sneakers, jeans, and t-shirt.

The lieutenant, flanked by soldiers, approached the group, demanding in Spanish, "Who is in charge of this ship?"

Bin Shadid answered through the interpreter. "This is my ship. Is there a problem? We are merely taking on supplies and cargo. We have permission from your government."

"What is this cargo you are loading?" The lieutenant gestured to the trucks. "The harbor master informed me that you have come from the Middle East. What cargo could you want from Cuba?"

"We are loading pipes, pumps, other equipment. Again, I have been given permission from your government." Bin Shadid did not say that the permission had been given after a substantial sum of money had been transferred to the Cuban Minister of Transportation.

The lieutenant scanned the ship's deck and the men brought by Badour, who were disappearing into the cabins. "I suspect that those people you are taking on board are dissidents you are smuggling out of the country. And perhaps your ship holds supplies, perhaps even weapons, that you are giving the dissidents."

"As I said, we are merely loading equipment."

"We will inspect the trucks. We will inspect your ship for dissidents and weapons." The lieutenant issued a curt command to the sergeant standing beside him. The sergeant moved back to the massed soldiers, ordering one group to move toward the ship, and another to approach the trucks.

"Before your men commit acts that will get them *imprisoned* you should inspect the ship yourself." Bin Shadid instructed his interpreter to convey the message loudly, and she voiced it so that the soldiers could hear. They stopped their movement and looked nervously from the sergeant to the lieutenant.

The lieutenant's eyes widened, and after a long pause, he curtly instructed his sergeant to hold.

"What do you mean imprisoned?" he asked.

"I have been in direct contact with your Minister of Transportation. We obtained his expressed permission to dock and take on cargo. To countermand that permission would constitute disobeying your own government."

"Why would the Minister—"

"Just come on board yourself and see for yourself that the men who arrived are not dissidents. It is the most efficient thing to do."

The lieutenant shifted uneasily back and forth from one foot to the other. Then abruptly, he nodded and stalked up the gangplank onto the ship, followed by bin Shadid and the interpreter. Bin Shadid escorted the soldier to his quarters in the cargo hold, where the lieutenant smiled and shook his head in wonder at the lush decor on the otherwise seedy freighter. Rahnim accompanied them, unfastening the leather strap holding his pistol in the holster.

Bin Shadid poured himself a glass of ice water and offered one to the lieutenant, who declined with an impatient wave.

After taking a sip, bin Shadid said, "I know you are a busy man, so I would suggest that you do not need to conduct a full search of the ship or my trucks. I think I can satisfy your curiosity right here and now."

"I'm not sure exactly how you could accomplish that," said the lieutenant.

Bin Shadid nodded at Rahnim, who pulled a small canvas satchel from a safe.

"I find that curiosity can be allayed, and consequences avoided, by the offering of a gift," he said, gesturing for the satchel to be handed to the lieutenant.

The lieutenant opened it to reveal bundled stacks of one-hundred-dollar bills. He stared silently at the money, seeming to ponder the calculus of his next decision. Clearing his throat, he zipped the bag shut, and announced, "I am done here." He pivoted about and left.

Bin Shadid, Rahnim, and the interpreter followed him out to hear him bark orders to his men, who loaded back into the trucks. He climbed into his own vehicle, which executed a quick U-turn and sped away down the dock, followed by the troop trucks.

"Load quickly, so we can get out of port," said bin Shadid, who took up a position on the deck to watch, Badour coming to stand beside him.

For the next hour, the ships cranes hoisted pallets of crates and metal cases into the ship's hold. Three of the new men hauled an air compressor, dive tanks, and other scuba equipment up the gangplank and onto the deck.

"The men are all loyal?" bin Shadid asked Badour, watching the men.

"Yes, Agha bin Shadid. The four marine engineers have been with us for decades. They worked around the clock, executed the Russian blueprints perfectly. They deeply feel your pain for your family, for our people. They seek the same revenge as you. And the divers, too. They are our best."

Bin Shadid was silent, nodding slowly in appreciation.

Then came the lift of three large-diameter twenty-foot cylinders off the trucks, and bin Shadid descended with Badour into the hold, watching intently, jaw set, as they ponderously lowered.

Finally, the hold's massive overhead hatches creaked closed, leaving only the glare of the work lights to illuminate the interior.

Resting on three steel cradles were the three cylinders that had just been loaded. Beside them sat the bomb, surrounded only by its steel frame, its Styrofoam packing removed revealing its electronics, nuclear trigger, and second and third stages.

The four Iraqi marine engineers and the three Korean nuclear engineers were intently inspecting the three cylinders, talking quietly among themselves. The interpreter, now more modestly dressed in an abaya, had difficulty keeping up with the translation between Kurdish and Korean.

"Tell me what I am looking at," said bin Shadid. "I examined the Russian plans, but I want to make sure."

Badour smiled in quiet pride. "Agha bin Shadid, you are looking at the three sections of a Status-6 drone torpedo. . . Poseidon, the Russians call it. Our engineers brilliantly adapted the plans you procured so that the bomb can fit into the middle section. The nose section contains guidance and navigation mechanisms. The tail section contains the batteries and ramjet propulsion system. It has no propellers, so it runs silent. Undetectable."

"Did the adaption affect performance?"

"Not at all. Since Russians designed the torpedo to carry a nuclear payload, its speed and maneuverability will be unaffected by having the bomb installed. However, range is affected because we had to use batteries for propulsion, rather than the nuclear reactor in the Russian plans. But the range is perfectly adequate for your purposes."

"What's next?"

"I will check." Badour excused himself and moved off to huddle with the engineers. After several minutes, he returned.

"Agha bin Shadid, the engineers say they need a week to assemble and bench test the drone," he said. "By then, we will have made it to our position closer to the target. Once there, they propose to load it with ballast to mimic the mass of the bomb. Then, we will conduct a sea trial."

"And if the trial is successful?"

"Then we mate it with the bomb. We test the entire system. Then we can proceed to target."

***

"*Azzy, Where the hell are you? How the hell did you get there? What the hell do you think you can accomplish?*"

Ben launched the rapid-fire questions at Azariah without waiting for a reply. He scowled at her image on his cell phone, as she shrugged in seeming nonchalance. She was dressed in a head scarf, sitting on a couch. He remembered to keep his voice down. He, Carrie, and the nuclear weapons team had just landed in Baghdad after a flight from the Saudi port of Jeddah. Ben moved away from Carrie and the others who might overhear.

"As I promised, dear brother, I'm in Erbil," she answered. "An old boyfriend, Jonas, from my time in Israel smuggled me across the

Turkish border. He's with Mossad now. As luck would have it, he was stationed in Iraq. Please don't tell Albert. He'll get jealous, the dear man. You know how he is, he—"

"Again, what the hell do you hope to accomplish?"

"When I told him what was going on, my guy hooked me up with a local Mossad operative. We're going to—"

"You told him? You told Israeli intelligence that we're tracking a hydrogen bomb?"

"It sure got his attention. And it got me cooperation."

"Cooperation to do what?"

"To stop this monster."

Ben paused, steadying himself as the enormity of what his sister planned to do sank in. It confirmed his worst fear. She was putting herself in mortal danger. He couldn't possibly let her proceed. But then the horrifying memory of finding Abby's body returned. And the heartbreaking memory of her sweet smile, her laugh, their last warm embrace and the feel of her pregnant belly. His dark rage renewed itself.

"What is your plan?" he asked coldly. He knew his sister's history as a soldier. He knew she was fully capable of killing.

"Jonas has contacts in Erbil who can locate bin Shadid's home and his office. I've also got some ideas about how to get close."

"Just ideas? Azzy, please, please promise me that you will only do this if you are sure you can get out alive. Promise me that."

"My dearest brother, I do not want to subject you and Mom and Dad to losing two family members. This local guy is good. And you know I've got the training."

"Promise, Azzy!"

"I can promise I'll only go in if I have a good chance of accomplishing the mission and getting out."

"Look, I know the man. . . better than you do. At least promise me that you'll contact me when you're there and if possible let me see everything that's going on."

"Then kill him?"

Ben paused, beset by moral qualms. But then he took a deep tremulous breath, remembered the evil behind the tragedy he had suffered, felt his anger rise, a fire in his soul, and whispered, "Kill him."

CHAPTER FOURTEEN

"*Oh, sweet Jesus!*" whispered Grinell. He was perched on the edge of the desk in the Baghdad CIA station, staring up at one of the wall screens. "The pieces fit."

"What pieces?" asked Carrie. She had entered carrying a tray of coffees for her, Grinell, and Ben. They were still bleary-eyed from their travels and spending hours poring over images from the decoy ships.

"Carrie, what country represents the worst-case scenario for getting the hydrogen bomb?" asked Grinell.

"North Korea, no doubt," she answered. "They have the nuclear technology to engineer one. And they're beginning to have the missile technology to deliver a warhead."

"Well, bin Shadid is almost certain to give them the bomb technology."

Ben came up beside him, looking at the screen, shaking his head. "It does fit with his psychology and his goal of revenge."

"What makes you say North Korea will get the technology?" asked Carrie.

Grinell gestured at the screen showing an array of emails and graphs. "This is the intelligence thread from our operatives. We had the first inkling North Korea was involved from some really odd data from China. Our station chief there said his operative in China had seen a big spike in flow through the oil pipeline into North Korea."

"So, China was being generous to North Korea?" asked Carrie.

"China is *never* generous. I figured the oil had to come from somewhere. On a hunch, I asked our analysts for their data on bin Shadid's ships. Sure enough, he redirected five tankers from Basra to China. We did a calculation, and that matches the increase in flow to North Korea."

"Why would he do that?" asked Ben.

"Well, we couldn't figure how in hell could bin Shadid hope to restore that bomb. He needed experts. Knowledgeable engineers. Iran was one source, but like you said, Carrie, North Korea would be the best. They already have nuclear weapon technology. And they would be drooling for plans for a thermonuclear bomb."

"So, he would be looking for North Korean engineers?" asked Ben.

"Yup, and you can be sure they would help him. And in return, they would be allowed to gather the specs and plans to let their country build a thermonuclear weapon. That development would exponentially increase the global nuclear threat."

"We need more intel from China," said Carrie. "Can we find out whether there's been any significant activity along the China-North Korean border?"

"No, we're blind in that area now."

"Why?"

"Our operative disappeared. As far as we know North Korean nuclear engineers are already working for bin Shadid."

"I agree with your reaction," said Carrie. "Sweet Jesus."

***

"Faint," Jonas instructed Azariah. She and the dark-eyed, thickly bearded young Mossad agent had just reached the gate in front of bin Shadid's sprawling stucco villa. Azariah was disguised in a long abaya with a veil hiding her face.

Azariah obediently crumpled to the pavement baking in the hundred-degree Iraqi summer. She was sure that the camera mounted above the gate had captured the scene.

Jonas assumed a stricken look, as he pushed the button to the intercom and knocked on the gate, pleading in fluent Kurdish,

"My wife! She has become ill from the heat! Please help us! She is with child!"

A voice from the intercom said, "Take her to hospital."

"I need to cool her down immediately! Please! By the grace of Allah, please! She is my wife!"

After several minutes, a black-suited security man appeared at the gate, frowning down at Azariah. His frown vanished when he saw Jonas, who was dressed as a Muslim cleric.

"As-salamu alaikum," said Jonas.

"Wa alaikum assalaam," replied the guard quickly. "Imam, I am so sorry about your wife. Please come in." He opened the gate and stood back, bowing.

"You are most merciful," said Jonas, lifting Azariah up and helping her through the gate. She stumbled and panted, as Jonas half-carried her through the ornately carved mahogany door and into the two-story, marble-floored entry. "May we please have privacy so that she may remove her abaya?" he asked as he slipped off his shoes and helped Azariah do the same. "Her modesty demands it."

"Of course," said the security man solicitously, leading them up the curved staircase to the second floor. They entered a bedroom hung with Persian tapestries and with a massive four-poster bed. "Shall I call a physician?"

"Let me just cool her. Then we will continue our journey. May I trouble you for water?"

"Yes, Imam. I will send some up. Would you like tea? Refreshments? Would you like to stay overnight?"

"Water will be sufficient, my son," said Jonas. "And your offer of lodging is most kind, but we are on our way to a mosque where I have been assigned."

The bedroom door closed, and Azariah tore off the veil and the abaya, moving quickly to the window. She wore a gray jumpsuit, and strapped to her chest was a compact AR-15 pistol. Jonas moved up beside her, also surveying the scene.

"Jackpot!" she exclaimed "My God, jackpot!" The window looked out over a large swimming pool, and lounging beneath the shade of the mansion's portico was Saadallah bin Shadid. Glaring at the man, Azariah unstrapped the AR-15 pistol, unfolded its stock, and pulled a silencer from her pocket, screwing it on. She pulled out the magazine, checked the cartridges and snapped it back in. She quietly opened the window.

"I've got a great shot. I can get him center mass, and he won't make a sound. They won't even know he's dead, and we can get out."

Jonas clasped his hand on her shoulder. "Okay, but remember what you promised your brother."

Azariah took a deep, frustrated breath and groaned. "Yeah, yeah."

A knock at the door interrupted them, and Jonas moved to open it just wide enough to take a tray with a pitcher of ice water and a glass.

Azariah took the time to connect with her brother on video. After a moment, his worried face appeared on the screen.

"Where are you?" he demanded.

"Jonas and I made it into his house," said Azariah. "I've got eyes on bin Shadid. I've got a perfect shot."

"How did you manage that?"

Azariah swung the phone around to show the Mossad agent. "Jonas posed as my husband. He dressed as a cleric. I wore a veil and pretended to have heat exhaustion. It got us in. I need to kill the bastard, and get out."

"Look, Azzy, I'm in Baghdad with Carrie. Grinell has just arrived." The phone image showed Ben pausing and looking up from the phone. "Um, actually, I'm *not* with them anymore. When they heard 'kill', they left. CIA doesn't sanction killing of foreign nationals. They had argued like hell against it, but I told them it was not their business."

"Okay, so I'm taking the shot."

"Not until you show me the scene. *Azzy, just hold off!*"

"*Drek!*" she exclaimed. Then, "Okay." Azariah pointed the cell phone to show bin Shadid lounging by the pool.

"Now can I kill him?"

"Zoom in."

"*Shit!*" she whispered, but did so. The magnified scene centered on the man's tanned torso and face, his eyes hidden behind sunglasses.

"What's he doing?"

"He's just lying there having a glass of wine."

"You sure that's wine?"

Azariah paused to scrutinize the scene. "Yeah, there's an ice bucket beside him with a bottle in it."

"Azzy, tell me everything that happened when you got into the house."

"*Will you let me take the goddamned shot?*"

"*Not until you tell me, Azzy!*"

"Like I said, the guard let us in because he thought Jonas was an imam. And I was his pregnant wife. He showed us to this bedroom. He brought ice water. That's it. Now can I take the shot?"

"*Azzy, that is not bin Shadid! I repeat, that is not bin Shadid!*"

"But he looks exactly like the picture you gave me."

"The guy at the pool must be a double. Azzy, the real bin Shadid is a devout Muslim. He doesn't drink alcohol. In fact, it's certain bin Shadid isn't in residence, because he wouldn't have even allowed liquor in the house. The guy must have sneaked the wine in. Also, if bin Shadid had been in the house, the guard would have told him about the cleric, and he would have come to greet him personally. Azzy! *Get the hell out!*"

"Okay, okay. But what does this mean?" she asked.

"It solves a big mystery. Now I'm sure bin Shadid is with the bomb. That means if we can track him, we can find it!

***

The crack of a rifle shot brought bin Shadid rushing to the starboard side of the ship, leaning over the railing. He joined the Korean and Iraqi engineers anxiously watching the scene.

The rolling swells of the ocean sent the ship heaving, as bin Shadid scanned the sea surface. Even with his sunglasses on, he squinted against the reflected glare of sunlight.

Below, two wet-suited divers were struggling to shove the massive drone torpedo away from the ship's hull, so it could be launched on its sea trial. They had just unhitched the drone from the steel brackets connecting it to the thick cables of the ship's heavy-lift crane.

The rifle shot had come from the third diver, who had remained on board as a lookout for sharks. He was stationed a dozen feet away on the railing.

When bin Shadid gave him a questioning look, he pointed to the area off the boat's stern. The massive gray body of a Great White shark thrashed the water in its death throes, dark blood flowing from the bullet wound.

"Sir, we must get them out!" shouted the diver. "Others will come soon!"

"Is the drone safe?" asked bin Shadid. "Is it clear of the ship?"

Two shark fins surfaced farther out from the ship, slicing through the waves as the sharks headed toward the divers. The divers gave the drone one last shove and leaped into the inflatable boat. One started the engine, and they managed to wedge it between the ship's hull and the drone. As the drone slammed against the inflatable boat, the other diver gestured urgently to bin Shadid. He took up his two-way radio and commanded,

"Start it up! Now!"

This would be the ultimate test of the drone. The Korean and Iraqi engineers had worked on it around the clock since the ship *Trireme* had made its way closer to its target.

A gush of water erupted from the tail of the drone as its ramjet propulsion came to life with a loud hiss. The explosive burst of water engulfed the divers, and the sixty-foot-long black torpedo moved ponderously away from the ship.

Bin Shadid bounded up the metal stairs to the bridge, where his chief engineer Badour and the head Korean engineer watched a computer screen. Beside them stood the interpreter, quietly translating their clipped conversation.

Badour handed bin Shadid a tablet computer, saying, "You should be able to control all functions from here."

"Navigation? Targeting? Detonation?" asked Bin Shadid, scanning the tablet's screen.

"Yes, Agha bin Shadid, all functions."

"And the ballast in the torpedo?"

"I double-checked, as you instructed. It matches the weight of the bomb. I recommend that you navigate the torpedo out four kilometers and return four kilometers to the ship. Start with the low speed, which gives it stealth, then end the last kilometer with high speed, which makes it not able to be intercepted."

With Badour's coaching, bin Shadid entered the commands into the tablet. They intently watched the computer screen, as the map showed the glowing dot marking the drone move slowly away from the ship. They followed its course intently for an hour, when the dot reversed and began the return leg.

"This will amaze you, Agha bin Shadid," declared Badour. "Bring the torpedo to the surface, and go outside, if you please."

Bin Shadid entered the commands, and he, the interpreter, Badour, and the Korean engineer moved outside and down the steps to the railing.

Badour said, "Now you will see it in high-speed mode, where it will randomly alter course to evade interception."

They scanned the surging ocean in the direction of the torpedo. Suddenly, a boiling eruption of spray marked the torpedo's location, and they could see its black shape accelerating toward them. It swerved left for a minute, bursting through the waves, then swerved right. It accelerated toward the ship, finally slowing two hundred yards out, its momentum carrying it to within fifty yards of the ship.

The divers, who had been resting aboard the ship, climbed down into the inflatable boat and sped out to the torpedo, hooking a cable to it, and beginning to tow the massive drone slowly back toward the ship. The heavy-lift crane whined to life, swinging over the starboard side and lowering its twin cables to the water.

As the divers hooked the drone to the crane, bin Shadid turned to the Korean engineer. "Are you satisfied?" he asked.

The engineer nodded, his answer translated as, "Yes, sir, the delivery system worked perfectly. Now, we can install the weapon."

Bin Shadid glanced briefly heavenward. Allah was blessing his labors with continued success. He would go below and pray for ultimate victory.

***

The portly, middle-aged man with the thatch of curly, gray hair cursed at the Iraqi soldiers as they shoved him into the CIA interrogation room. He was still dressed in a robe and slippers. Early that morning, they had burst into his penthouse apartment in Baghdad, handcuffed him, and driven him into the fortress that was the American Embassy in the sprawling Green Zone.

He also cursed Ben, Carrie, Grinell, and the Baghdad CIA station chief, as he was shoved onto a chair across the table from them, his hands bound in plastic cuffs.

"You are Barahim bin Ramezani?" asked Grinell.

"You are Americans?" he asked in heavily accented English. "What do you want with me?"

"Are you bin Ramezani?" asked Grinell again.

"You know who I am. And I know you are CIA scum, yes? You are ones who came in before war and kidnap and interrogate and torture us. And you . . . what is word? *Doublecross* us. We want to surrender, but your general says 'No, we make war.' I was in Iraqi intelligence. We knew about you."

"We're more interested in your friend Saadallah bin Shadid."

Bin Ramezani paused, stiffening. "I only know the name."

"Bullshit," said Grinell. He slapped a photo on the table. It showed eleven grinning young men dressed in soccer uniforms. Circled in red were two of the men standing beside one another with their arms linked. "You went to school with him. You played soccer together. You were at his wedding."

Bin Ramezani laughed sarcastically. "Oh, *that* Saadallah bin Shadid."

"And seven of his ships are registered in *your* name."

"His ships? No, I am successful businessman. I can buy my own ships."

Carrie leaned in toward bin Ramezani, and he shifted uncomfortably at having a woman so close to him. "Is he on one of those ships?"

"He has his own ships. He does not need mine."

"Which ship?" asked Carrie.

"Do you know what he plans to do with that ship?" asked Grinell.

"He has his own ships to do whatever he wants."

Ben had sat through the exchange, glaring at the jowly man. Ben got up and circled around behind bin Ramezani. He bent down and said with cold menace into bin Ramezani's ear, "He intends to use it to commit a horrific terrorist act that will kill massive numbers of people. And he killed my wife and my unborn son. Imagine the vengeance I will extract on you, and even on your family, if you do not tell what you know."

Grinell stood up and said to Carrie. "I think perhaps we will take a breather, get a cup of coffee. And leave Ben and Mr. bin Ramezani to chat." He turned to go, then stopped and turned back. "By the way, if you aren't persuaded by Mr. Webber, think about this. By not telling us what we need to know, if Saadallah bin Shadid carries out his act, we will *disappear* you. You will spend the rest of your life at a black site. Someplace not very nice. I'm thinking Thailand. Actually, the rest of your life might not be that long." He nodded to Ben and opened the door.

"Wait!" exclaimed bin Ramezani, jerking his head back and forth between Ben and Grinell, his eyes wide. Beads of sweat appeared on his brow. And in a frightened whisper, he said,

"*Trireme.*"

***

"The ship disappeared, went dark," said Carrie, striding up and down before a series of glowing wall screens in the CIA's Baghdad Operations Center. The screens displayed a world map, in which the oceans were cluttered with red dots marking the positions of ships. Sitting across from the screens was a row of computer terminals being intently scrutinized by CIA analysts. A hushed murmur pervaded the large, darkened room, as if the analysts believed that to speak at a normal level would somehow cause secrets to leak out.

"What do you mean 'disappeared'?" asked Ben.

"The *Trireme* just vanished from the tracking system after it left port. Ships use an automatic identification and location system. It works anywhere on Earth, since it transmits to satellites. But the *Trireme* turned off its AIS transponder after it left Istanbul."

Said Grinell, "That means we'll have to rely on humint. . . human intelligence. . . to find it." He moved off to confer with the Ops Center officers sitting at desks on the far side of the room.

"Any idea where it could have gone?" asked Ben.

"Anywhere," said Carrie. "Whether bin Shadid meant to or not, he was smart to pick Istanbul. From there, the ship could have gone through the Mediterranean and the Strait of Gibraltar to the Atlantic. Or through the Suez Canal to the Red Sea and on to the Pacific. Hell, with his contacts and resources, he could even have switched ships. He could have taken it off the ship, moved it through Turkey and down to Basra and put it on another of his secretly owned ships in the Persian Gulf. That way his buddy bin Ramezani would be giving us false information without even knowing it."

"Then we should take another run at him," said Ben. "Maybe he knows more than he thinks about what another ship might be."

"You did scare him," said Carrie. She smiled conspiratorially. "Did you really mean what you said about revenge. . . going after his family?"

"It was a tactic I thought would work. My studies of the *Quran*, helped me get inside bin Shadid's head. To Muslims, revenge is more acceptable than in western religions. So, bin Ramezani would take my threat more to heart. I was counting on that."

Grinell returned, shaking his head. He scanned the screens, saying nothing.

"So, what's the plan?" asked Carrie.

"The goddamned ship could be anywhere," he answered. "We're putting out a global alert to all our operatives, and sending a classified message to Interpol. We're telling them the *Trireme* is carrying contraband. We're *not* telling them that there's a thermonuclear bomb on the ship. If that got out, the world would go nuts. Not only that, but every pirate, terrorist, and rogue state would be looking to hijack that ship to try to get hold of the bomb. And if bin Shadid finds out he's been identified, he might just put into the nearest port and detonate the bomb."

"Meantime?" asked Carrie.

"We pray that somehow, somewhere, somebody sees something. We pray hard."

CHAPTER FIFTEEN

"We are talking to the bomb," said the chief engineer Badour, with a faint, proud smile. "And it is talking back."

He patted the sonar-absorbing rubber tiles shrouding the hull of the sixty-foot drone torpedo. The huge cylinder rested on four steel cradles in the hold of the *Trireme*. Badour's other hand held a tablet computer, and he offered it to bin Shadid, who took it almost reverently in both hands, staring solemnly at it.

"What does tell you?" he asked.

Badour pointed to numbers in one part of the display. "Here, it is telling you its GPS coordinates. Here is where the coordinates of the target will be displayed, although it is blank now. Here is where—"

"I will enter the target coordinates now."

Badour paused, his eyes widening. "Very well, Agha bin Shadid. You know them?"

"I memorized them long ago." With that, bin Shadid touched the tablet screen to bring up the keypad, entering longitude and latitude down to four decimal places. "Tell me the rest of the controls," he said.

Badour paused before replying. His hand trembled slightly as he pointed out the other elements of the display. It had been so jarringly casual, this momentous step in the targeting of this unimaginably destructive weapon.

"You can enter a time to detonation here. So, if the drone does not reach its target, the bomb will still detonate."

Still holding the tablet, bin Shadid walked the length of the drone, nose to tail, sliding his palm along its smooth surface. He reached the tail, where the exit ports for the ramjet propulsion jutted from the body. The Korean engineers were carefully bolting down the covering over the turbine, in a final step to seal the torpedo's hull.

Bin Shadid gestured for the interpreter to approach, and he told the Koreans through her, "You have done well. Your work here is done."

A worried expression on his face, the North Korean engineer bowed three times and thanked him, just as Badour's satellite phone emitted the tone signaling a call. He stepped away to take it, and after ten minutes returned, his expression grim.

"Bin Ramezani was abducted in Baghdad," he told bin Shadid. "My security man traced him to the Green Zone. My source inside said he was taken to the US Embassy. The CIA station is there, and I'm sure that's where he is. We can also be sure that he has told them of the *Trireme*. What will you have me do, Agha bin Shadid?"

"Ready the drone for launch. Set a course for the target."

***

The Cuban CIA agent shoved open the door to the cluttered, paper-littered office of the Havana harbormaster and marched in. The slight, wrinkled harbormaster with the deep tan sat bolt upright when the imposing, beefy man with a thick walrus mustache and an imposing, unruly mop of graying curls stood looming above him. The harbormaster was also intimidated by the agent's uniform identifying him as a sergeant in the Revolutionary Armed Forces. It had been a useful cover for the agent before, and it would serve very well now. He found that his rank was perfect for his purpose. He was not an officer, so that his activities would draw attention. But he had authority, especially with civilians like the harbormaster.

"You had a ship here last week, the *Trireme*, no?" the agent demanded.

The man stammered, "Um, I would have to check my—"

"Tell me when they came in, when they left, and what cargo they loaded."

The harbormaster opened his mouth as if to object, glanced down at the pistol on the sergeant's hip, and began typing away on his ancient computer with its smudged keyboard.

"Yes, yes, I see it here. It arrived a week ago Friday and stayed in port only two days."

"Loading what?" demanded the sergeant.

"There is no cargo manifest listed for loading," said the harbormaster, scrutinizing the computer screen.

"Then what the hell was it doing here?"

"I don't—"

"Find out. I am reporting to my lieutenant, who is reporting to the captain, who is reporting the colonel, who is reporting to the general. Do you want them all to come down on you?"

"Oh no! No! I can find out." The harbormaster snatched up the phone. He dialed, and when the other party answered, proceeded to quiz him on the *Trireme*'s cargo. He hung up and turned back to the sergeant. "I called the dock supervisor. He remembers the ship because soldiers came to inspect it. You could check—'

"I will not check with anyone. You will tell me what you know."

"Well, uh, the supervisor said that he saw men board with equipment, including diving equipment. And big cases, like for weapons. And he saw them load pipe."

"Pipe? Like water pipe? Oil pipeline pipe?"

"No, he said it was neither. He worked in the oilfields in Venezuela. He said it was only three pieces, and they were much larger than oil pipes. They were, he said, maybe twice as big."

"And where did these men and these big pipes come from?"

"I didn't ask," said the harbormaster, snatching up the phone again and making a second call. After a brief conversation, he hung up and turned back to the sergeant. "He said he wasn't sure. But he heard one of the men say something about a long flight. I hope—"

But the sergeant had already turned to leave. Outside the harbormaster's tin shack, he climbed into his utility vehicle and drove to Jose Marti airport, inflicting the same intimidating military presence on the cargo supervisor there. It took only a little pressure for the nervous man to check his flight manifest and discover that an Egyptian cargo plane had arrived the day the *Trireme* docked, and had unloaded men, equipment, and cargo. The flight had almost certainly been carrying cargo originating in Iraq.

The sergeant returned to his day's duties at the barracks. That night over a beer, he transmitted a coded document via his cell phone revealing all he had learned that day. He emphasized the unusual diameter and weight of the pipes loaded onto the ship. And also, the unusual number, only three.

***

"Just be quiet and do as you're told," loudly commanded the Israeli Mossad agent Jonas, as they approached the auto repair shop on the busy Erbil street. The command was meant to be overheard.

Azariah merely nodded meekly, as Jonas had coached her to do. It was not in her nature to remain mute, but she didn't know Kurdish, so silent assent was the best tactic with the mechanics. She was dressed in baggy fatigues and a head scarf, carrying a small canvas bag.

For this mission, Jonas was no longer her "husband". He was now her "supervisor". Dressed in an Iraqi army uniform, he strode into the garage, demanding "Where is the owner? I need to talk to the owner."

A middle-aged, gray-bearded man hurried up, wiping his hands with a greasy rag, smiling obsequiously. "Sir, I am the owner. How may I help you?"

"We have received intelligence that terrorists may be installing bombs in the vehicles of prominent people in Erbil. I am checking garages to ascertain their level of security."

"Oh, sir, we have the very highest level. I can assure you of that."

"And who does this limousine belong to?" asked Jonas, waving his hand at the black car.

"Agha Saadallah bin Shadid. His driver brings it in each week for servicing and cleaning."

"And do you watch such vehicles around the clock?"

The garage owner grimaced. "Well, we lock them up at night."

Jonas glared at the man. "Not good enough. I need to have my technician, this woman here, inspect the vehicle, to see whether it has been tampered with."

Jonas nodded at Azariah, who moved toward the limousine.

"Oh, sir, I am not sure that the driver would allow that. I should call—"

"You are preventing my technician from inspecting the car? That is suspicious, to say the least. I am calling in guards. We are shutting down your garage." He took out his cell phone, poised to punch in a number.

"Oh, please!" pleaded the garage owner. "Tell her to go ahead."

Jonas slipped the phone back into his pocket. "I will want to see your records. Take me to them."

As the owner led Jonas away to the office, Azariah made a show of sliding under the limousine, inspecting its undercarriage. A mechanic approached, saying something in Kurdish. Azariah froze for a moment, then remembered that she was an "army official." From her position on her back, she waved the mechanic off, with an imperious gesture. She used the only Kurdish she had been taught for this mission.

"Min tenê bihêle Divê ez bixebitim!"

The mechanic, at being scolded to leave her to work, put up his hands in a gesture of supplication and moved off.

Taking up her canvas bag, Azariah opened the limousine's passenger-side, crawled in and wedged herself beneath the dashboard. She reached into the bag, and brought out a tablet computer and connector cable, plugging it into the vehicle's onboard computer. Tapping the screen, she began to download data.

She heard a voice outside the limousine and looked up. It was the mechanic, and he was peering into the side window, looking directly down at her. He began jabbering urgently in Kurdish.

Azariah checked the screen, seeing that it had was only halfway through its download. She reached into the bag, clutching the pistol with its silencer.

The mechanic waved his hands in alarm, and Azariah began to withdraw the pistol from the bag. They might have to shoot their way out. There might be bodies to dispose of.

The commanding voice of Jonas arose behind the mechanic, and he retreated as Jonas harangued him in Kurdish. The mechanic attempted to answer, but Jonas cut him off, turning to the owner, declaring in Kurdish,

"Your man does not understand our inspection procedure. If he continues to interfere, I will have him arrested. I will have *you* arrested!"

The owner scolded his mechanic, who pointed at Azariah, still crouched in the front seat. She checked the tablet's screen. The download was almost complete. She gave Jonas a worried look, and he increased the volume of his harangue, shooing the mechanic and the owner away. He returned to give Azariah a glare that said "finish!"

She checked the screen again. The download was complete. She stuffed the tablet and the cable into her bag, stood up and nodded emphatically to Jonas, who told the owner,

"We have completed our inspection. See that this vehicle and all others you service are guarded twenty-four hours a day. Is that clear?"

"Yes, sir! We will! Thank you!"

Jonas strode out of the garage, followed by Azariah. Once they had reached the safety of their car, he asked, "Get it?"

She grinned, taking out the tablet. "Yup. Looks like we got the GPS data on the limo for the last six months. We'll know every place this *farzeenish* went."

"Yes, 'monster' is the right thing to call him," said Jonas. "But Azzy, you probably shouldn't use yiddish terms around here. You're in a Muslim country."

***

"We have no idea where the ship is," said Grinell, shaking his head grimly, as he watched one of the wall screens in the Baghdad CIA Ops Center. "We can only guess."

"Okay, then let's at least try educated guessing," said Carrie.

Ben contemplated the map, declaring, "I need to do some thinking on that. I know he'll want to make a broader statement. And he's smart. He'll have a plan to do that. I've got to look at his history more. It's up to me. It's up to me." The last sentence was a frustrated whisper. He took a deep breath, lowering his head.

Carrie shook her head, her lips pursed in frustration, saying, "Okay, he's smart, but is it smart to think he can just run that ship into some harbor and detonate the bomb? He'd be stopped immediately.

We'll put the Coast Guard on alert. And if he did detonate the bomb, he'd be committing suicide."

"No, that's not like him, either," said Ben. "He wants to see the impact. He wants the satisfaction of revenge, which means he has to stay alive. And to Muslims, suicide is a cardinal sin."

"Then, what's he gonna do?" Carrie asked spreading her hands wide in frustration. "Is he going to load a twenty-seven-ton bomb onto some speedboat and have some suicide bomber run it?"

Said Ben, "There's got to be clues in what he brought on board in Cuba. I mean, look, he flew men and equipment halfway across the world."

Ben's phone buzzed, and it was Azariah. He put the phone on speaker.

"Are you home yet?" he asked.

Azariah replied with a seeming non sequitur. "Dear brother, did you know bin Shadid's limo is serviced every week?"

"What does that have to do with anything? Azzy, are you still in Erbil?"

"Are you on speaker? Is everybody there?" she asked.

"Yes, Azzy, what the hell?"

"Listen, Jonas got me into the garage that services bin Shadid's limo. I downloaded his GPS history. We've taken a first look. Ben, he was there!"

"Where?" asked Ben.

"Berlin! The bastard was in Berlin when Abby was killed. The GPS showed the limo took him to the Erbil airport early that morning. It then returned to his villa. Flight records showed his jet went to Berlin. Then, it returned late on the night Abby was killed. Then, his limo picked him up at the airport."

Ben's hand began to shake, tears welling in his eyes. He said nothing. Carrie took his arm, speaking for him. Azariah's news brought back the agonizing sorrow, like a dark mass pressing on his chest.

"What else did you find out?" she asked.

"We traced where the limo went, checked addresses to see what they are." said Azariah. "Lots of restaurants and offices. A few places that seem odd. We're going to check them out."

"Send us the list," said Grinell. "We'll see what else it can tell us."

Ben ended the call, trembling with rage. "I have to. . ." he began, but couldn't finish the sentence. He left the op center, waving off Carrie's offer to go with him.

***

One sobbed piteously, as the three North Korean engineers begged for their lives. Their pleas in Korean went untranslated, but their message was clear. Rahnim the guard said nothing, as he herded them up out of the ship's hold, up the metal stairs and onto the deck of the *Trireme*. Waiting for them was the Iraqi engineer Fayez Badour and bin Shadid.

Said the lead engineer, "We know that those who came before did not return. But please, we have done as you asked. Please allow us to leave."

"We are not going to kill you," said bin Shadid through the interpreter. "We are sending you home. As agreed, once we deploy the drone, I will allow you to leave. And as agreed, you will have the plans, data, and specifications for the weapon."

The begging turned to relieved smiles and profuse thanks in Korean.

Bin Shadid pointed out over the sunlit ocean, where a mile off the port side could be seen the elongated hull of a North Korean freighter, with four cranes jutting from its deck for loading bulk cargo.

"It is the *Dae Jang*, and we made contact with it this morning," he told the engineers. "It is carrying a cargo of sugar from Cuba to North Korea, and it will be your transport home."

The North Koreans chattered among themselves in relief, the chief engineer replying, "We apologize deeply for doubting you, sir. We were happy to have served Dear Leader by serving you."

"You will still serve both of us by taking this," said bin Shadid, handing the engineer a thumb drive. "These are the plans for the bomb and for the drone. It is payment for your work and a gift to your leader."

"We do not need drone plans," said the chief engineer loudly, scowling. "We have our own drone, called Haeil-5-23. It is fully—"

"I know better," interrupted bin Shahid. "My intelligence says that your drone is only experimental. You know that the Russian one is superior."

The engineer said nothing, his expression now an impassive mask. He had dutifully spouted the official party line within hearing of the other engineers, at least one of whom was undoubtedly a spy for the government. "Just as a reference, I will take the plans," he said. He took the thumb drive and followed the other two over the side of the ship and down a swaying rope ladder to a waiting inflatable boat. The boat's motor roared to life and the craft accelerated away toward the distant ship, cresting the sunlit ocean swells.

"Agha bin Shadid, surely you know that giving them the technology will have grave consequences," said Badour. He spoke deferentially, ducking his head, cautious about questioning the wisdom of his master's actions.

"The bomb will kill millions," bin Shadid replied, watching the receding boat, his voice a cold, quiet monotone. "This has the potential to kill millions more. It is my even greater vengeance."

***

"My dear, this could be the perfect place for us," announced Jonas haughtily. He had escorted Azariah through the glass doors and into the marble-sheathed lobby of the gleaming high-rise apartment building Baya Towers. Now, he was playing the part of "wealthy husband" to a fashionable Azariah. He wore expensive slacks and a tailored sports jacket and Azariah wore a beige linen pantsuit.

Her eyes hidden behind large sunglasses, Azariah merely nodded.

The concierge came to attention behind his counter and smiled. "Sir, may I be of service to you?" he asked in Kurdish.

"Perhaps," said Jonas. "But first, do you happen to know English? My wife is British, and she prefers that language."

"I do, sir," said the concierge, now in English.

"We are seeking a place here in Erbil, to come in winter. My wife does not like London or Paris in winter."

"Well, sir, Baya Towers is a premiere residence," said the concierge, smiling and nodding. "You would find it most comfortable."

Azariah took off her sunglasses, saying, "Our dear friend Saadallah bin Shadid recommended it. He has visited here and it impressed him. He was visiting. . ." She assumed a puzzled expression, waving the hand holding the sunglasses ". . . Oh, I don't remember the name. The party was so loud we couldn't hear the name. It was. . . um . . ."

"Arkady Yahontov," volunteered the concierge. "Agha bin Shadid has visited Mr. Yahontov."

"Ah, yes, that was the name." She turned to Jonas. "You know, I think we should see Mr. Yahontov. Ask how he likes the place."

"Well, he is not here," said the concierge. He lowered his voice to a conspiratorial whisper. "Indeed, I do believe he may be leaving. That might mean his penthouse would become available."

"Oh, too bad he is not here," said Azariah. "What makes you think he is leaving?"

"I haven't seen him in a month, maybe more. And a while back, some delivery men came. They had a wooden crate with them that they said was a gift. They took it up to his apartment. But then they brought it back and loaded it into a van. I asked them why. They said that Mr. Yahontov wanted it shipped elsewhere."

Said Jonas, "Ah, well then, we will contact him directly. The penthouse might be the perfect place for us, right, dear?"

"I wish to see the penthouse before we commit," said Azariah, looking dubiously around the lobby. "I would hope the penthouse would be more richly appointed than this space. It needs a designer."

The concierge wrinkled his brow in hesitation. On the one hand, his tenant would not like him showing the penthouse. But on the other hand, and more importantly, he knew he would get a fat commission if he managed to rent a vacant unit, especially the penthouse.

"Well, let me see, let me see. Um. . . let me make a call." He called the penthouse, letting the phone ring for minutes before hanging up and announcing cheerily, "I think it would be fine if I took you up to inspect it."

He called one of the porters to take over his desk, led them into a private elevator lined with wine-colored leather upholstery, and took them to the penthouse.

They entered the penthouse through the black-lacquered door with its gold-leaf trim. It was a sprawling two-story apartment with marble floors and floor-to-ceiling windows looking out over the park.

Azariah scanned the living room, nodding noncommittally. "Oh, we would definitely have to redecorate." When the concierge looked away, she gave a quick nod of her head toward the kitchen. Jonas got the signal, and told the concierge,

"I need to see the kitchen. We have a chef, and I would want to ensure that the facility is adequate. And we have a maid."

The concierge led him away, and Azariah immediately began inspecting the room. She emitted a surprised "humph" when she saw on the coffee table a glass with the dregs of what had been a drink.

Somebody had left in a hurry, or had been taken, she thought to herself. She moved quickly to the kitchen door and caught Jonas's eye, pointing upstairs. He nodded and continued to hold the concierge's attention with questions about the appliances.

She hurried up the curved staircase to the upper hallway, ducking in and out of doors, until she found the main bedroom. It held a richly carved, king-size four-poster bed flanked by bedside tables, a mahogany dressing table and bureau, and a large sofa. Sunlight streamed through the floor-to-ceiling windows.

She hmphed even more emphatically when she saw what sat on one of the bedside tables: an extremely expensive watch and a vial of blue pills.

This guy would never go anywhere without his little blue pills. And his cell phone, she thought. Indeed, the other bedside table held a cell phone resting on its charger. This could give them invaluable intel on who this guy had contacted. She picked up the phone.

"*What are you doing?*" came an indignant voice behind her.

She whirled around, holding the cell phone, to see the concierge glaring at her. She froze.

"You should not be up here, madam! This is a private home, after all."

She recovered, holding up the phone. He had not actually seen her pick it up, so she declared coldly, "I am making a call. I require privacy. *Leave!*"

The concierge's accusing scowl transformed to an embarrassed smile. He raised his hands in a placating gesture, backing away.

Azariah strode toward him, backing him away even farther, as she announced into the phone, "We will require the jet at three o'clock. Madrid. And obtain that champagne we had in Paris. The nineteen-ninety-five Krug Clos d'Ambonnay. I suppose we could make do with a two-thousand-and-two Dom Perignon, if we have to."

She silently congratulated herself for having remembered the lessons in wine she had learned from an ex-boyfriend.

They left the apartment, and as they reached the lobby, the concierge said obsequiously, "Sir, madam, if you give me your contact information, I can let you know if his penthouse, or another apartment, becomes available."

"No need. We will return at the appropriate time," said Jonas, as they pushed through the glass doors and into the blazing sunlit day.

The moment they entered the rented limousine, Azariah whipped out the stolen cell phone.

"I assume your tech guy, or the CIA's can get into this thing. Now, we'll find out what this Russian was up to!"

CHAPTER SIXTEEN

"That Russian was a busy man. . . before he was made to disappear," sighed Grinell, fatigue shading his words, rubbing his eyes. He looked haggard, as did Ben and Carrie. They had spent the previous three days and nights in Baghdad analyzing the Russian oil executive Arkady Yahontov's cell phone logs with National Security Agency analysts.

That was followed by the near-sleepless flight to CIA headquarters in Virginia. They had moved the intelligence operation, and the FBI's Nuclear Emergency Support Team to a conference room deep within the massive complex

Now, they stood staring at the room's wall screen. The conference table was crowded with laptops and piles of folders, its chairs occupied by the team members. And around the periphery sat their staff members.

Despite the crowd of people, the room was dead silent, except for the delicate clacking of keyboards and the swish of shuffled papers.

All were intently scrutinizing the display of phone calls and texts Yahontov had made and received in the weeks before his disappearance.

"Any pattern?" asked Ben.

"Well, there's a positive pattern and a negative one," said Grinell, sinking into his chair.

"Okay, what's that mean?"

"The positive pattern is that he was in repeated contact with a Russian assistant minister of defense. Our Moscow operative says that minister oversees advanced technology for the Russian navy. He was up to something with the guy."

"And the negative pattern?"

"Shortly after he met with bin Shadid, he went totally dark. No phone calls, no texts, no evidence that he was at his apartment, even though his phone was."

Carrie paced the room, shaking her head. "I just feel like I've got pieces of a puzzle here, but I can't figure out how they fit together."

"Okay, what are the pieces?" asked Ben.

"First, we know bin Shadid is very, very rich," she said, ticking off points on her fingers. "So, he can buy whatever he wants, to exact his revenge. Second, he has enormous international contacts through his business. He can reach out to whoever he needs. Finally, he is technically sophisticated. He knew how to put together a team of engineers that could not only restore the bomb, but build really convincing decoys."

"Okay, what's the takeaway?" asked Ben. "When I'm trying to piece together some historical scenario, I back away and look at what lesson I need to take away."

"It's that bin Shadid would never, ever expect to just sail into a harbor and detonate the weapon. He would somehow build technology that would enable him to accomplish his goal. He needed something from Yahontov."

"So, what might that be?"

"A fast, stealthy delivery system," she answered.

"And what would that delivery system consist of?"

"Yeah, that's a missing piece." Carrie grew quiet for several minutes, frowning in thought. Then, she stopped short in her pacing. "*Pipes!*" she exclaimed. Then, "Pipes, pipes, *pipes!*"

"What about the pipes?"

"The ones they loaded onto the *Trireme* were maybe seven feet in diameter. The bomb is about seven feet in diameter. The bomb will fit inside." Carrie slumped against the wall, exclaiming, "*Dear Lord, they weren't pipes, they were hull components of a torpedo! Status-6!*"

"And what is a Status-6?" asked Ben.

"It's a stealth drone torpedo that the Russians have built that carries a nuclear warhead! We've known about it for a few years."

Now Grinell chimed in. "Bin Shadid probably paid Yahontov a huge chunk of money to use his contacts in the Russian Ministry of Defense to get him plans for a Status-6. And he got his engineers to build it."

"Again, what's the takeaway?" asked Ben.

"It means that if he deploys the bomb on a Status-6 torpedo, we can't detect it." Carrie sighed and stared forlornly into space.

"It means we could be standing here one moment. And the next moment we would be blasted into vapor."

***

Carrie arrived the next morning with two large containers of coffee to find Ben slumped on his desk in the cubicle he had been assigned.

"You asleep?" she asked.

He looked up and smiled blearily, taking the coffee. "Well, a combination of sleep, thought, and prayer."

He gestured at his computer screen, which displayed a map of the radius of a blast and fallout of a 100-megaton explosion in Washington, DC. The map showed concentric red and orange circles marking the area obliterated or damaged by the blast. Surrounding them was a much larger yellow tail stretching to the east, showing the cloud of radioactive contamination.

"You think his target is D.C.?" she asked.

"Almost certainly." Ben rubbed his bearded face blearily. He took a long gulp of coffee. "I spent last night trying to get into his head and assessing the characteristics of every major city. I assumed the target would be the United States, since we're the ones who killed his family."

"Why DC in particular?"

"It fits his immediate objective to do enormous damage and kill vast numbers of people. But it also fits his strategy to punish the country responsible. The whole country."

"How so?"

Ben put his finger on the screen, tracing the yellow tail of radiation eastward. "Okay, the initial blast would decapitate the government, destroying DC. But then, the prevailing winds would carry a lethal radioactive cloud up the entire eastern seaboard all the way to New York and on to Boston. So, with one bomb, he could decimate a huge swath of the country."

Carrie took a deep breath and let it out. "That's not all. Then there's global impacts."

"Global, really?" asked a voice behind them, as Grinell entered the room.

Carrie continued. "Yup. The team consulted with some climatologists about the broader effects from a blast. The hundred-megaton bomb is about seven thousand times bigger than the Hiroshima bomb. They've calculated that a ground burst would send about thirty-five billion metric tons of soot into the atmosphere. It would cause protective ozone levels to plunge, letting through UV radiation that would damage human health, crops, and ecosystems. And global surface temperatures would drop to the lowest levels in a thousand years, causing worldwide famine for decades. A thermonuclear winter."

"Dear God!" breathed Ben.

Grinell said hopefully, "Okay, maybe he couldn't get the sea drone to D.C. It's inland. Maybe it would be stuck at sea, where he wouldn't want to set it off."

Ben shook his head, answering, "He could direct the sea drone all the way through Chesapeake Bay to the Potomac River and the center of the city. Then he could detonate it within a stone's throw of the capitol. It means if we're to intercept the *Trireme*, we should concentrate in the waters off the East Coast. But it's a big area."

"I can narrow it down," said Carrie. "A nuclear-powered Status-6 has unlimited range, but I'm sure his engineers didn't have access to the technology to build a small nuclear reactor. So, they had to make do with battery power. That limits the range and thus the area to be searched."

Said Grinell, "It's time to run this up the chain of command. *All* the way."

"Okay, but for now, it's just a hunch," warned Ben. "We could be dead wrong."

Grinell chuckled. "And you could be dead right. I need to brief the director." He left, as Carrie and Ben set out to review their data.

After half an hour, Grinell returned, his expression somber.

"So?" asked Carrie. "How did they take it?"

"Well, we're set in motion a very, *very* quiet machinery. They decided to take your hunch seriously. But more important, we've found a ship."

"The *Trireme*?" Asked Ben bolting up from his chair.

"No, but one that's important. We were monitoring traffic in the region by satellite, and we found a freighter that was spoofing another freighter."

"Spoofing?" asked Carrie.

"It falsified its electronic signature to be another freighter we knew was still in port. It looked hinky, so we had a Global Hawk drone do a flyover. It's the *Dae Jang*. North Korean. It supposedly carries sugar from Cuba. But the navy suspects it's one of North Korea's ships that smuggles Russian military hardware to Cuba. Falsifying its identity makes it legally a pirate ship, so we have the right to board it."

"So, why is it important?"

"It may have met up with the *Trireme*. When we found it, it was off a direct course to North Korea. Maybe, just *maybe*, it had diverted to take on some very important passengers with some very important data."

"The nuclear engineers!" exclaimed Carrie. "They could have the plans for the bomb. . . for the drone!"

"Bingo! And we're going after them. And we need you and your folks to be there."

***

The assistant to the director of the Central Intelligence Agency sat down on the bench along the sprawling Washington, DC mall, watching the noontime joggers pass by. A slim middle-aged woman, she had the serene look of someone who prided herself on a calm, efficient demeanor. And an absolute discretion. She unwrapped the deli turkey sandwich that would be her lunch. She took a deep breath of the cool autumn air, opened her metal water bottle and took a sip.

She was shortly joined by the assistant to the Chief of Staff of the President of the United States. She was a similarly demur middle-aged woman, wearing a dark blue pantsuit. She opened the Cobb salad that was her lunch, and unscrewed the top on her bottle of iced tea. They smiled and greeted to one another, and began to chat amiably about the weather, a sale at the local Nordstrom, and the doings of their families.

Nobody gave them any notice, a sharp contrast to the intense interest if their bosses had similarly picnicked. Or, the notice if they had suddenly scheduled a last-minute official meeting along with their staffs.

After their pleasant lunch, the assistant to the director of the Central Intelligence Agency, stood to deposit her trash. She looked down at the assistant to the Chief of Staff of the President of the United States and said, "Y'know, Camp David is very nice in the fall." She pointedly turned and walked away.

That afternoon, the Chief of Staff announced that the President and her family had decided to spend a week at Camp David. Also, the members of the Joint Chiefs of Staff left for the underground Raven Rock Mountain Complex—the sprawling military command and control center linked by a six-and-a-half-mile tunnel to a bunker 140 feet beneath Camp David.

Their families quietly left their homes in the area on family vacations, to visit sick relatives, or on business trips.

***

The helicopter from CIA headquarters touched down on the tarmac of a Norfolk Naval Station helicopter runway carrying Ben, and the CIA nuclear weapons team. Nearby, the Osprey tiltrotor aircraft was roaring to life, its thick rotors beginning to spin.

Rousing themselves from the exhausted sleep they had lapsed into, they climbed out and sprinted to board the Osprey. They hurried up its rear ramp, squeezing past the 50-caliber machine gun mounted there. The flight engineer who would man the gun already sat in the nearest seat.

Ben and Carrie moved quickly forward through the Osprey's interior, sitting near the other flight engineer who manned the craft's belly gun. They donned headsets to communicate.

He nodded in greeting, but quickly returned his gaze to a monitor screen. It showed him the aim of the Osprey's remote-controlled six-barrel gatling gun. One pull of the trigger would spew 3,000 rounds per minute, shredding any target. The gunner tested the joystick aiming controls, and the gun, mounted in the belly, obediently swiveled beneath him. He pressed a button to retract the mini-gun into the Osprey's hull.

The flight engineers left their seats to make sure Ben, Carrie, and the others were strapped in. One of the flight engineers briefed them on the mission.

"We're flying direct to target," he said, as the noise rose in the passenger compartment and the rear ramp whined shut. "We're gonna meet up with a SEAL team from the carrier. They'll be dropped off on the ship by another Osprey. We'll approach without firing. If they fire first, we can both legally engage. And when the target is secure, it's all yours."

Carrie leaned over to Ben and said, "When we board, we'll all split up. Better to find the engineers. Then interrogate them for what they know about the *Trireme*'s course."

"Yeah, and the attack strategy," Ben answered, shaking his head. "Long shot. We miss the mark, and. . . " his voice trailed off, conveying his fatigue and horror at the prospect of not being able to stop a thermonuclear holocaust.

She patted his knee in reassurance, as the engine roar increased and they felt the Osprey lift off. After hovering briefly, the craft tilted forward and gained speed, its engines smoothly rotating forward for level flight.

The Osprey skimmed over the gray-green ocean for two hours, as a smothering fatigue once more enveloped them. Ben managed to sleep fitfully, his head lolling, his dreams dark visions of explosions and death.

He startled awake to the voice of the pilot announcing, "Target ahead," as the Osprey slowed to a hover. The rear ramp whined open, and Ben felt his strength and resolve flood back, as he saw the North Korean ship, below. It was a rust-stained hulk, its only superstructure being the white bridge and its tall cranes. The ship was vulnerable, only the bridge giving the crew, and the engineers, anywhere to take cover.

Its crew was scrambling onto the deck, peering up at the Osprey. Their attention riveted by the looming aircraft, they didn't notice the inflatable raft on the other side of the ship carrying the SEAL team. Three of the ship's crew pulled out assault rifles and loosed a volley of fire at the Osprey.

"Clear to engage," Ben heard over his headset from the pilot. The flight engineer in the tail swung the machine gun into place, cocking it. One of the North Korean sailors shouted, pointing to a grappling hook sailing over the railing, snagging itself on a rail. It grew taut with the weight of a climbing SEAL. The sailor rushed to the railing, carrying an assault rifle, leaning over the side, aiming it at the climbing SEAL.

The tail gunner loosed a fusillade of rounds at him, filling the passenger compartment with an ear-splitting roar and the metallic tattoo of spent casings clattering to the floor and off the ramp.

The sailor's body collapsed to the deck, shredded to a near-unrecognizable mound of bloody flesh, as the SEAL vaulted over the railing, bringing up his assault rifle. Meanwhile, the second Osprey zoomed into view, its rear ramp open, its tail gunner in place.

The staccato crack of automatic gunfire from the crew echoed from the bridge, as the other sailors began peppering the two Ospreys. Ben and the others ducked at the metallic thunk of rounds against the armor of the Osprey. One round erupted through the aft doorway and slammed into the ceiling of the passenger compartment.

The tail gunners on both Ospreys answered with a devastating barrage of gunfire. The fusillade raked the bridge and deck of the freighter and sent the crew's bodies collapsing to the deck as the rounds impacted them.

The eight members of the SEAL team had all made it onto the deck. They fanned out, targeting armed crew members with precise volleys from their assault rifles.

Abruptly the gunfire from the ship stopped, and the remaining crew threw down their weapons and raised their hands. The SEALs moved on them, binding their hands, then spreading out to secure the ship.

The tail gunner swung the machine gun out of the way and hauled out a small L-shaped seat used with the Osprey's hoist in the ceiling. He pulled out a steel cable from a hoist and attached the chair.

He turned to Ben, Carrie, and others, announcing, "Y'all ready for a little ride? We're gonna let y'all off and go refuel."

Ben quickly moved aft, where the tail gunner strapped him onto the seat, and switched on the hoist to let out the cable. Ben swung out of the door, suspended a hundred feet above the pitching deck of the freighter. Any fear of dangling in midair above an enemy freighter was suppressed beneath his utter determination to confront the men who had restored the most dangerous weapon in history.

As he reached the ship, he slammed down twice on the heaving deck before he was able to find his legs and unbelt himself. As the chair was hoisted aloft, he did not wait for Carrie to come down, but turned to another of the SEALs, asking,

"The engineers? Are they alive? Do you have them?"

"Pretty sure," came the terse answer. "We've got three guys in the crew mess that don't look like sailors."

"Take me to them." Ben turned to the SEAL managing the hoist. "Tell Carrie where I've gone."

Ben followed the SEAL down a ladder and through a narrow, dingy passageway that smelled of diesel fuel and sweat. They passed through a hatch into a small room with metal tables and benches. There, a SEAL held three men, who stood against the metal bulkhead, their hands bound in front of them. They wore white shirts and black trousers, unlike the faded coveralls of the crew members. The spare men stood with their heads bowed, shoulders slumped in fear.

"Any of you speak English?" asked Ben.

The men looked at him blankly.

He turned to the SEAL guarding the men and winked. "Shoot one of them."

The middle of the three men gasped, wide-eyed.

"So, you speak English," said Ben to him.

"Yes. Little," admitted the man.

"I'm sure you have the plans for the bomb and the drone. Where are they?"

The man shrugged, saying, "We have no plans."

Carrie, appearing beside him, asking, "Any progress?"

"A little," he answered. Then to the North Korean. "We know you are the nuclear engineers. Again, where are the plans?"

"No plans! No plans!" answered the man, shaking his head in denial.

"Search them," said Ben, and the SEAL roughly patted down each man, turning his pockets out. The SEAL shrugged.

Carrie shook her head in frustration. "What do we do now?"

"Well, here's what I think," said Ben. "If I was them, I'd expect the freighter to be seized and they wouldn't have access to any hiding place on it. But they know eventually, they'll be returned home. After all, they're civilians, and on the high seas, and we don't have evidence that they've done anything. So, my bet is that the plans are on a thumb drive, likely a very small one, easily hidden."

"But where would they hide it?" asked Carrie.

"I'd bet one of them swallowed it. We know damned well they won't talk. We need that thumb drive immediately. We can't wait the day it'll take to work itself through his. . . system."

"So—?"

"So we slit them open."

"NO!" shouted the middle Korean, translating the threat to the others, causing them to cry out in panic.

"*You can't do that!*" exclaimed Carrie. "*That is barbaric!*"

"Oh, I couldn't," said Ben. He nodded to the SEAL guarding the men. "But *he* could."

His expression a mask of cold-blooded determination, the SEAL pulled out his six-inch knife, its stainless-steel blade glimmering in the sun streaming through a porthole. He grasped it underhanded and moved toward the men.

"UP BACK!" shouted the middle North Korean, pointing to his rear. "UP IN BACK!"

The SEAL grinned, saying "Well, looks like he didn't do a top-down hide, but a bottom-up." He sheathed his knife and shoved the engineer out of the room for an extraction of the thumb drive.

"*Dear God, you really would have had him cut open?*" asked Carrie.

"No," said Ben. "But I knew they would absolutely believe it. They live under a brutal regime where something like that would be routine. I counted on that."

After ten minutes, the SEAL returned holding a small thumb drive in his gloved hand. The engineer hobbled in front of him, wincing with each step.

"I wasn't real gentle," said the SEAL, handing it to Carrie. "Good thing he put the thing in a baggie before shoving it up his ass."

She shook her head in relief, pulling out her laptop. "Okay, let's see what that monster has built."

***

"*Any idea how the damn drone works?*" demanded Grinell, pacing back and forth at the front of the aircraft carrier's pilot briefing room. "*Any idea at all?*" He clenched his jaw in frustration and scanned the dozen members of the CIA, DOE, and FBI teams. They sat in the rows of chairs, their laptops open, offering only head-shaking and shrugging.

The room's large wall screen displayed the drone's circuit diagrams, cross-sections, and computer code. Ben and Carrie had arrived only two hours ago with the plans for the thermonuclear bomb and the drone torpedo. They had been downloaded quickly from the thumb drive, and the weapons engineers had loaded different segments of the data onto their laptops. Carrie and Ben stood beside Grinell at the front of the room scanning the wall screen.

One engineer said, "Well, if we had time—"

"We don't have goddamned time!" exclaimed Grinell. "For all we know, the drone is already sitting off the East Coast and ready to take out the whole goddamned area."

Ben asked, "Have the North Korean engineers revealed anything about bin Shadid's plans?"

Grinell shot a questioning glance at one of the CIA agents. The agent had headphones on, listening to interrogations of the engineers. His laptop displayed images of three small rooms in the carrier. Each one showed a North Korean shackled to a metal table, being questioned by an agent and an interpreter.

The agent shrugged. "So far, all they've said is that they had mated the bomb to the drone. And that both were operational when they left the ship."

"Oh, hell," interrupted one of the engineers softly. He sent his laptop display to the wall screen. It showed a circuit diagram of the drone's electronics. "I've found a seismic sensor in the drone. Looks like if the drone is subjected to any kind of violent jolt, the bomb detonates."

"So, we can't just blow it out of the water?" asked Grinell.

"Nope," was the resigned answer.

"We can't open it up either," said another engineer, sending a magnified cross-section of the drone to the wall screen. "All the access ports have switches that activated when the covers were closed, to trigger detonation if they're opened again."

"So, even if we intercept it. . . which we can't because it's stealthy . . . we can't open it up."

"No way," came that engineer's answer.

"So, we can only pray that we get to his ship before he launches it."

A quiet chorus of "Yes" arose from the group.

"Any good news?" asked Grinell, almost rhetorically. "Any at all?"

One engineer raised his hand. "The drone plans include the design of the nuclear propulsion system that powers the Russian version, and—"

"C'mon, that's good news?" asked Grinell sarcastically.

"Yeah, sort of," said the engineer. "As Carrie said, bin Shadid's engineers don't have the technology to construct the nuclear propulsion system, even with the plans. So, they certainly substituted batteries. And with the plans showing the space allowed for nuclear propulsion, I calculated how many batteries they could fit in the torpedo. And from that, its range, which tells me where they have to launch from, which is fairly close to the coast."

"Okay, okay, then, good. That gives us a limited area to search. I'll let the recon people know. That'll help with the satellite and drone searches." Grinell took up his cell phone, punching in a number.

The meeting ended with the engineers scrutinizing their laptop screens and Grinell moving from one to the other, quizzing them.

Ben and Carrie left the room, walking together down the hall to the carrier's mess hall. Ben sagged into a metal chair at one of the long tables, his burst of energy from the raid spent. Carrie took packaged sandwiches from the buffet and set one down in front of him.

"Eat," she commanded.

"Can't," said Ben. "Besides all that. . ." He waved toward the briefing room, ". . . Azzy has gone dark. She's not answering her phone. Albert, her husband, hasn't heard from her. Neither have Mom and Dad. I kind of lied. Told them that Azzy was just probably busy. That she was on a research project. They know Azzy, though, so they knew I was lying." He took a deep breath. "*My God, she could be dead!*"

Carrie did not answer but rose, patted him on the shoulder, and fetched large cups of coffee.

"Now drink."

Ben managed a wan smile. "You are a lot like my sister, you know."

"Yeah, well, but she's interested in your welfare. I'm only interested in how effective you remain as part of this team."

"Liar." He took a drink of coffee and unwrapped the sandwich, taking a bite.

"Okay, maybe I'm a fibber." She shrugged and took a bite of her own sandwich.

"Heard from your wife?" Ben asked.

"Yes. We video-chatted early this morning. Got to see the little ones, too. Miss them horribly. I need so badly to see them and Beth, but at the same time, I recognize that they pick up on my anxiety. They—"

She was interrupted by shouts from down the hall. They rushed back to the briefing room to find the engineers standing staring at the wall screen. It showed an aerial view of a ship.

"Is that—" began Ben.

"His ship," said Grinell, not taking his eyes from the screen. "The drone found his ship. *We've got the son of a bitch!*"

***

Bin Shadid said to the North Korean nuclear weapons director on the screen, "As we agreed, your engineers are bringing you plans for a weapon that will give your country unprecedented power." He waited for his interpreter to translate his words to the man, who stared grimly at him from the wall screen in bin Shadid's quarters on the *Trireme*. The officer was dressed as before in a uniform covered with medals. Behind him as before stood a row of black-suited men.

"You are wrong. The engineers are not coming," replied the officer.

"What do you mean?" Bin Shadid allowed himself a mildly puzzled expression.

"I received a transmission from the *Dae Jang* before we lost contact. They were under attack by American forces. I must assume that our engineers were captured or killed. So you have not fulfilled your side of the agreement."

Bin Shadid spat a curse under his breath. After a pause of a full minute, he declared, "You *will* have the plans." He paused again, trying to formulate a strategy, determined that this key element of his revenge would not fail. "I will send the plans by way of my own security chief, Khalid Rasul. He will make it to China. I have contacts who can get him to the North Korean border. Send me details on where he is to go and how you will get him across."

Bin Shadid ended the video call, sent the interpreter back to her quarters, and quickly made another call. Within minutes, the swarthy face of Khalid Rasul appeared on the screen, in the background the marble walls of bin Shadid's Erbil villa.

"You will receive an encrypted download soon," he told Rasul. "It will consist of the plans for the bomb and the torpedo. You have the code key. Decode it, copy it to a thumb drive and scrub the computer. Then take the large jet to China. I will give you the destination."

"Agha bin Shadid, I will do so," replied Rasul. "Are you safe?"

"That does not matter, Khalid, my dear friend. The transmission will also include the information to give you access to all my accounts. Use my resources as you need to. I am trusting you with this mission as I have trusted you so many times before. Promise me you will do this no matter what. *No matter what happens to me, Šamšir.* "

Rasul paused before answering, his expression somber. "Sir, I must know, are you in danger? Will you—"

"*No matter what!*" exclaimed bin Shadid.

"No matter what," echoed Rasul. "As always, I am your Šamšir."

CHAPTER SEVENTEEN

"This here mission is a *real* nasty, critter," warned the Osprey flight engineer to Ben, Carrie, and the rest of the team. Wearing headsets, they were harnessed into the Osprey as it roared aloft from the carrier deck. "The drone shows the ship is well defended, and they've got a shitload of ordnance."

The Osprey's passengers had already taken the warning. They were bulked up with Kevlar vests and flotation jackets. They wore helmets and carried sidearms. Ben and Carrie now sat aft in the passenger compartment to be first out the door.

The flight time to the freighter *Trireme* was much shorter than to the North Korean freighter. The ominous portent of that fact was not lost on Ben and Carrie.

"They're closer to a launch point," Carrie said to the group over the headset radios they all wore. Some nodded in recognition of the fact, some bowed their heads, some directed their gaze at the ceiling.

"*Ten minutes to target,*" they heard over the radio from the pilot. "*Pucker factor to maximum.*"

The aft ramp lowered, to reveal the open Atlantic sliding past below, and the tail gunner swiveled the fifty-caliber machine gun into place. Farther forward, the belly gunner pressed buttons to deploy the minigun beneath the Osprey's hull.

The Osprey slowed to a hover and swung around to give the tail gunner a field of fire at the ship.

As the *Trireme* swung into view out the aft door, there rose a distant rattle of automatic gunfire and the thunk of rounds against the hull. The tail gunner had just fired his first burst when the pilot bellowed "*INCOMING!*"

The Osprey careened violently to port, slamming the passengers against the seats. A crackling hiss told of decoy flares erupting from the craft. Ben could see the flares arcing downward.

From the ship's deck spewed a white contrail marking the trajectory of an approaching shoulder-mounted missile. A thundering blast erupted near the Osprey, and it jerked sideways before righting itself.

"We're okay," said the pilot over the radio his voice dead calm. "The flares diverted the missile." Then, to the gunners, "Bring the pain!"

The belly gunner unleashed a hurricane of rounds from the minigun, a cascade of metal that ripped across the ship's deck, shredding bodies and leaving the deck a pockmarked ruin. Ben could see that the other Osprey had done the same.

After pausing to check for further resistance, the Osprey hovered closer to the ship, to prepare for unloading its passengers. As before, Ben saw the attacking SEALs hurdling over the ship railing, spreading out across the deck strewn with corpses. This time, he thought, they would have little to target, given that no enemy could possibly have survived the onslaught.

But one did. A crewman leaped out of the bridge hatch to the railing, brought up his missile, and fired.

Before the pilot could react, the missile slammed into the Osprey's starboard engine, the deafening explosion shattered it into shards of flying metal, and the craft flipped on its side and plummeted toward the ocean.

The violent impact violently sent the passengers' limbs flailing like those of rag dolls, but their harnesses held them fast. The Osprey slammed into the ocean on its port side, its rotor thrashing the water. As its fuselage settled onto the ocean surface, a tidal wave of seawater rushed into the interior.

The belly gunner's body flopped lifelessly in its harness, a piece of the engine having sliced through the minigun hatch and torn away his leg.

Stunned from the blast and the crash, Ben was only vaguely aware of the other flight engineer unhitching him from his harness. He looked down to see a shard of metal embedded in his life jacket. It had punched through the jacket, stopped by his bulletproof vest.

"*The bird'll float for a while!*" he shouted to Ben over the groans of the others and the rush of water. "You got time, but we need to get people out quick."

Ben nodded dully, shook his head to clear it, and pulled himself up. He yanked the shard of metal out of his life jacket and waded through icy, knee-deep water to begin freeing the other team members. He saw that Carrie was already up and hauling people toward the rear ramp. Ice water was rising in the cabin, so the flight engineer unlatched the overhead escape hatch, hefting one of the team members out. He turned to Carrie, but she waved him off.

"*My team first!*" she exclaimed.

Ben, Carrie, and the flight engineer lifted team members through the hatch, as the water rose to their waists. Ben could see out the rear ramp a SEAL in an inflatable raft, hauling people on board.

He looked back to see the pilot dragging the co-pilot out the front doorway. The co-pilot did not move.

Finally, the engineer and Ben lifted Carrie out, following themselves. They launched themselves into the frigid waters, swimming awkwardly toward the raft. The SEAL pulled him aboard.

"You okay?" asked the SEAL. "You hurt?"

"*Get me on board!*" exclaimed Ben. "I've got to get to him before the others." He reached down to grasp his pistol. It was still in its holster.

Carrie crouched in the bow of the boat as it leaped forward, speeding toward the ship. A ladder dangled from the deck, and she began to climb up. Two other team members followed, then Ben had his turn, and he hauled his dripping, sodden body up and onto the deck.

"We're going to look for the bomb," Carrie told him, gathering the team members to head for the cargo hold.

Ben had other plans. He pulled his cell phone from a waterproof pouch and brought up his photo of bin Shadid. He moved rapidly down the deck, stopping one SEAL after another, asking, "Seen him? It's critical I find him!" Finally, one of the SEALs pointed to the freighter's superstructure.

"Bridge," he said. "Think I saw him on the bridge."

Ben tore off his life jacket and his bulletproof vest and ran toward the ladder to the bridge, hauling himself up. An engulfing fury overcame the trauma of the crash. His target was within reach.

He reached the bridge, swung open the metal hatch and ducked inside. A SEAL held a single figure at gunpoint. It was bin Shadid! Dressed in a fraying brown sweater and stained pants, bin Shadid stood against the wall of the bridge, his hands up, next to an open window. Beside him was a metal table, on it a tablet computer.

Ben pulled his pistol, leveling it at bin Shadid. "I got him," he told the SEAL. "I need to question him. You've got better things to do."

"You sure? Want me to cuff him?"

"No. I got him." Ben wanted bin Shadid's hands free when he shot him. The horrific image of his dead Abby rose hauntingly in his mind.

The SEAL left, and Ben said, "I've waited for this. I've waited to watch you die. You killed her. You were there."

Bin Shadid lowered his hands, waving them in a placating gesture.

"I did not kill your wife," he said quietly. "I did not kill your unborn child. I would not."

"Then your man did. You told him to get the documents and kill anyone in the way. I know you did."

"No. No. I did not tell him to do that. He was not my man. He was hired. He killed them on his own."

Ben cocked the pistol, his breathing heavy, his jaw clenched. He would fire, and he would not stop firing until the pistol was empty and bin Shadid was a bloody corpse. His finger tightened on the trigger. A slight pull, would bring his revenge. His heart pounded in his chest, and tears welled in his eyes.

"You're lying," he choked out.

"I do not lie."

Ben felt an inkling of doubt corroding his resolve. "Is the man here? On the ship?"

"He is dead. I had him killed."

"How do I know that?"

"I would do it because, just as was your wife, my family was murdered. I would have no mercy on anyone who would kill a family. I had it done."

"Prove it."

"I cannot." Bin Shadid slowly picked up the tablet and held it out the window. "This is the controller for the drone and for the bomb. Kill me and it goes into the ocean. Spare me, and I give it to you."

Ben tried to steady his trembling hand for the shots. Carrie's voice came from behind him, pleading, "Ben, don't! The bomb's not here! It's not here! *For God's sake, Ben, please don't!*"

Ben said nothing, glaring at his enemy, his finger still tight against the trigger.

Said Carrie, "We need the information he has. And if you kill him, you will make him a martyr. It will inspire others."

Ben took a deep breath. His hand steadied. He took his finger from the trigger. "Give it to her," he said to bin Shadid.

"You won't kill me?"

"No. My word. I know you want to live to see the success of your monstrous act. But no, I won't. Give it to her."

Bin Shadid slowly handed the tablet to Carrie, who bent to scrutinizing its screen. After a long moment, she said in a trembling voice,

"Oh, God! The drone's gone! It's been launched! You just launched it! How?"

"We were towing it behind the ship, just in case. We released it when we saw you coming." Now bin Shadid's hands were clasped in front of him, his expression one of dark hatred.

Carrie held up the tablet. "Show me how to stop it. For the sake of millions of innocent people . . . families, children, please show me."

"It is irretrievable," he said coldly. "The display will show you where it is. You can watch it go to its target. But you can't stop it. It's stealthy, so you can't pinpoint it. And it maneuvers randomly."

Carrie held up the tablet so Ben could see it. One window in the display showed steadily changing GPS coordinates, as the drone headed away from the ship. Another window showed the target GPS coordinates: "38.8899° N, 77.0091° W." Another recorded the torpedo's depth. The most ominous window showed a countdown clock. It was going down, minute by minute, second by second, from "06:24:13."

"We have little time," she said, her voice catching with emotion. "So very little time."

***

"How do we stop it?" asked Carrie, almost to herself, as she, Ben, and the DOE, CIA, and FBI nuclear weapons teams crowded around the metal tables in the *Trireme*'s mess hall. She stared at the tablet's screen as if it might yield an answer. Bin Shadid had been handcuffed to the bunk in the captain's cabin, refusing to yield any more information.

"How do we stop it? How do we stop it?" She repeated, standing and slumping back against the bulkhead, head bowed.

"Just blow it up?" asked one team member.

"Remember, seismic sensor," countered the head of the DOE team, absentmindedly scratching his thick beard. "It'll detonate."

"Besides," said another. "We're not sure we can even locate it, even with the GPS coordinates. It's always moving and randomly."

"People, we've got to think of something now!" exclaimed Carrie. She consulted the tablet. "The torpedo's thirty miles from the ship, and time is down to five hours."

Ben asked, "How does it know where it is?"

"GPS coordinates," answered a team member.

"And how does it get its GPS location?" he asked.

"Radio signal," said one of the DOE engineers. "It must be near enough to the surface to deploy an antenna."

"Can you jam it? What would happen if you jammed it?"

The scientists and engineers looked at each other in wrinkled-brow puzzlement.

Said Carrie to one of the engineers, "Hey, you traced the trigger electronics. What do you think?"

"Well. . ." The sallow-faced young man paused to open his laptop and scrutinize its screen. "Hmm . . . well. . . it would maybe . . . "

"*Dude!*" exclaimed the DOE team leader. "*Give us an answer before we're all toast!*"

"I think the torpedo would just stop until it could reacquire," said the young man.

"You *think?*" asked Carrie. "You *think?*"

"Well, I'm looking at the circuitry. And I'm looking at the code in the control chip. I don't see a detonate trigger if navigation is lost. But I'd bet bin Shadid wouldn't want the bomb to blow up just because of a glitch in reception. It would still be on its timer, though."

"Well, in any case, looks like the only recourse we have is to get near it, jam it, and pray that we don't end up as clouds of vapor in a thermonuclear blast."

CHAPTER EIGHTEEN

"*Uh, Cap'n Jimmy, we're being attacked!*" The young first mate of the Atlantic fishing trawler *Amanda June* poked his head down into the main cabin, rousing the captain, Jimmy DeCarlo, from his afternoon nap. Behind the mate, a thundering roar filtered into the cabin.

"What the hell?" answered the captain, pulling his lean form up from his bunk and donning his frayed, black Red Sox baseball cap.

Answered the first mate, "There's this big damn whatchacallit. Helicopter-looking thing, and it's—" He gave up the rest of the sentence as his voice was drowned out and a gale whipped at his clothes, making his ponytail flap madly like the tail of a happy dog.

Captain Jimmy bounded up the stairs onto the deck, holding onto his cap and staring up at the massive Osprey looming overhead.

"*Shitfire!*" he exclaimed. He rushed to the aft deck, just as a SEAL in battle gear plummeted down on a cable from the back ramp of the Osprey. The SEAL unhooked himself from the chair's safety belt. He turned and waved for it to be reeled in, then turned back to the captain.

"Sir, we need your trawler," said the SEAL. "We're tracking a torpedo, and you're the closest craft for an intercept."

"Shitfire! A torpedo? Listen, I don't want to get my ship blown up! I don't—"

"Sir, just wait until the other people get down here. They'll explain."

191

The SEAL guided Jimmy to the rail, while the hoist lowered Carrie, Ben, and two of the nuclear weapons team onto the small, pitching deck. The trawler's crew of three stood behind the captain, mute in their shock at what was happening. The invaders introduced themselves, as the Osprey lifted away, accelerating to the west to search for the torpedo.

Carrie stuck out her small hand as the roar of the Osprey faded, replaced by the quiet slap of the ocean waves against the hull of the boat. "I'm Carrie. I'm a weapons expert with the government." She introduced Ben and the others. "We badly need your help. There is a torpedo headed for Washington, D.C., and you're the only craft that can enable us to intercept it."

"The soldier guy said torpedo," said Jimmy. "Who would be dumb enough to send a torpedo against a whole city."

"Sir—"

"Call me Jimmy. Nobody calls me sir but people who don't know me."

"Jimmy, this is an incredibly dangerous torpedo."

"Yeah, well, you've got the navy to help you. You don't need my boat. I'm gonna call—"

Ben stepped forward. "Jimmy, we're going to need your help because this torpedo is carrying a thermonuclear bomb that could wipe out the entire region. Kill millions of people."

Jimmy's eyes widened. He gasped, "Ah, what? Thermo-what? My wife, my kids, my mom are—"

"A terrorist launched it."

Jimmy took off his cap, looked back at his crew, scanned his boat, and declared, "*Yeah? Well, hell, tell me what you need!*"

"I have to warn you. We're going to try to jam its signal. You have to understand that we're not sure what will happen. It might detonate. Understand?"

Jimmy's expression grew grim. "Then I gotta let the guys vote. I can't ask my crew to get killed without that."

He moved to gather the crew, talking to them in a low voice. One slumped against the railing as he heard the news. Another made the sign of the cross. After a moment, all three nodded somberly. Jimmy returned to Carrie.

"We only ask one thing. We need to call our families."

"I sympathize, I really do" said Carrie. "But that would generate a panic and as the word spread globally, possibly even a nuclear war. We need to concentrate on stopping the torpedo." She showed him bin Shadid's tablet computer. "Look, as fast as possible, we need to get somewhere on a line due west of these coordinates. That's where the torpedo is headed."

"Yeah, yeah, I get it," said Jimmy, shaking his head sadly at the crew. He ducked into the wheelhouse and started the boat's engine. He slammed the throttle forward to launch it with a roar. An eruption of foam at the stern marked its acceleration, and it began to tear through the chop of the ocean waves. Jimmy consulted the trawler's GPS display, spinning the boat's wheel to bring it to a western heading.

Carrie followed Ben into the wheelhouse. "Once we get ahead of it, we're going to ask you to deploy your nets," she said.

"You want us to catch a damn torpedo? Seriously?"

"The GPS isn't accurate enough to intercept, and it's not on the surface. So yes."

Shaking his head in astonishment, Jimmy declared, "Well, lady, you got one hell of a lot of confidence in our seamanship!" He turned to his mate. "Get the nets ready, Joaquin. We're gonna try and catch us a big damn fish!"

The mate joined the other crew members on the deck, hauling on the mound of nets, readying them to be deployed overboard.

After an hour, they saw the Osprey hovering over the water in the distance. Carrie radioed the pilot and after a brief conversation reported, "We're in luck! The Osprey found it. It's going to use its electronic warfare system to jam the GPS signal." She relayed the pilot's countdown. "Five, four, three, two, one . . ." She paused, taking Ben's arm. They both held their breath, peering at the hovering Osprey.

Finally, Ben let out a relieved exhalation. "No—" he began.

Carrie finished the sentence. "—detonation." But then she added, "Yet. But it stopped!"

At Carrie's direction, Jimmy piloted the trawler to the west of the Osprey and directed the crew to begin paying out the boat's nets, as the trawler slowed. He spun the wheel to bring the boat to port, circling the position of the hovering Osprey.

After twenty minutes, the first mate shouted up over the roar of the Osprey's engines, *"Cap'n, we caught something!"*

Carrie radioed the Osprey and it lowered closer to the ocean surface. Four SEALs in wetsuits and scuba gear plunged into the water.

The mate switched on the boat's winch to begin hauling in the net. The winch's motor whined in complaint under the load of the mass entangled in the net.

Carrie and Ben rushed to the stern, joining the rest of the nuclear weapons team, peering out to the spot where the SEALs had splashed down. The winch continued to reel in the net, creating a large, wet pile on the deck.

A massive, black, glistening object heaved to the ocean surface, fishing net wrapped around it, the four SEALs clinging to its side. The people on the deck variously cursed in wonder and invoked the heavens.

"Jesus," breathed Carrie. "Now what the hell do we do?" She consulted the tablet. It said "3:42:14" and counting down.

"We can't just tow it out to sea," said Ben. "We can't get far enough out. It'll still devastate the East Coast. The blast, the radiation, the tidal wave . . ."

"And, of course, we'll all die," said Carrie. She moved off to consult with the nuclear engineers, both shaking their heads. She returned to find Ben staring at the huge torpedo One of the SEALs attached a box to its surface, as he clung to one of the four brackets on its hull. Ben stared at the torpedo, then down into the water.

Carrie returned to scrutinizing the tablet as if it would yield some revelation. "Best we can think of is to lash it to the boat, head out to sea and just—"

"How deep is the ocean here?" he interrupted.

"Why?" asked Carrie.

Ben didn't answer, but went into the wheelhouse, followed by Carrie, asking the captain the same question.

"Well, around here . . ." Scowling in concentration, the captain scrutinized the fathometer ". . . maybe a thousand feet."

"How deep water can you get us to in, say, an hour?"

"Damned deep. East of here is Norfolk Canyon. It's more than five thousand feet."

"Is the edge steep?"

"Yeah, real steep, narrow canyon. Leads out to deep ocean."

Ben turned to Carrie. "*We sink it! We somehow attach a mass to it, and we sink it in deep water!*"

Carrie furrowed her brow in thought. Ben continued.

"It'll be down in a submarine canyon. The water will contain the blast. And the canyon walls will deflect the it to the east, away from land."

Carrie shook her head. "Still, there's an ethical problem. A blast underwater would transmit energy for huge distances. The blast could well devastate the ecology of a huge region of the Atlantic. Then there's the likelihood of a tidal wave. All the way across the Atlantic. I just don't know . . ."

Ben grasped her shoulders, shaking his head. "Carrie, I understand that we're stuck figuring out which is the lesser of two catastrophic evils. We need a vote."

Carrie finally nodded, and they left the wheelhouse and explained the issue to the two engineers. They radioed the others onboard the *Trireme*. Voices were raised, objections were voiced, even shouted. Tears were shed. Finally, Carrie called for a vote.

The tally in, she switched on the radio and asked the Osprey pilot, "How much can an Osprey lift?" she asked him.

The answer came back over the radio. "About seven tons. Why?"

"We need the heaviest thing an Osprey can lift that will sink. We want to attach a weight to the torpedo and sink it. Can you do that?"

After a brief pause, in which voices were heard in the background, the pilot replied, "*Oh, hell yes!* I'll radio the carrier. Another Osprey can bring it. I need to get people off the *Trireme*." The Osprey lifted from the trawler, its engines rotating to propel it forward, sending it speeding away.

"*Wait!*" exclaimed Carrie over the radio. "Will it stay jammed? The torpedo?"

"The SEALs attached a portable jammer," came the pilot's reply. "We're good."

She moved to the stern, shouting to the SEALS, "Stay with the torpedo, get it free of the net." Then to the trawler captain, "Can you get us close to the torpedo?"

Jimmy nodded and began to gently maneuver the boat nearer to the SEALs and the black, glistening torpedo floating in the waves.

Soon it was alongside, and Carrie and Ben moved to the port side, crowding along the railing with the rest of the team.

The SEALs clung to the brackets, as the waves lapped at the side of the torpedo. They shouted to the crew to let out the boat's winch, wrapping its cable around the torpedo to secure it, as they freed it from the net.

Carrie checked the time on the tablet. "02:02:33."

"*C'mon! C'mon!*" she whispered, as they all stared with growing alarm at the horizon toward the carrier, fervently willing for the other Osprey.

Just as the tablet read "01:43:14" they heard the distant roar of its engines, as the Osprey appeared in the distance. It descended from the sky, slung beneath its belly a massive jet engine.

Over the radio came the pilot's voice: "They weren't real happy about our taking one of their engines, but it's two thousand pounds, so it'll probably do."

Two of the SEALs hauled themselves aboard the trawler, shrugging off their scuba tanks, signaling upward to the Osprey.

The Osprey payed out the thick cargo cable from its belly, lowering the engine onto the boat. The SEALs detached its cargo net and the weight of the engine, caused the trawler to settle heavily lower in the water, waves lapping over its deck. The SEALs detached the cable from the boat's winch, unleashing the torpedo, and used the cable to fasten the engine to the front bracket on the torpedo.

The Osprey lowered its rear hoist and another SEAL pulled himself aboard and began to help the nuclear team be lifted away.

One of the SEALs approached Carrie, shaking his head and speaking quietly. She returned to the wheelhouse, telling the captain.

"We'll have to scuttle the boat. I'm sorry."

"*Jesus, my boat? You can't just sink my damn boat!*"

"Well, if the bomb goes off, the boat will be destroyed."

"Yeah, and if it doesn't, my boat will have been sunk for nothing."

"I'm sure you'll get compensation."

"Yeah, well, there's no compensation for thirty years of my life."

"Please. It could save millions. It could save your family."

Jimmy took a deep breath, and let out a deep sigh. "Yeah, you're right. Sink her."

Carrie checked the tablet. It said "01:14:12."

The captain shut down the trawler's engine and followed Carrie and Ben out to the deck, where the last of the nuclear team and the boat's crew were being hoisted into the Osprey. The chair lowered down, and the trawler captain strapped himself in and was lifted away. He was followed by Carrie and Ben and finally the SEALs.

In the Osprey's passenger compartment, Carrie and Ben found seats near the rear doorway, where they could see the trawler below and the torpedo, which was now attached only to the massive jet engine, its metal cowling gleaming in the sun. The torpedo sank slowly beneath the waves, still visible beneath the brown waters, and the cable attached to the jet engine zinged to tautness.

Ben turned back into the passenger compartment, as he donned a headset. He fixed an icy stare on bin Shadid, who had been brought from the *Trireme*. He sat with his head down, his hands cuffed in front of him, harnessed into his seat. He had been brought in case he relented, willing to help avert the cataclysm he would cause.

"You have lost," he told bin Shadid. "You have failed."

Bin Shadid looked up, glowering. "Not yet," he said.

Through the headset, Ben heard the pilot command, "Sink her."

The belly gunner leaned over his display, using the joysticks to aim the minigun. He pressed the trigger and the gun emitted a high-pitched buzz, as hundreds of rounds spewed from its barrel. The gunner had aimed below the water line on the trawler's port side, and the fusillade ate a gaping hole in its hull. The *Amanda June* heeled over, its deck awash.

As the Osprey gained altitude, the jet engine slid ponderously down, caught briefly on the trawler's low railing, then splashed into the water, instantly sinking. The torpedo's tail lifted above the rolling swells, then knifed out of sight.

"Jesus, we've only got twenty minutes for it to get to the bottom," said Carrie. She held up the tablet, pointing to the depth display. "We're at three hundred meters. We need a mile! Four hundred meters, five hundred, six hundred. . ."

She continued to read off the depth as the jet engine dragged the torpedo into the depths.

At 1100 meters, Ben said, "Maybe five thousand feet is crush depth."

Carrie shook her head resignedly. "It won't crush. The torpedo was designed to hide itself on the ocean floor, so its hull will withstand any depth. In fact, if the pressure change triggers the seismometer it could—"

A booming, skull-rattling roar engulfed the passenger compartment, drowning out even the Osprey's engines.

***

"WE'RE GOING DOWN!" bellowed one of the nuclear team members.

"*Nossir!*" They heard the pilot exclaim over their headset. "*By God, It looks like the ocean's coming up!*"

Out the Osprey's side window, Ben could see the ocean bulging upward all the way to the horizon. The surface began to churn, as if some gargantuan sea creature was heaving up from the depths.

The sea surface erupted into a foaming boil, launching geysers of steaming ocean water, some of which lanced upward as high as the Osprey.

The pilot vaulted the Osprey into the cloudless sky to escape the rising ocean. Below, Ben could see the doomed trawler *Amanda June* bobbing about like a toy in a bathtub, as it disappeared beneath the seething waters.

A figure tore past Ben toward the rear door. It was bin Shadid! He had freed himself from his harness and was trying to jump!

Ben managed to catch one leg, but bin Shadid kicked free, stumbling onto his knees. His fall delayed him long enough for Ben to free himself, leap out of his seat, and tackle the terrorist. The tail gunner grabbed for bin Shadid, but missed.

His wrists still handcuffed in front, bin Shadid punched and kicked, his boot smashing Ben in the face, stunning him for a moment. Freed, bin Shadid launched himself again crawling toward the door and death in the boiling ocean.

"*You are not going to die!*" Ben shouted. "*I will not let you be a martyr!*"

He managed to leap up to clutch bin Shadid once more, but the man grabbed at the pylon holding the rear machine gun and pulled himself ever closer to the door. He managed to hook his hands around the ramp, hauling himself to its edge.

"*Let me die! You wanted me to!*" he shouted over the roar of the Osprey's engines.

Kicking Ben with a glancing blow to the head, he hauled his torso over the back edge of the ramp, suspended above the ocean. Ben scrambled forward, blood streaming into his eyes. He realized that now he would be in danger of plunging off the aircraft along with the terrorist. He felt a sharp yank behind him, and the tail gunner's voice shouted, "*You're hooked! Stop the son of a bitch!*"

Ben knew the gunner had attached him to a restraining belt, and he took the advantage to crawl forward over bin Shadid's body clasping his hands around his chest, trying to pull him back inside.

But Ben had no leverage, and bin Shadid carried him plunging over the edge of the ramp.

He and the terrorist now dangled from the restraining strap beneath the Osprey, the boiling ocean below, the roar of its engines filling their ears, the gale from its propellers tearing at them. Ben managed to wrap his legs around bin Shadid's body.

"NO!" he bellowed. "GODDAMMIT, NO!"

Bin Shadid reached up and tore one of Ben's hands from its grip. He clawed at the other. His body pitched forward, beginning to slip away, but Ben tightened the grip of his legs. He grasped bin Shadid's jacket, hauled his body up and clasped his arms around the man's chest. A sharp pain knifed through his left arm where he had been wounded weeks earlier, but he held on.

"*Don't move!*" he heard shouted from above. It was the tail gunner. "*The strap's not meant to hold two people! Don't move!*"

Exclaimed bin Shadid, "You don't want to die! You don't want to die just to save me!"

"*You will not become a martyr!*" Ben felt a jerk. Was the strap failing? Below them, the ocean seethed. His face was being scalded by the rising steam, the salty smell of hot brine smothering him.

He made a decision. He would never let go. He took a deep breath, coughing at the searing steam entering his lungs. He tightened his grip on the terrorist, the pain in his arm becoming agonizing. But he held on. He felt the man's breathing. And he felt a soul-deep satisfaction at knowing breath would remain in bin Shadid's body until justice was done.

A form loomed beside him, and he managed to turn his head to see the tail gunner strapped into the chair of the Osprey's lift. He reached out to Ben.

Ben shook his head emphatically. "*Take him first!*"

"*Let the bastard go!*" shouted the tail gunner.

"*Take him first!*" Ben repeated.

The tail gunner bellowed a curse, swung over, and grabbed bin Shadid, circling a line around his body. The hoist reeled them in, and Ben was left swinging alone by the strap, staring down at the boiling ocean. If he died now, he decided, it would have been worth it for Abby and for the many the terrorist had killed.

But then he felt another jerk on the restraining strap, and he was being hauled upward. He felt arms clutching at him, heaving him back into the aircraft. He lay on the ramp, panting. Carrie's face appeared above him. She helped him up and got him harnessed back into his seat and his headset put back on.

The rear gunner appeared with a medical kit and began to daub the blood from his face and scalp, applying a clotting sponge. The bleeding stopped, and the marine cleaned and disinfected the wound, closing it with surgical glue.

"He didn't die," was all Ben could murmur. "I didn't let him die. He will face what he has done."

"He will," said Carrie, embracing him.

"And he will see how he failed."

"Not completely failed," came a tense voice over the headset. One of the physicists waved from his seat at the front of the passenger compartment. He had his laptop open.

"What do you mean?" asked Carrie.

"You saw the ocean rise up," he said. "I did some quick calculations. The detonation will generate a tsunami, maybe twenty, maybe *thirty* feet!"

Carrie rushed over, scrutinizing the man's computer screen. "How long do we have?" she asked.

"Almost immediately to the East Coast. Maybe six hours to Africa. Longer to Spain, France and the UK," was the answer.

Carrie moved up behind the pilot. "You heard?" she asked him. He nodded. "Radio the Coast Guard," she told him. "Tell them and get hold of FEMA, Homeland Security, and anybody else you can think of. People need to get far enough inland, or high enough. And tell them to alert the Atlantic coastal countries."

The physicist said, "We should monitor the wave so we can better warn the rest of the world. We won't be able to make it to the coast in time. The wave'll move at hundreds of miles an hour. But at least we can get some sense of the aftermath."

The pilot, having heard the conversation, pushed the small thumb wheel on his joystick to rotate the craft's engines into a horizontal flight mode, launching the craft roaring toward the Atlantic coast.

An hour's flight brought them over Chesapeake Bay, where they flew over a jumble of boats tossed onto the shore like toys. The tsunami had sent the water coursing through low-lying areas, carrying away cars and ripping small buildings to pieces. They could see people on rooftops being rescued by boats and huge military trucks plowing through the floodwaters.

The team members were quiet as they crowded around the Osprey's windows and peered out the rear door at the devastation.

Carrie radioed the Coast Guard for an update, reporting back, "It's bad. Virginia Beach was inundated. Also Norfolk. The naval base is underwater. The wave went up into the Potomac and flooded along the river. Lots of water rescues going on."

"We'll have to divert to Dulles Airport," said the pilot.

As the Osprey hovered over the flooded base with swamped aircraft and buildings, Ben shook his head. "True, he failed at the nuclear attack. But he is very smart, very strategic. The effective terrorists I've studied always had many points of attack. Guerrilla warfare doesn't mean just one attack."

Carrie took a deep breath and blew it out in a relieved sigh. "Well, it's hard to imagine anything worse than this weapon. Surely, the worst is over."

***

Khalid Rasul sat alone in the darkened room of the Erbil villa, slumped over in his chair. His head was bowed, tears welled in his eyes. The only light came from the glow of the TV screen, which showed an aerial scene of flooding along the US Atlantic coast.

But that devastation, or even the deep-ocean thermonuclear blast that caused it, did not give him comfort. The news had leaked that the mastermind behind the attack, Saadallah bin Shadid, had been captured, his full revenge thwarted. Rasul feared that his revered commander, his dear friend since childhood, would surely be murdered by the Americans he loathed. Just as they had murdered his family.

For decades, Rasul had been his friend's šamšir, his sword. But this time he had been useless. He had failed. He had been unable to protect bin Shadid. He had been unable to ensure that bin Shadid could avenge his family's murder.

Rasul looked down at his hands. Even years later, his fingertips still held scars from when he had clawed desperately through the rubble of the collapsed building, hoping to find bin Shadid's family alive.

Bin Shadid had crouched beside him, also frantically tearing at the concrete blocks to uncover mangled body after body. They had narrowly escaped their own death because they had been late to the wedding, having flown into the city after a business trip. Driving toward the wedding hall, they had seen the explosion and the rising column of white smoke when they had been only a kilometer away.

When they came upon the horrific site, they had leaped from the vehicle, joining the shouting, sobbing crowd of townspeople in the rescue effort.

But before that horrific day, Rasul had taken such joy in seeing how happy bin Shadid was with his gentle wife Faiza, his sweet children Hakeem and Isra. The little ones called him uncle, and he was so proud of the title.

He had been the one who had found little Isra in the rubble. He had been the one who had carried her limp, shattered body to her father, and they had cried together. They had cried when Faiza's body was uncovered with Hakeem's.

Rasul picked up the thumb drive that held the files transmitted from bin Shadid. He had studied them. He knew what they contained. Their data were a weapon that could be far more devastating than even the bomb. They could enable the North Koreans to inflict a holocaust on all of America for causing such tragedy to bin Shadid's family, and beyond that to Iraq.

They were a weapon that he would dedicate himself to delivering to the North Koreans. That would be his tribute to Saadallah bin Shadid and to his family.

The door to the room opened slowly, and one of the security men cautiously entered. He approached slowly, holding a laptop, hesitant to intrude on Rasul's grief.

"Sir, may I show you something important?"

Rasul nodded.

"The concierge at Baya Towers called. You had asked that he tell you of anything unusual, any suspicious visitors. He said that a man and a woman came there. They went into the Russian's apartment."

"So?"

"Well, we obtained security camera footage. Can I show it to you?"

Again, Rasul nodded.

The security man set the laptop in front of Rasul, who at first only distractedly viewed it. Then uttering a curse, he leaned forward and clutched the laptop.

"*Him!*" He pointed at the man. "He was here in this house! He was with the woman who collapsed in front of the house. He was dressed as an imam. I allowed them in for her to recover. She was veiled, so I didn't see her face. But it must have been her . . . the sister of Benjamin Webber. . . the one we abducted . . . the one who killed our men and escaped!"

"What does this mean, sir?"

"She was here to kill bin Shadid. But she did not. She must have realized that Faisal was a double . . . that he was not Agha bin Shadid. *She was the one who told the Americans they should look for him elsewhere!*"

"What do you wish done?"

"She is probably still here in Erbil. Find her. She will be useful in my mission, and after that . . ." The guard nodded. Rasul did not need to finish the sentence.

CHAPTER NINETEEN

"**B**en, dear Ben! You're safe!" Azariah clutched the satellite phone, exhaling a sigh of relief. She smiled over at Jonas, as they sat in the battered gray Toyota driving slowly down Bharka Road In Erbil. The narrow road passed an anonymous block of walled gardens that hid modest stucco houses. They pulled up beside a bare park of baked earth, across from one of the houses. Old men sat on worn benches beneath a metal canopy, watching young boys kicking about a soccer ball. Azariah put the phone on speaker.

"Did you see the news?" asked Ben.

"The bomb? Yes, it went off underwater?"

"We managed to sink it in a mile of ocean. It created a devastating tidal wave, but it could have been worse."

"And the terrorist?" she asked.

"Tried to jump into the ocean."

"Tried?"

"I stopped him."

"Jesus, you should have let him."

"I wanted him to face justice. Not be a martyr."

"Benjamin you're a better man than me."

"I'm going home, Azzy. You come home, too."

"Soon, I promise. We've got unfinished business. Jonas wants to trace bin Shadid's network. There are still a lot of bad actors out there. And who knows what mischief they could cause." She nodded over at

Jonas, and the dark-eyed, slim young man with the thick beard nodded back in agreement.

"Can't they do it themselves?"

"Ben, I've come this far. I need to see it through. And I know the players."

After some gossip about the family, she ended the call. They had parked across from the address of one of bin Shadid's guards.

"Think he'll tell us anything?" she asked.

Jonas shrugged and took a sip of his Coke. "Well, he could have—"

Three bullets erupted through the rear window, two slamming into Jonas's head, exploding away his face. His head snapped forward, and fragments of his skull and brain painted a splatter of red on the car windshield.

Azariah screamed in horror, recovering enough to reach for the pistol in the car's door pocket. But before she could bring it to bear on the unseen shooter who had murdered Jonas, the side window shattered, showering her with glittering glass fragments. A hand thrust through the window, slapping a cloth over her nose and mouth; another hand clutched the back of her head. She struggled, clawing at the hand, gagging at the stench of chloroform before her arms sank limply to her side, and her head lolled forward.

A hulking, black-garbed man wrenched open the car door and hauled out her limp body, zip-tying her hands behind her and stuffing her into the trunk of the black sedan that had pulled up. The kidnapper slammed the trunk shut, and the two leaped into the car. With a throaty roar, it accelerated away down the street.

***

"This is just about as bad as it could get," said Carrie quietly. She sat with Ben, Grinell, and the nuclear team in the CIA conference room. "Boy, was I ever wrong, thinking we were okay."

On an animated map on a wall screen a sequence of lines traced the jagged route of a data transmission from the *Trireme* to Erbil, Iraq.

"Looks like bin Shadid sent a huge, coded file over his private network, ricocheting across a series of servers to his villa in Erbil," she said.

"How is that 'as bad as it gets'?" asked Grinell.

"Well, the NSA couldn't crack the code, but they could tell the file was the same size as the files on the thumb drive we took from the North Koreans. That almost certainly means that bin Shadid transmitted the plans for the bomb and the torpedo to Erbil. It could be a greater disaster than even the bomb."

"How?" asked Ben. "I don't understand."

"The file not only has plans for a thermonuclear bomb, which would give North Korea a weapon thousands of times more destructive than their nuclear weapons. It also has plans for a delivery system that could clandestinely carry the bomb anywhere in the world. The plans include how to build the small nuclear reactor that could give the torpedo practically unlimited range. It's a poor-man's ICBM."

Grinell said, "The implications are horrendous. With North Korea's technology, they could build dozens of nuclear-powered, nuclear-tipped torpedoes. They could launch them without detection, and over months they could make their way to the coast of any country in the world. They could lurk there, waiting to be detonated."

"Actually, they don't even have to do that," said Carrie. "They could just build one and set it off in the middle of an ocean, just to show that they have the capability. Then they can make whatever demands they want, and the countries . . . America included . . . would be forced to accede."

Ben said, "But wouldn't it be suicide to attack the US or any of its allies?"

"No country would take that chance," said Grinell. "Dear Leader is a sociopath. The safest thing would be to give him money, food, technology. . . whatever. Hell, he could even set off a bomb to punish one country, and the others wouldn't do a thing."

"Well, I can't figure out why he didn't just transmit the files to North Korea in the first place," said Carrie.

Ben leaned back in his chair, staring at the ceiling for a long moment. "Two reasons. One is that North Korea's internet is closed to the outside world. But the main reason is that his culture is one that depends on personal interactions. It would give him great satisfaction knowing that one of his people personally handed over the data to a North Korean general, even their leader."

"Then we've got our work cut out to find out who's carrying the data and intercept them," said Grinell.

Ben pulled himself out of his chair, saying, "Well, I need to go to Erbil and pry my sister loose from whatever she's doing. And we've got to get our lies straight that we're going to tell Albert, Mom, and Dad."

Carrie smiled. "Given it's your sister, that'll take a lot of prying, a lot of lying."

They walked together out of the CIA headquarters. In the parking lot, they embraced, holding each other for a long time.

"Are you okay?" she asked softly.

Ben shrugged. "Still got scars. I'll always have the scars."

"Yeah, and I know you don't mean the physical ones. Come see us when you get back. I want you to meet Beth and the kids."

"Yeah, that will—" Ben's phone buzzed and he answered it. He listened for a long moment. "No," he whispered in shock. "*No! God! No! No! Where?*"

He ended the call, turning to Carrie, his expression stricken.

"What?" asked Carrie.

"Jonas is dead. Murdered. Azzy is missing."

***

Azariah emerged slowly from the mottled, gray shroud of unconsciousness to feel herself belted into a leather chair. The steady, low roar of engines told her she was on a plane. She opened her eyes to see sitting across from her the same muscular security man she and Jonas had encountered at bin Shadid's villa. He was dressed simply, in dark trousers and a white dress shirt, his sleeves rolled up. He looked up from his laptop to scowl at her. Beside him on the desk between them was a small black box.

"You," she said blearily. "You son of a bitch, you killed Jonas."

"Not me. People who work for me," he said.

"Same damned thing."

She realized that her hands were free. She also realized that the only thing keeping her from attacking him was the seat belt. She took a deep breath to clear her head, to prepare herself. She rehearsed what she would do. Then she did it. She reached down unfastened the seat belt and began to launch herself toward him.

He pressed buttons on the black box. It beeped, and a jolt slammed her as if she had been kicked in the gut. She grunted and writhed in agony, her body jerking spasmodically. She collapsed back into the seat.

"Fifty thousand volts," said the man, holding up the control box. "Check your waist."

Azariah managed to recover enough to feel around her waist, finding a thick black belt fastened tightly around it.

"What—" she began.

"Stun belt," he interrupted. "We saw what you did to our people who took you last time. We wanted a more effective means of control."

He waved the hand with the control box, and a guard appeared at his side. He handed the guard the control. "He will be watching. If you attempt any sort of attack . . . if you do not obey every command . . . you will be neutralized in the same way."

Azariah looked at her blood-caked hands, her blood-stained clothes, remembering the source of the blood that spattered them.

"Can I wash? Can I change?"

"No. I want you to carry the mark of what we did to your friend. I want you to carry it to your death at our destination."

"Where are we going? What are you going to do?"

The man reached in his shirt pocket and brought out a thumb drive.

"I will deliver this. It is the plans for the bomb, for the torpedo, for everything the North Koreans need to achieve the revenge for the death of my friend Agha bin Shadid's family."

"Then what?"

"Then, when you have witnessed that goal achieved, I will kill you. You were one who helped cause my friend's failure. You will see his ultimate success."

"He is your friend? That monster is your friend? Who are you?"

"My name is Khalid Rasul. As a boy, I lived on the street of Baghdad. I starved, I ate rats. Then one day I saw another boy being attacked by a gang. It was the same gang that had once attacked me. I had an iron pipe. I attacked them, and they fled. . . those who could still walk. The boy was Saadallah bin Shadid, the son of a Baghdad merchant. His family took me in, fed me, clothed me, educated me. I owe them my life. I pledged to protect bin Shadid, to be his šamšir, his sword."

"But even so, why would you do something that would cost millions of innocent lives? They have done nothing to you."

Rasul put the thumb drive back in his pocket and leaned forward, glaring at her. He held out his hands.

"I carried his little dead daughter away from the building that Americans had bombed. It was a wedding. I helped him bury that daughter, his beloved wife, his son. They were my family almost as much as his."

"Where are we going?"

"Northern China. People in Dandong will transport us across the border. The North Koreans are expecting me." Rasul gestured to his laptop. "Bin Shadid has given me control of all his resources. I will use them to achieve his revenge. I will still serve him as his šamšir."

***

A stricken Ben stood beside the Mossad agent, staring in shock into the gray Toyota that had held Jonas and Azariah. The driver-side door and seat were covered in caked blood. The driver-side windshield showed three bullet holes where bullets had exited and was splattered with dried blood and brain matter. But the passenger side showed only a few blood specks and no bullet holes.

The car sat in the concrete block building that was the Iraqi police garage, near the mammoth Erbil police station. Standing with them was CIA agent Henderson Skolnick. He was a man of medium build, medium height, unremarkable brown hair, unremarkable brown eyes, and unremarkable features. He was dressed plainly in brown slacks and a tan polo shirt. In short, he presented a perfect anonymous image for a CIA agent who had spent two decades infiltrating terrorist groups, leading insurgents, and assassinating an unknown number of people who threatened his country.

"See the void?" asked the Mossad agent.

"Void?" asked Ben.

"The passenger seat shows a void in the blood splatter where your sister was sitting. There is no blood on the seat. And there is no blood on the windshield. She was not hit."

"God! That means she was taken!"

"Yes, but more positively, that means they didn't want her dead," said Skolnick.

"She's alive?"

"Almost certainly," he said.

"Any information where she is?"

The Mossad agent said, "One of bin Shadid's planes took off an hour after the attack. We have an informant at the airport who saw them carry an unconscious woman on board. Two men were on the plane, and he identified Khalid Rasul as one of them. They filed a flight plan to Beijing, but we suspect they're going elsewhere."

"Where?" asked Ben.

Skolnick said, "Likely somewhere along the China-North Korean border. It's nine hundred miles and could be anywhere. But I have a couple of hunches. In any case, the NSA will track the plane."

"Then I'm going to China," said Ben quietly.

"I understand you have a personal stake in this," said Skolnick. "And I saw by your CIA record that you've seen action. But you've not seen hard-core action. And you've not been in China. I've been stationed here. I'm going in alone. I'll keep you apprised—"

"Yes, I do have a personal stake," said Ben. "That's why I'm the best person to have beside you in this thing. As for not seeing hard-core action, ask your people what I did in the field in Berlin and in California."

Skolnick shot him an annoyed look and moved to a corner of the garage, taking out his satellite phone. He could be heard arguing with whoever was on the other end.

Questioning the Mossad agent about Azariah's and Jonas's activities in Erbil, Ben learned that they had been tracing the bin Shadid organization.

After fifteen minutes, Skolnick returned, his expression a frown of frustration, announcing, "Okay, look. You will follow my orders in China. You will not go off half-cocked. Is that understood?"

"Got it. You do your part; I'll do mine. Rescue my sister and stop Rasul. And stop a holocaust."

CHAPTER TWENTY

"I am here," announced Rasul into the phone. He squinted into the late afternoon sun, seeing that the private area of China's Dandong airport was deserted. So, he signaled back at the plane for the guard to haul Azariah off the plane and into the black SUV. He was sure they hadn't been traced because they had not landed in bin Shadid's airplane. They had switched to another private plane in Beijing.

A van pulled up, and three hulking, buzz-cut men and one smaller man got out holding stubby Chinese QBZ-95 assault rifles in tattooed hands. They wore black windbreakers with the orange and red sunrise logo of the China National Petroleum Corporation. But Rasul knew they were members of the Triad gang in the pay of the company.

"You have your instructions?" he asked in broken Cantonese.

"We do," said the smaller man in perfect English, who was missing an ear, a sign of punishment in the gang. "But do you have our compensation?"

"Of course." Rasul signaled to the jet, and the pilot emerged holding a black satchel, handing it to the one-eared man, who took the satchel with a hand missing its little finger.

Rasul listened to the voice at the other end of the phone, then announced, "The patrol boat has been dispatched. We are to meet it at dusk."

He climbed into the SUV passenger seat, turning back to Azariah. "I have just spoken to the director of the North Korean nuclear program. Soon they will have the plans. You will see the transfer. But you will not live to see the result."

***

His expression grim, Ben peered out the windshield, as Skolnick drove the SUV down the deserted road along the route of the Yalu River. He felt a seething fury at the thug Rasul, who had taken his sister. He remembered seeing Rasul with bin Shadid in Istanbul. He was no doubt somehow complicity in Abby's murder. He would *not* lose another loved one to the monster.

"The patrol boat is on the river," said Skolnick, consulting his tablet computer as he pulled over and got out of the SUV. "Satellite image shows it coming across to this side." He pulled a duffel bag out of the back of the vehicle, motioning for Ben to do the same with a second.

"So you're sure this is where the North Koreans will pick up Rasul and Azzy?"

"Well, we know there's been suspicious activity at this crossing. And it's not just because the pipeline is here, and that the North Koreans guard it heavily. Our asset went missing here. Likely killed. And it's unusual for a North Korean patrol boat to come to this side of the river."

As the sun set, they hauled the duffel bags through the brush-choked woods, emerging at the water's edge. They were upstream from the looming 48-inch oil pipeline that was North Korea's major oil source from China. It ran overhead, slung beneath the massive iron Friendship Bridge that spanned the river near Dandong, China.

Skolnick zipped open one of the duffels and pulled out an MK 12 sniper rifle and an M4 assault rifle, handing the latter to Ben.

"You know how to use one of these?"

"Of course. CIA trained me." Ben pulled out the rifle's magazine, checked that it was full, slapped it back in, and chambered a round.

He would not hesitate to kill Rasul or any other human who got in the way of rescuing his sister.

Dusk began gathering on the wide river, as they saw the North Korean patrol boat make its way slowly to the shore under the shadow of the pipeline. It was perhaps half a mile away.

"We need to stop them!" exclaimed Ben. He shouldered the rifle, took up the duffel, got to his feet, and headed toward the landing spot.

"Seriously?" asked Skolnick. "You mean go up against a patrol boat with a fifty-caliber machine gun and a dozen soldiers?"

"If that's what it takes." Ben plunged away into the brush.

"Shit! Just wait!" Skolnick called after him. "Just let's get close and see what's possible. I've got plenty of ordnance, even a shoulder-mounted missile. But we need to be strategic."

"You be strategic. I'm going to save my sister."

Skolnick uttered a curse and followed. As they neared the landing spot, the sound of the idling engine of the patrol boat grew louder. But just as they reached the small clearing, that sound abruptly grew into a throaty rumble, as the engine throttled up. The boat accelerated away from the bank into the river, and they could see outside the boat's small cabin in the gathering gloom, standing next to two soldiers, the tall figure of Khalid Rasul.

"*Where's Azzy?*" asked Ben in anguish.

"They must have put her in the cabin," said Skolnick.

"*They're gone! God, they're gone!*" exclaimed Ben. His desperation clawed at him, leaving him casting about wildly for a plan. "Somehow, we've got to stop that boat!"

"We've only got one option," said Skolnick. He reached into his duffel and pulled out the shoulder-mounted missile, flipping off its cover and safety tab.

"No, damnit! We don't have just one option!" Ben dug into the duffel he was carrying, finding the flare gun he had seen there earlier. "We engage them. Draw their fire."

"Are you nuts?" Before Skolnick could stop him, Ben fired a flare, which arced into the sky, casting its yellow light on the receding boat and the river.

"What the hell makes you think they're going to come back to fight you?" asked Skolnick.

"Because Rasul will know it's me. He knows I'm the one who stopped bin Shadid. He will want to kill me. And he can damned well try." To make sure Rasul knew it was him, he stood up, the flare casting its glow on him.

Sure enough, he heard shouting over the boat's engine, which swerved to head back toward them. The crack of rifle fire erupted from the boat, followed by the louder staccato rattle of machine gun fire.

Bullets raked the shore, splintering the trees and impacting a nearby boulder, blasting away chips of rock.

Ben and Skolnick dove behind the boulder, and Skolnick brought up the sniper rifle. He quickly stood up, sighted, and squeezed off a round. A shout came from the boat.

"One down," he said, chambering another round, waiting for another opportunity.

Ben flipped his rifle to automatic fire, positioned himself prone beside the boulder and loosed a volley that peppered the boat. He uttered a silent prayer that the bullets wouldn't penetrate the cabin.

The thud of an explosion sounded behind them, and at first Ben was confused. Did the boat carry a mortar?

"That was our SUV!" exclaimed Skolnick. "Somebody just blew up our SUV!"

As the gunfire from the boat tore at the boulder, a burst of fire erupted from the woods behind them.

Ben reversed his position, scanning the darkening woods for the new attacker. He fired a burst into the woods, but it was blind. More machine gun fire came from the patrol boat, which had stopped several hundred yards away.

"We're dead," said Skolnick solemnly, as withering fire struck from both sides. "They'll kill her, too, dump her body in the river. They won't want the complication of an American prisoner. All they want are the plans."

Ben froze in agonizing indecision. *All would be lost! What should he do? He couldn't kill his sister! God, what would Azzy want him to do? What should he do!* He took a deep trembling breath. He clutched the rifle, and decided.

He choked out, "She wouldn't want them to give the weapon to the North Koreans. She wouldn't want her life—" He was interrupted by more volleys from both sides. "*The missile! Fire it!*" he exclaimed.

Skolnick took a deep breath, shouldered the launcher and leaped up, but then crouched back down, shaking his head. His action was answered with more rounds from the boat's machine gun tearing away at the boulder. More rounds from behind them struck the rock on their side.

"It's too far!" he said. "Damn! Can't get an accurate shot at that range. I've only got one."

Ben leaped up and scanned the scene, then crouched back down, driven to ground by the incoming barrage.

"Can you hit the pipeline?"

"What the hell for?"

Ben held up the flare gun.

"Yeah, that'll do it." Skolnick nodded, shrugged, took a deep breath, leaped up, and launched the missile. It erupted with a whoosh from the launcher, flashed toward the pipeline and exploded. From the pipeline burst a roiling gush of black oil that cascaded onto the patrol boat and spread in a dark slick on the brown waters of the river.

Bellowed shouts replaced gunfire from the boat.

Ben stood and fired the flare gun, and it arced at a low angle skittering into the oil-slicked water. The oil ignited with a crackling roar, yellow flames throwing up billowing clouds of smoke blacker than even the darkening sky. The flames raced across the water, reaching the patrol boat and engulfing it.

The screams of burning men echoed across the water, followed by a wave of searing heat, along with the acrid pungency of burning oil.

Ben stood up, his jaw clenched, tears streaming down his face, watching the inferno and the flailing men engulfed in flames. He was heedless of the lethal enemy behind him. He was ready for his own death. He had brought justice for the murder of his beloved Abby and his unborn son. He had ended the horror. As agonizing as the decision had been, he knew it would have been his sister's wishes. His dear sister. He remembered her kindness, her courage. He remembered her wry smile, her warmth.

"Ben, you okay?" came a voice behind him. *Dear God, it was Azzy's!*

He whirled around to see her push her way out of the thick brush, followed by three hulking Chinese men and one smaller one, all in black windbreakers holding assault rifles. Skolnick stood up, dropped the missile launcher, and raised his hands.

"WHAT? HOW? YOU'RE—" Ben managed to shout.

"Yup, it's me in the flesh."

"How?" He didn't wait for an answer but embraced her, holding her tightly, as if she would vanish if he let her go.

"Well, these men were supposed to kill me," she managed to say in the tight embrace. "Y'see, the schmuck Rasul wanted to kill me on the boat. They were originally going to do that. But the North Koreans got cold feet. They only wanted the plans for the bomb and the torpedo. They didn't want complications. And they didn't have the okay from their commander. Killing an American citizen, was a complication. So, they refused. So, Rasul settled for having these guys do it here, on the China side."

The four Chinese stared impassively at Ben, Azariah, and Skolnick. The smaller man uttered a phrase in Chinese and raised the hand missing the little finger. All four brought their rifles up.

"Why didn't they kill you?"

"Well, turns out, they're Triad. Organized crime. They like money. . . a *lot*. Fortunately, the little one-eared guy, the leader, speaks English. I told him if they didn't kill us, they'd each get a million dollars."

Skolnick said, "And you're expecting the CIA to come up with it?"

"You're CIA, I take it?" asked Azariah. Skolnick nodded. "Mister spook, I showed these guys how to set up untraceable accounts online in a Cook Island bank."

"And you expect me to fill up those accounts with a million dollars?" asked Skolnick.

"Million dollars *each*," said Azariah. "If you want us to stay alive, you'll do it."

"And why wouldn't they just take the money and kill us, anyway?" asked Skolnick.

"Yeah, well, if they killed Americans, especially CIA agents, the Agency would be all over their asses. These guys' Triad bosses would make sure they didn't live long after such a royal screw up. But if they help us, besides getting rich, they become CIA assets. They'll work for you, and you'll be a mensch with your spy buddies because you recruited very useful Chinese gangsters. I told them you'd even teach them the secret CIA handshake. And I also told them if they worked for you, you'd give them a get-out-of-jail-free card. . . asylum, if they ever needed it. I told them they should try for Miami, or LA."

Ben, still embracing Azariah, asked "Okay, why were they shooting at us?"

"Just for show," she said. "They didn't aim to hit you. They wanted to make sure the North Koreans didn't tell their bosses they'd not done their duty. They take Korean money, too."

The four Chinese each handed Skolnick their phones. He uttered a wry curse and took them. He leaned against the bullet-scarred boulder, took out his satellite phone, and began a call.

After explaining the situation to the person on the other end, he launched into an argument. "Yeah, you heard me," he said. "Four million. Hell, take it out of the petty cash! I don't give a shit where you get it! You want our blood on your hands? Wouldn't look good on your action report, right?"

He hung up, and after a tense half an hour in which the Chinese still wielded their rifles, Skolnick used their phones to transfer a million dollars to each account. The four scrutinized their phones, smiled, and shouldered their rifles. They turned to leave, but Azariah held up a hand to stop them.

"Say, look, you guys blew up their car. How about you give us a ride to the airport?"

CHAPTER TWENTY-ONE

"*Four point three billion dollars!*" exclaimed Azariah, plopping into the wing chair across from Ben, who sat on the couch in her living room. She had been in her study in a long phone conversation with her Mossad contact in Iraq.

"Amazing!" exclaimed Ben. A month after their battle in China, he still looked a bit haggard, but had recovered considerably while ensconced in Azariah's and husband Albert's handsome colonial house on Long Island. He absentmindedly reached up to scratch his beard, still unused to his newly clean-shaven face, as well as his shorter haircut. They were symbols of his emergence from a spiritual darkness into a recovery from Abby's death and the ordeal that followed. Abby would have wished that for him.

Azariah peeked through the living room doorway to make sure Albert and their mother and father were out of hearing range, occupied in the kitchen making dinner. She was reassured by the clank of pots and pans and the sounds of friendly squabbling over how long to cook the green beans.

"Bin Shadid really had that much money? Billions?" asked Ben, leaning forward on the couch, a wine glass in his hand.

"Yup, they managed to trace just about all of his funds. And the Iraqi government was all too willing to let the money be used as relief for the victims of the tsunamis around the world. It helped get Iraq off the hook for having harbored the schmuck who set off a nuclear bomb."

"Anything about the people who . . ." He did not finish the sentence. Azariah knew he meant the men who had murdered Jason and kidnapped her.

She shrugged in mock puzzlement. "Um. . . the funniest thing. Funny-strange, that is. It seems that two men in Erbil who had worked for bin Shadid were found dead. They were shot through the head. The Iraqi police ruled it suicide."

"Good detective work, I'd say," Ben said, his tone ironic.

"Yes, and they've rounded up all bin Shadid's people who were involved in engineering the bomb and the torpedo. But one other strange thing. Somebody blew up the warehouse where the gardener said he kept his equipment and chemicals. The gardener and his sons were okay. He said it was probably a rival, and he was targeted because he wasn't protected by bin Shadid. Poor guy, out of a job and all."

Ben shook his head sadly, as Azariah got up to pour more wine into his glass. He took a sip, letting its warmth suffuse his body. Being surrounded by family helped greatly to heal physically from the trauma and violence he had suffered. But he knew he would never completely heal from the psychic scars.

They spent the next half hour talking over plans for bin Shadid's upcoming trial. Ben reassured her, under yet another round of loving interrogation from his sister, that he was recovered enough, for the days of testimony he would have to give.

The doorbell rang and Azariah answered it. From the foyer came the happy sounds of greeting. Carrie entered the living room, holding the hand of a little girl with silky brown hair, whom she introduced as her daughter Diana. Ben rose and warmly embraced Carrie. Her welcome presence brought him another measure of comfort.

Carrie was followed by their two-year-old toddler, introduced as Lewis, who marched in proudly displaying a truck he had brought with him.

Finally came Carrie's wife Beth, a petite, dark-haired, dark-eyed woman with a ready smile. She held a baby swaddled in a pink blanket.

Ben said, "We'll introduce you to Azzy's husband Albert, and mom and dad, after they finish making dinner." He smiled down at the baby in Beth's arms, letting the little girl grasp his finger with a tiny hand. "And who is this little one?"

"Well, we want to talk to you about her," said Carrie. "But first I need to know how you're doing."

"Fine," said Ben. "I'm starting back at the university in a month. I'll be working on the book on hidden monsters with a much greater insight."

"Hard-won insight," said Carrie.

"True. I think my work will help stop future terrorists. Certainly, Khalid Rasul was a classic hidden monster, who enabled bin Shadid. And, of course he . . ." Ben did not finish the sentence. He reminded himself that the China operation that thwarted the transfer of the nuclear plans was classified. Beth didn't know about the disaster that had been averted. Instead, he said "We were so happy to hear that you wanted to come visit. I sensed that you had a reason, though. Was it to show off your new baby?"

"Well, more than that," said Carrie, smiling over at Beth. "First, we think you should hold her."

"Delighted," said Ben. Beth gently nestled the baby into his arms. He smiled happily. "Nothing like a baby to remind you what's important," he declared with an emotion-thickened voice.

"We just adopted her a week ago," said Carrie. "We were already approved and on the adoption list. We found out she was orphaned in Africa from the tidal wave. Her family was killed but by some miracle, they found her alive. We said yes immediately!"

"Wow!" breathed Ben. "How great for her and for you!"

Carrie took Beth's hand and both smiled. "Well, Ben, the reason we wanted to come here was to ask you something important. Will you be her godfather?"

Ben laughed in surprise and declared "Oh, my God, yes! That would be such an honor!"

"Wonderful! So, Ben, I'd like you to meet your goddaughter Abigail. Abby, meet the best godfather ever!"